TENSIO

"Do not even ask me to escort you there," Lieutenant Du'kai said in a firm voice. "I am charged with proving I am a better man than poor Jamie Lansdale, and I am determined to do so."

Averie laughed. "And what if I defied you?" she asked. "Jumped down and went running through the streets as fast as I could? You are always so proper—I cannot picture you snatching me up and throwing me back into the wagon."

He laughed as well, but there was something in his eyes that gave her pause. "I think you misread me to some extent, Lady Averie. I am a soldier. I am capable of a certain ruthlessness when the situation requires."

She arched her eyebrows. "I had better not test you, I suppose."

"Are you in the habit of testing people?" he asked softly.

OTHER BOOKS YOU MAY ENJOY

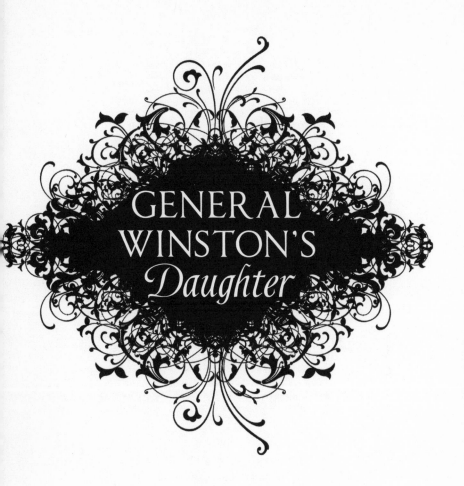

GENERAL WINSTON'S *Daughter*

SHARON SHINN

speak

An Imprint of Penguin Group (USA) Inc.

SPEAK

Published by the Penguin Group

Penguin Group (USA) Inc., 345 Hudson Street, New York, New York 10014, U.S.A.
Penguin Group (Canada), 90 Eglinton Avenue East, Suite 700, Toronto, Ontario, Canada M4P 2Y3
(a division of Pearson Penguin Canada Inc.)
Penguin Books Ltd, 80 Strand, London WC2R 0RL, England
Penguin Ireland, 25 St Stephen's Green, Dublin 2, Ireland (a division of Penguin Books Ltd)
Penguin Group (Australia), 250 Camberwell Road, Camberwell, Victoria 3124, Australia
(a division of Pearson Australia Group Pty Ltd)
Penguin Books India Pvt Ltd, 11 Community Centre, Panchsheel Park, New Delhi - 110 017, India
Penguin Group (NZ), 67 Apollo Drive, Rosedale, North Shore 0632, New Zealand
(a division of Pearson New Zealand Ltd)
Penguin Books (South Africa) (Pty) Ltd, 24 Sturdee Avenue, Rosebank, Johannesburg 2196, South Africa

Registered Offices: Penguin Books Ltd, 80 Strand, London WC2R 0RL, England

First published in the United States of America by Viking, a member of Penguin Group (USA) Inc., 2007
Published by Speak, an imprint of Penguin Group (USA) Inc., 2009

1   3   5   7   9   10   8   6   4   2

THE LIBRARY OF CONGRESS HAS CATALOGED THE VIKING EDITION AS FOLLOWS:
Shinn, Sharon.
General Winston's daughter / Sharon Shinn.
p. cm.
Summary: Seventeen-year-old heiress Averie Winston travels with her guardian to faraway Chiarrin,
a country her father's army has occupied, and once she arrives and is reunited with her fiancé,
she discovers that her notions about politics, propriety, the military, and even her fiancé have changed.
ISBN: 978-0-670-06248-5 (hardcover)
[I. Coming of age—Fiction. 2. Military occupation—Fiction. 3. War—Fiction.
4. Social classes—Fiction. 5. Soldiers— Fiction. 6. Betrayal—Fiction.] I. Title.
PZ7.S5572Ge 2007
[Fic]—dc22
2007014703

Speak ISBN 978-0-14-241346-3

Printed in the United States of America

Set in Cg Cloister   Book design by Jim Hoover

To my agent,
Ethan Ellenberg,
who loved this book
from the very beginning.

CHAPTER ONE

I t seemed like the voyage to Chiarrin would take forever. Three weeks out of Port Elise, Averie could hardly remember a time she had not lived aboard ship, sharing cramped quarters with Lady Selkirk, eating progressively less interesting meals in the captain's private dining room, and spending hours at the stern watching the water unfold. Her books and sewing projects could entertain her for only a few hours a day, and she and Lady Selkirk could exhaust their common topics of conversation before breakfast.

If she had not had Lieutenant Du'kai's companionship, she truly thought she might have gone mad.

At first, Lady Selkirk had not been sure Lieutenant Du'kai was suitable company for a gently bred young girl. Averie had watched with some amusement as her chaperone visibly weighed up his advantages and drawbacks. Against him was the fact that he was Xantish, with that characteristic brown skin and curly dark hair, and completely without ties to any of the prominent families in Xan'tai. In his favor was the fact that he was an officer in the Aeberelle army with a promising future before him.

What ultimately made Lady Selkirk welcome him into their circle, Averie thought, was the sheer unrelenting boredom of the journey. There were so few people to talk to aboard the frigate, and certainly no one who could offer entertaining conversation. Lieutenant Du'kai had been a godsend. By the second week out, neither Averie nor Lady Selkirk would think to sit down to dinner without inviting him to join them.

"You only want to take your meals with us because our food is so much better than what they serve the enlisted men," Averie said playfully one night.

The accusation made him smile. He had a particularly attractive smile, which lit his whole face and made his warm brown eyes seem even warmer. "I would gladly accept a dinner invitation from you if you were serving fried cat and desert grass," he said gallantly. His Aebrian was as fluent as hers, though he spoke with a faint accent, exotic and appealing. "It is the company, not the food, that draws me back."

Averie giggled, but Lady Selkirk nodded. "Very properly said," she approved. She was dressed tonight in a gown of dark purple; she seemed, by her bulk, to be anchoring the table to the floor. Her iron-gray hair was pulled back into a no-nonsense bun, but she had allowed herself the frivolity of earrings and a single gold necklace.

Lieutenant Du'kai, of course, was very neat in his dark blue uniform with its silver buttons. But Averie had not bothered to take much trouble with her appearance. She was wearing a thin pink cotton dress, and even that seemed heavy for the weather, which grew hotter and more humid the farther south they traveled. She had dispensed with the underdress she would have been ex-pected to wear in Port Elise. Her blonde hair hung in a careless braid over her left shoulder, long enough to brush the table. If she'd thought Lady Selkirk would have allowed it, she'd have come barefoot to the meal.

"Well, I wouldn't eat fried cat with *anyone*, even if I liked him," Averie said.

Lieutenant Du'kai smiled at her again. "Ah, if you plan to travel the world, you will have to accustom your-self to eating much worse meals."

Averie spooned mashed apples onto her plate. "Such as?" she demanded.

"Some cultures consider insects a delicacy," he said.

"To *eat*?" she exclaimed. "I don't believe you."

"I assure you, it is true. Ants and locusts and crick-ets."

Lady Selkirk looked horrified, but Averie was intrigued. "How do they taste?"

"It depends on what sauces and seasonings you use to prepare them. Crickets, I know, can be covered in chocolate and eaten as a dessert. Very crunchy."

"You've *tried* them?"

"I was in Khovstu for a year. I ate them often. Quite tasty."

"I don't want to eat crickets no matter what they're covered with," Averie said.

Lady Selkirk sniffed. She was a champion sniffer. It was the way she signaled that she considered a topic, or an outfit, or a situation, so far from genteel that it should not even be acknowledged. "This apple compote is very good," she said pointedly.

"It is," Lieutenant Du'kai agreed.

But Averie was not willing to see the subject turned. "Do you eat insects in Xan'tai?" she wanted to know.

"No, indeed, we eat many of the same foods you enjoy in Aeberelle," he replied. "There are variations, of course. We do not grow much wheat, so we make our bread with a different grain. And we grow spices that are unfamiliar to you northern folk."

"Not anymore!" Averie said. "Everyone has been using ma'het in their meat dishes lately. I like it very much."

"Much more subtle than salt," Lady Selkirk said.

Lieutenant Du'kai was smiling again. "Yes, and the Aebrians' taste for ma'het is proving to be quite a boon to the farmers in the eastern provinces of Xan'tai," he said. "It has made a handful of old families very rich."

"What else is different?" Averie wanted to know. "In Xan'tai?" They had talked very little about his home country in all these days, she suddenly realized. She had not even thought to question him about the country where he had been born.

"Oh, that is a conversation that could take days!" he said in a teasing voice.

Averie thought, *He does not want to talk about it. Or at least he does not want to talk about it with us.* Which piqued her interest even more. "No, truly, tell us something," she urged. "I know that it is much warmer there, and that you have many rivers and flatlands. But I don't know anything about the people or what they do."

He considered her briefly, and for a moment she saw something in his dark eyes that startled her—sadness, perhaps, or weariness, or resignation. It surprised her even more than his reluctance to talk. What did Lieutenant Du'kai have to be unhappy about? "Or what they eat or what they wear," he added. "There is too much to tell."

"One thing," she wheedled.

He glanced around the room, as if looking for something that would spark an idea, and his gaze rested briefly on her left hand, lifted to hold a teacup. "Your ring," he said.

She set down the cup and wiggled her hand, so the large ruby on her fourth finger sparkled in the candlelight. "It's very pretty, isn't it?" she said. "It belonged to Morgan's mother."

Lieutenant Du'kai nodded and said, "And it indicates that you and Colonel Stode are betrothed."

Averie dimpled. She still liked to hear the words said aloud. "Yes, but we have been engaged forever. I think I was eight when I decided I would marry him. He was seventeen and thought I was just a horrid little girl, but I always knew. I was probably fifteen before he began to fall in love with me, but it was a year before he proposed."

"That's hardly forever," Lieutenant Du'kai said. "You're only seventeen now."

"Eighteen!" she exclaimed. "I had my birthday right before we set sail. But what were you going to say about my ring?"

"In Xan'tai, couples do not exchange jewelry to signify that they are married or about to be," said Lieutenant Du'kai. "Nor is it as easy to tell by dress what a man's station in life is."

That made Lady Selkirk sniff again. She was a great believer in being able to determine a person's worth by his clothing and appearance. But Averie was curious.

"It's not? Then how do you find out about people?"

"They tell you!" he said with a laugh. "The first time you are introduced to someone, he will give you his whole history in a few sentences. 'I am Ket Du'kai. I am twenty-five years old. I have no wife; my parents are both still living. I have no independent fortune, but I am honorably employed as a soldier in the Aeberelle army.' And you nod, and then you give him your own history in return."

"I am Averie Winston, *eighteen* years old. My mother is dead, but my father is alive and he is the top general in the Aeberelle army," she rattled off, although Lady Selkirk turned a scandalized look upon her. One simply did not *discuss* one's attributes; one just assumed everyone knew them. "I have quite an impressive fortune, actually—"

"Averie!" Lady Selkirk hissed.

Averie continued blithely. "Although it won't be mine until I'm twenty-one. Or until my father dies, and then I'd be quite rich, but of course I'd be very sad."

"Averie Agatha Winston!" Lady Selkirk exclaimed. She was aghast.

"It's not like Lieutenant Du'kai doesn't know I'm an heiress," Averie said.

"It is cheap and vulgar to say so aloud," Lady Selkirk said in a crushing voice.

"But not to Lieutenant Du'kai," Averie reminded her.

"I was just pretending I was meeting him for the first time in Xan'tai."

Lady Selkirk turned her hard gray eyes toward the corporal. "Forgive her lapse in manners," she said. "She is something of a hoyden, despite my best efforts."

"I am not at all offended," he assured her. He spoke gravely, but Averie thought he was hiding a smile. "In fact, she has not finished telling me her status."

"What? What else should I have said?"

"You should have mentioned that you are engaged. A young man in Xan'tai who meets you for the first time will want to know if you are eligible for courting."

Averie smiled. "I am engaged to be married to Colonel Morgan Stode—now, do I tell you *his* status, too?"

"You don't have to, but it would generally be of interest to your listeners."

"He doesn't have a fortune, but he's been in the army for nearly ten years, and he's risen quite rapidly through the ranks," she said.

"His family is of the highest respectability, but there was a tragedy involving his father," Lady Selkirk broke in to explain. Obviously she couldn't stand the thought of anyone thinking Averie would marry a penniless man of no particular breeding.

"Shot himself and left behind nothing but debts," Averie explained.

"*Averie!*"

"Well, Lieutenant Du'kai doesn't care," Averie said. "I don't either. And it's not like it was Morgan's fault. He was only ten or eleven when his father died. His sisters went to be governesses," she added, "but as soon as he had enough income, he bought them a little house in the country and they didn't have to work anymore. I like them both a great deal, but they're always criticizing my behavior."

"Perhaps if you behaved better, they would have no incentive to do so," Lady Selkirk shot out. She turned her mortified face toward their guest. "You must be quite shocked this evening, Lieutenant, at Averie's irrepressible mood. I assure you, she is not always so wild."

"I'm not *wild*! I haven't done anything wrong! What have I done?"

Lieutenant Du'kai gave Lady Selkirk a little bow. He was seated across from her at the small table, still cluttered with all their plates and dishes. "Indeed, I would never find her high spirits out of place. In fact, I was about to be bold enough to ask you about your own history, for I do not know how you became Lady Averie's chaperone. I would not expect you to give me a Xantish introduction, of course! Just some details."

His gentle tone mollified her, as it always did, and Lady Selkirk responded with a smile that was almost pleased. "Oh, my own story is very ordinary. I married a fine man and had two sons. I have known the Winstons forever—my father's property runs alongside their principal estate—and General Winston's dear wife died when Averie was only ten. There was no one else to take care of this child."

"There were plenty of people," Averie said with a scowl. In fact, she hadn't noticed much of a difference in her life once her mother died, except that she had even more freedom. Her mother had been vain, beautiful, and mostly absent. Averie had been left to roam the estates pretty much on her own, which had suited her just fine.

"My husband had died a few years before," Lady Selkirk went on. "So when General Winston asked me if I would help raise Averie, I happily agreed. At first, I was installed at Weymire Estate, but lately we have spent more time in Port Elise, where I have tried to prepare Averie for the life she will lead when she is wed." She sighed. "It has not been an easy task."

Averie took her turn to sniff. "It could have been easier," she informed her chaperone. "*I* didn't care about deportment or learning how to speak Weskish! When am I ever going to go to Weskolia, anyway, since we've been at war with them forever! And Morgan wouldn't care, either, if I was not so *accomplished* in all those silly social arts."

Lady Selkirk turned that cool gaze on her. "Indeed, Colonel Stode would care a great deal," she said in a steely voice. "He is an ambitious man, and he could have a spectacular political career ahead of him once he leaves the army. He will need a wife of much charm and social skill to aid him in that career."

Averie glared down at her plate, suddenly in a bad mood, for Lady Selkirk was right. Morgan *was* ambitious. He *did* hope to have a career in government. Averie eventually would have to learn how to be a political wife.

"I cannot see that either of you has a thing to worry about," Lieutenant Du'kai said in a soothing voice. "From what I can tell, Lady Averie is both well mannered and absolutely genuine, and I would think she would win friends for Colonel Stode no matter what company they find themselves in."

Such a remark could not help but please both members of his audience, and Averie and Lady Selkirk both found themselves beaming. At that very moment, the cook's assistant squeezed into the dining room, bearing a tray of lemon tarts. Sugar was bound to improve anyone's mood, and they ended the meal quite in charity with one another. Averie was already looking forward to tomorrow night's dinner.

CHAPTER
TWO

But Averie did not have to wait for dinner to resume her conversation with Lieutenant Du'kai, for she unexpectedly encountered him the following afternoon. The hot weather had driven her out of the cramped cabin and to the upper deck, where the breeze of passage at least made the sticky heat bearable. In the weeks at sea, she had grown used to the constant rock and motion of the frigate, the incessant sounds of creaking wood and flapping sails. Now she picked her way across the deck, where sailors were busy sanding the wood and coiling ropes. None of them spoke to her. Lady Selkirk and the ship's captain had made it very clear they were to keep their distance from Lady Averie Winston.

She was delighted to find Lieutenant Du'kai standing at the stern of the ship, his hands wrapped around the railing to help him keep his balance. He moved over a little to make room for her, and she said, "I see you have found my favorite spot on this entire ship—the place where I can look backward at the land I have left behind."

"Are you so sad to be leaving Port Elise behind, then?" he asked.

She considered that. "It's not so much that I miss Port Elise," she said. "It's more that I am a little apprehensive about visiting Chiarrin. What if I don't like the food and I can't bear the heat? Morgan will be in the army a long time, and I hope to travel with him as much as I can. But what if I am sickly and ill at ease? I will be a liability then."

Lieutenant Du'kai smiled down at her. He was lean and fine-boned, only two or three inches taller than she was—a comfortable size, she thought. Morgan was well over six feet, and muscular. He tended to make Averie feel dainty, which she liked, but he also tended to overlook her sometimes, which she didn't. "Lady Selkirk's dire predictions to the contrary, I can imagine few situations in which you would be a liability to anyone," he assured her. "See how well you have withstood the ship's journey! I don't think you need to worry about how well you will take to Chiarrin, or any other place Colonel Stode is posted. You strike me as someone who possesses both physical strength and intellectual curiosity, and those are excellent characteristics for a traveler."

Lieutenant Du'kai always knew just what to say to make her feel pleased with herself, Averie reflected. She smiled. "And do you possess those characteristics, Lieutenant?" she asked. "For you have traveled very far from home as well."

He made an indeterminate gesture with one hand. "Ah, well, my reasons for leaving my home were much different from yours," he replied.

She was intrigued now. "And those reasons were?"

He glanced down at her, hesitated, and then smiled. "I was a young man who wanted to see the world," he said. "What better way than to join the Aebrian army?"

She tilted her head to one side, considering him, wondering if that was the whole truth. "I left dinner last night with a number of questions about you," she said.

He showed her a laughing face. "Truly? Then ask them."

"You called yourself Ket Du'kai. Would I call you Ket if we were friends?"

He swept her a graceful bow. "In Xan'tai, I would introduce myself as Ket Du'kai M'lesh," he said. "My father's name is Du'kai, my mother's is M'lesh, and I am known to my friends and family as Ket. My father's name is Du'kai Chorav Shotay, and my mother's is M'lesh Sovain Taz."

Averie was fascinated but confused. "So then—when we call you Lieutenant Du'kai, we are calling you by your father's name? It is not your name at all!"

"In a way it is. And I have been called Ket Du'kai for much of my life, and so the words have a familiar ring to them."

"And? If we were friends, I would call you Ket?"

"We *are* friends," he said with his usual gallantry, "but I feel certain Lady Selkirk would not want you calling me Ket any more than she would want me to use your first name freely."

Averie could not help laughing at that. He was absolutely right. Before she could answer, he spoke again. "I must say, I do not entirely understand your own naming conventions. Why are you Lady Averie, while Lady Selkirk goes by her last name?"

Averie bubbled with laughter again. "I am Lady Averie because I am a lord's unmarried daughter. If I never marry, I will be called Lady Averie forever. Once I marry Morgan, I will be Mrs. Stode, unless he is given a title, as he might be. Then he would be, say, Lord Markham and I would be Lady Markham."

"So naming depends on your age and status. As does everything in the world."

"May I ask another question?"

"Please do."

"Why didn't you want to talk to us about Xan'tai last night?"

That surprised him, she could tell, and he gazed down

at her a moment in silence. "What would you like to know? I will tell you anything you ask," he said at last.

"I don't even know enough to ask a decent question!"

"That is hardly a surprise," he said, his voice somewhat clipped, and turned his head so that he was looking out at the sea.

Averie absorbed that a moment in silence, losing her balance a little as the ship rocked heavily, as the mood of the conversation shifted from playful to tense. Lieutenant Du'kai was angry because she was ignorant about his home country? "I didn't mean to offend you," she said in a tentative voice. "I suppose I *am* something of a hoyden, as Lady Selkirk says. I am sure everyone else knows so much more about Xan'tai than I do, but I *am* interested. I would *like* you to tell me, but I don't want to vex you."

For a moment he stood beside her, rigid and facing the sea, while the constant wind of passage ruffled his dark curls. Finally, he sighed and relaxed. Shifting against the railing, he faced her again, smiling with some sadness.

"No, Lady Averie, in fact, you are about average for individuals of your rank and station. You know only that Xan'tai exists, that it supplies certain delicacies, that its people are dark-skinned, and that various Aebrians have made a fortune by going into trade there. Oh, and perhaps you know that, seventy-five years ago, Aebrian

armies invaded Xan'tai, which had been a peaceful country with no military might, and took land from landown-
ers, commerce from shopkeepers, wealth from the rich,
hope from the poor, and pride from everybody. But I see
by your face," he ended, "that you don't."

Averie felt almost as shocked and unable to breathe
as if he'd tossed her off the deck into the cold ocean.
"But—but—yes, I mean—of course I know the Aebrians invaded Xan'tai," she stammered. "But—we were—I
mean, Xan'tai was a backward country! Everyone said
so! The Aebrians brought industry and trade and—and—
a governmental system—"

"Is that what they teach the Aebrian schoolchildren?"
he asked. "That you did a good deed by coming in and
wresting away our land? That you found us desperately
in need of guidance and instruction, unable to run our
own lives until you stepped in?"

She stared at him. "Well—I can't recall precisely if
that's how it was phrased—but I—I just thought—I mean,
otherwise—"

"Otherwise, your fathers and your brothers and your
uncles and your friends who joined the army and sailed
to Xan'tai and overran our country and killed our young
men could not be justified in their actions?" he said.

Averie simply stared at him.

Lieutenant Du'kai watched her a moment in silence,
his face again unreadable, and then he turned and gazed

out at the ocean again. "Xan'tai was a placid, thriving, and beautiful land seventy-five years ago," he said in a calmer voice. "Xan'tai used to trade its produce with countries around the world. Xantish sailors were the first to find Khovstu, the first to sign a treaty with Larall. We even traded with the Aebrians when they first sailed into our harbor."

He glanced down at her, then looked back out at the ocean. "We were in no need of schooling from the Aebrian empire. The Aebrians invaded because they wanted what was ours, and for no other reason. That is the reason men the world over take up arms to dominate another race. Because they want to, and because they can."

Averie felt sick to her stomach—because he was saying it, because he was so angry, and because she somehow knew it all to be true. It had never occurred to her to question the fact that Aeberelle had armies in place all over the world, in countries with unpronounceable names. She had heard tales of skirmishes won and had grieved over lives lost. She had flirted with more than her share of soldiers in the last two years. But she had never thought to question why they had gone to battle.

Lieutenant Du'kai glanced down at her again, his expression softer. "Why am I so passionate on this topic, you might wonder, since I was born fifty years after the occupation began?" he said. "I have never known anything but Aebrian rule—nor has my father—though my grandmother used to tell stories about the life she led before the ships began unloading Aebrian soldiers. And, I must confess, life under Aebrian occupation has not been all bad. Our transportation systems were rudimentary until the Aebrians came along, and we now have excellent roads and rail systems. We learned a great deal about medicine from your doctors. We learned more about trade from your businessmen. Once the fighting ended, we did not suffer so much.

"But do you understand what I am telling you, Lady Averie? This was not the course we chose. We had our own destiny, and we were content to follow it. Even today, there are factions who argue for home rule and who will not rest until the Aebrians are banished from our country. I am not so sure I think they are wrong."

"But you," she said softly. "If you hate Aeberelle so much, what are you doing—wearing an Aebrian uniform and fighting under an Aebrian flag?"

For a moment his face showed that same sad expression she had seen last night and not known how to interpret. "That is a most excellent question," he replied. "And sometimes I hate myself for the uniform on my back."

She exclaimed aloud at that, and he shook his head and went on. "A young man in Xan'tai today does not have many options. He can become a laborer at one of the ma'het farms. He can go into civil service, helping our Aebrian overseers run the country. If his family has money and is active in trade, he can work with his father to try and earn his fortune. He can be a sailor. Or he can go into the army." He glanced at her fleetingly again. "An officer earns a good salary, he is respectable, and he travels around the empire. No Xantish man can rise above the rank of captain, of course, but a Xantish soldier who has served in the Aebrian army has some status. Like Colonel Stode, I have political ambitions. And the army is a good place to foster them."

Averie's head was spinning, but she was determined to keep asking questions as long as he would answer them. "What ambitions?" she asked.

"Impossible ones," he said.

"What ambitions?" she repeated.

He gave a half shrug and turned his face back into the wind. "I would join those who fight for home rule, but I would do it from within the government organized by the Aebrians," he said. "I would work to pass laws restricting Aebrian influence. I would try for peaceful and civil means to dislodge Aeberelle, since violence has not worked. There are coalitions in place even now, working toward that end. I would join them."

"Why wait?" Averie demanded. "Why not go back to Xan'tai now?"

"Such a course takes money and connections," he

said. "I have neither. After a career in the Aebrian army, I will have some of both."

Averie was silent for a few moments, brooding. She leaned on the railing and watched the ocean falling back behind them, its calm surface broken only momentarily by the turmoil of their passage. "So if you feel so strongly about how your own country has been treated, how can you go off to Chiarrin and take away somebody else's land?"

"Yes, that thought is oppressing my spirits a great deal," he admitted. "When I joined the army, I did not expect to be part of a conquering force."

"What did you expect, then?"

He put his elbows on the railing. "I thought to be sent to Khovstu or Larall, where the army merely guards Aeberelle's commercial ventures. I didn't think to be going to a foreign land as the Aebrian army tore it apart."

She turned on him. "That's not fair! That's not what they're doing!"

He shrugged. "You are going to Chiarrin. You will see for yourself."

"Well, I will."

He looked down at her a moment, and she watched his face, trying to read his expression. Strange, until yesterday, she had always found Lieutenant Du'kai open and easy to understand. Today she had realized she probably didn't know the man at all, and the thought was very troubling. Whom else had she misunderstood, thought-lessly accepting their outward faces as their true ones?

"Now you hate me," he said.

She hunched a shoulder. "I don't."

"A little bit, you do. And you are angry with me."

"Not angry," she said. "Confused."

"Perhaps this night I should not join you and Lady Selkirk at dinner."

Even worse! First he was making her question all her comfortable notions of life; now he was abandoning her to the dreary company of Lady Selkirk. "You must do what seems right to you," she said stiffly.

He nodded and gave her a respectful bow. "I am glad we talked this afternoon, Lady Averie, even if you are not," he said. Before she could decide how to answer that, he spun smartly on his heel and strode away.

She looked after him a moment, resentful and unhappy, and then she turned back to watch the ocean again. She stood so long at the railing that her face grew quite flushed with the heat, and the salt air left her hair in untamable knots. Lady Selkirk exclaimed aloud when Averie returned to their cabin and spent the next half hour berating her. Averie tried to keep her expression contrite even though her heart was rebellious.

The lecture continued over dinner and expanded to cover the sorts of clothing Averie would be expected to wear, even in the Chiarrin heat, and the standards of behavior she would be expected to uphold, even in a savage land. Lady Selkirk could scold to her heart's content. Lieutenant Du'kai was not there to offer a change of topic.

But he joined them for dinner the following night, and everything seemed fine again. Averie had spent the intervening hours thinking very hard about what he'd said, and she'd come to the conclusion that she didn't understand the world very well. Invading another country and appropriating its lands sounded bad, but perhaps Lieutenant Du'kai didn't have all the information. He did not understand why it had been so important, why it had been *right,* that Aeberelle annex Chiarrin. Averie would ask Morgan, once they were there, and he would explain it all.

Having reached this cheerful conclusion, Averie was able to greet the lieutenant with her usual good humor. He sent her one quick look, but seemed reassured at her welcoming smile. Reassured and . . . disappointed?

"Lieutenant! I am so glad you were able to join us!" Lady Selkirk welcomed him. "Have you concluded the duties that kept you away from us last night?"

"Indeed I have," he said, taking his seat. "Tell me I did not miss anything too grand last night! In the common mess, we consumed a stew made of unidentifiable meat and some potatoes that must have been left over from this ship's *last* journey."

"No, our fare was quite ordinary," Lady Selkirk replied. "I believe we had some of the same potatoes. We will hope for better this evening."

Later, Averie was not able to remember what they ate, although it tasted fine to her. She just remembered how glad she was to have Lieutenant Du'kai back at the table with them, back in charity with her. They talked with great enthusiasm about their usual subjects—the journey, the heat, the people and places they knew back in Port Elise—before Lady Selkirk introduced a new topic late in the meal.

"I know very little about Chiarrin except that it will be blazingly hot," she said to the lieutenant. "You were there for a few months last year. What kind of place is it?"

"Hot and dry in the North, hot and humid in the South, where you will be," Lieutenant Du'kai confirmed. "The dividing line seems to be the Maekath Mountains, which are about a hundred miles north of the coastline."

"I understand that we will be staying in some sort of city, though most of the land is uncivilized," Lady Selkirk said.

"Chiarrin is not a tidy collection of cities and villages like Aeberelle is," he acknowledged. "And the city of Chesza is nothing like Port Elise, except that it, too, is a natural harbor. Unfortunately, the city has no nearby sources of fresh water, so for years Chesza stayed fairly small. Fifty or sixty years ago, the Chiarrizi built a system of aqueducts that carry water into the city from rivers many miles away. And as a consequence, the city has grown to about thirty thousand souls today."

"Tell us more about these aqueducts," Averie demanded.

He smiled. "They flow in from the northern quadrants of the city and pour into Mualota Fountain in the middle of Chesza. You can see people at the fountain at any time of the day, drawing water. I understand that an underground pipe takes the overflow water to wells and cisterns in various parts of the city."

Lady Selkirk was appalled. "Are you telling us that this fountain is the only place in the whole city to get water? Will be we sending our servants out every day to bring back enough water for drinking and cooking and bathing? How dreadful!"

Lieutenant Du'kai was grinning. "Indeed, some of the more prominent residents of Chesza felt exactly as you do, Lady Selkirk," he admitted. "Many years ago, the—the—perhaps you would call him mayor of the city—he arranged to have water diverted from the aqueduct to his own home. A few of the wealthier families followed suit. I do not know which house has been appropriated for your use by General Winston, but I am fairly confident that it will have this amenity, at least."

"Thank goodness," Lady Selkirk said.

Averie was troubled by his phrase *which house has been appropriated for your use.* He did not seem to notice her disquiet and continued with his travelogue. "The land outside the city is somewhat sparsely populated and does not have much industry," he said. "In some areas, the land is fertile enough to allow farming. In other areas, they raise hodee, which are much like goats. The Soldath Mountains in the Northeast produce emeralds. If you see a woman in Port Elise wearing an emerald necklace, the chances are good that the jewels were mined in Chiarrin. The Weskish are particularly fond of Chiarrizi emeralds and trade for them often."

"So we might find a few Weskish traders in Chesza?" Averie asked.

"Probably not now, with the Aebrian army in place," Lieutenant Du'kai answered. "But in the past, Weskolia had quite a presence there. In fact, the Weskish have their own name for Chesza—they call it 'City of Broken Gods.' I don't know why," he added. "No doubt there is a colorful tale about their deities."

Lady Selkirk sniffed. Proper Aebrians believed in the superiority of Aeberelle and the infallibility of the Aebrian government, and didn't have much time or use for capricious gods. Lady Selkirk was far more interested in human than divine interaction. "Tell me, Lieutenant!" she said. "Is there any society to be had? General

Winston led me to believe that a few of his senior officers had had their wives installed in Chiarrin. Do you know who is in residence?"

Averie gave her an indignant look, for who wanted to travel hundreds of miles from Aeberelle, only to be stuck drinking tea with the same boring people one had left behind? But Lieutenant Du'kai had already begun rattling off the names of some of the other women who had set up household in Chesza, and Lady Selkirk was nodding with satisfaction. Averie scowled down at her dirty dishes and thought life in Chiarrin would probably be just as dull as life in Port Elise.

CHAPTER
THREE

Three days later they sailed into Chesza Harbor. Averie was standing at the prow, gazing in fascination at the land drawing slowly closer. How warm and bright it looked, a sprawling mix of browns and tans and reds and dusty greens, so unlike Aeberelle, with its chilly shades of gray and blue. The port was a welter of boats, and behind it the city fanned out in a haphazard and inviting fashion. The buildings were all low to the ground and seemed to be constructed of a uniform reddish-brown material, while the roofs were copper and slate and verdigris. Even from shipboard, Averie could see the great white plume of the Mualota Fountain that Lieutenant Du'kai had described. It was the only thing in this entire vista that looked cool. Heat lay over the city like a sweltering fog, saturating the air, the buildings, clothing, hair, skin. Averie stood very still, breathing in the heavy air, feeling her palms start to perspire as she held tightly to the railing.

She was as far from home as she was ever likely to be, and it felt wonderful and terrifying at the same time.

It seemed to take forever before the ship docked, the gangplank dropped, and sailors began hauling their belongings from the cabin. Lady Selkirk insisted on watching as every box and crate was lifted out, issuing stern orders to the men, but Averie hurried down the swaying walkway. Almost immediately she spotted Sieffel, the burly ex-soldier who traveled with her father on every campaign. He and his wife, Grace, lived at the Port Elise house whenever her father was stationed in Aeberelle.

"Lady Averie," he greeted her. "I am glad to see you have safely arrived."

"Hello, Sieffel, it is good to see you!" she replied. "But where is everybody? My father? Morgan?"

"There was an incident this morning, and they both left early," he replied. "They said they would be back by dinnertime."

Morgan had been billeted in the same house as her father, which Averie thought was delightful. To be able to see him every day! It might be a tiny foretaste of what it would be like to live together when they were married. "Where is our house?" she asked, trying to see past the bustle of the harbor to the heart of the city. "Is it nice?"

"About two miles away. It is very nice indeed, though quite different from Weymire Estate or your home in Port Elise."

At that moment, Lady Selkirk came puffing up from below deck. She took one look at the swaying gangplank, said "Heavens," and then resolutely made her way down to shore. By the time she joined Averie and Sieffel, her face was gleaming with perspiration and she looked quite cross.

"If a single item we brought with us arrives intact, I shall be very much surprised," she said. "Sieffel! Take us instantly to the place we have been assigned. I cannot bear this wretched heat a moment longer."

Of course, they had to endure the heat for another forty-five minutes while they made a slow journey in an open wagon from the harbor to their new residence. Lady Selkirk complained bitterly the whole time, but Averie just stared around her with interest. The way was lined with more of those lovely buildings, which appeared to be made of a reddish mud smoothed over a framework of wood. The streets were crowded with people on foot and a few riders on horseback. Overhead, seabirds flew in lazy loops, calling to each other in mournful voices. No matter which direction they traveled, Averie could always see the great geyser of Mualota Fountain, shooting its white foam column into the air, reassuring the entire city that fresh water was only a few steps away.

They were a good half mile from the harbor when Averie realized that she had left the ship without saying farewell to Lieutenant Du'kai.

Sieffel called their new home "the governor's house," though Averie found herself wondering if "governor" was just a catchall Aebrian word to describe a high-ranking civil servant in Chesza. The building was long, lovely, and luxurious, a six-sided structure built around a central courtyard. Even Lady Selkirk liked it. Two wings comprised large bedrooms, airy but sparsely furnished. Another wing, apparently the primary common space of the house, was simply one open room crammed with furniture and shelves and potted plants. The kitchen wing was to its right, but they only peeked in and scented the air for its unfamiliar spices. The last two wings were areas that they probably never would have cause to visit—living quarters for hired laborers and a large area for storage.

Still, what they had been privileged to see was charming. The ceilings were low and the spaces were all rather dark, but the mudlike building material did something to absorb the heat, for it was wonderfully cool inside. All the windows facing out toward the city were covered with gauzy curtains to baffle the sun but allow air inside; the windows facing the courtyard were wide open and admitted a warm but pleasant breeze. And the courtyard! Most of the ground was covered by a colorful mosaic of smooth stones, though a circle of thin trees threw an umbrella of shade over the outer perimeter. At the center of the mosaic was a small fountain, a single jet of water falling with a musical clatter back into a scalloped basin. In a city that relied entirely on water imported over a great distance, such a fountain must represent the ultimate in wealth and extravagance, Averie knew. But she loved it instantly for its beauty and its uselessness.

"Can we go out and sit by the fountain?" she asked Sieffel. "Can I drink from it?"

He nodded. "Of course. It's the same water that is piped into the house."

Lady Selkirk sniffed. "Well, of course, none of this is exactly what we're used to, but it's much more endurable than I had dared to hope," she pronounced. "Come, Averie! Let us get settled in our rooms and wash off our travel grime. Then, Sieffel, may we have a light meal before dinner? You would not believe the rations we were served aboard ship. Those last few meals were very grim."

"Just come to the *maroya* when you're ready to eat," Sieffel said.

"The what?" Averie repeated, already liking the sound of the word.

"The *maroya*." He gestured at the long open room filled with so much furniture, though Averie didn't see a dining table. "This is where the general takes his meals."

"Then we will certainly eat here as well," Lady Selkirk said. "Come! Take us to our chambers, and we will rejoin you as soon as we can."

Averie's room looked out over the courtyard, so she was able to listen to the inviting melody of falling water as she surveyed the room. The bed was not as wide as her four-poster back at Weymire Estate, but the mattress looked plump and comfortable. A long, narrow mirror was set directly into the wall, edged with squares of red and blue tile; three straight-backed chairs were grouped beside a small table. One corner of the room held a tall, boxlike piece of wooden furniture that opened to reveal a row of deep shelves. Perhaps this was where she was supposed to store her clothes. She didn't see anything else that resembled a chest of drawers.

A door was set into one wall and she opened it, expecting a closet. Instead she found a small space entirely covered in red and blue octagonal tiles. Spigots protruded from the wall and one corner of the ceiling; a decorative drain was set in the middle of the floor. Averie began experimenting with the various knobs on the wall, and water gushed out from the overhead faucet. She clapped her hands together in delight at the thought of washing up in such a novel fashion.

She stepped out of the bathing room and impatiently

sorted through her bundles until she found a pale blue dress, lightweight and sleeveless. It was actually designed to be worn under a heavier outer garment. "But not in this heat," Averie muttered. "This will be just perfect for Chiarrin."

She quickly washed off in the marvelous bathing room, threw on the dress, and braided her wet hair. Slipping on a pair of shoes, she hurried out down the central corridor to the *maroya*. Sieffel and his wife were already there. Averie hugged Grace, who was thin and small and utterly imperturbable.

"So are just the two of you running the household, or have you hired some local help?" Averie asked after Grace had inquired about her trip.

"Just us day to day, though we'd like to hire Chiarrizi girls to help with laundry and cleaning," Grace replied. "Colonel Stode thinks you'll want to engage a personal maid."

"Oh, goodness, no, I'd rather *not* have a maid, if you want to know the truth," Averie said. How much easier to dress as she liked if no one was watching after her! She settled herself in a tall chair and asked, "When can I see the city?"

Sieffel shook his head. "That's for the general and Colonel Stode to decide."

Before she could ask any more questions, Lady Selkirk sailed into the room. She had not made much concession to the heat, for she was wearing her usual layered clothing and long sleeves. Her face was a little flushed, and her hair looked nowhere near as damp as Averie's. Possibly she hadn't bothered stepping naked under the water spigot.

"Is there food?" the chaperone asked pointedly as she climbed somewhat awkwardly into one of the tall chairs.

"Yes, my lady," Grace replied.

It was quite fun to learn how people ate in Chiarrin, Averie thought. Sieffel reached into a cache against the wall, pulled out two folded tables, and opened them up before Averie and Lady Selkirk. Grace brought in small trays and set food on each table. Averie's plate was filled with various kinds of produce and some dark brown bread.

"What's this?" Averie asked, taking a tentative bite of bulbous purple fruit. It was so juicy that liquid ran down her chin, so sweet that she closed her eyes in pleasure.

"It's a wikberry," Grace explained. "It's native to Chiarrin."

Lady Selkirk was looking at her own plate with a certain skepticism. "Are you sure this is safe for us to eat?"

"The general and Colonel Stode are very fond of wikberries," Grace replied.

Averie had already finished hers and was on to the

next item. This was a squat yellow plant that looked like a gourd but was much softer to the touch. "And this one?"

"A bumain," Grace replied. "It's very much favored by the people of Chesza, but the Aebrian officers and their wives do not like it so well. You peel it before you eat it, my lady," she added, as Averie was preparing to take a big bite.

So Averie folded back the thick skin and took her first taste of bumain. It was not nearly as sweet as the wikberry, and far chewier. "It tastes like something that would be good for you," she said, her mouth full. "Like potatoes, maybe."

Grace smiled. "Someone told me this is the first solid food that young mothers feed their babies," she said. "So it probably *is* good for you."

"It might be better if it was cooked in something else," Averie decided. "Something with some flavor."

"The bread is decent," Lady Selkirk announced, for she'd started with the most familiar item on her plate. "I would like some butter, though."

"We have native butter," Grace said apologetically. "Made from hodee milk."

Lady Selkirk shuddered. "Heavens, no. Jam, then."

"Wikberry jam?"

Lady Selkirk sighed. "Is there *nothing* here that reminds us of civilization?" she asked plaintively. It was clearly a rhetorical question; no one answered.

Averie finished all her produce before sampling the bread, which was mealier than the bread back in Aeberelle but very tasty even so. "That was very good," she complimented Grace. "And you made it all yourself, I suppose. You haven't even hired a Chiarrizi cook yet?"

"No, my lady. We have not found natives who wish to work in this house."

"But why not? I know my father pays excellent wages."

"Not too fond of the Aebrian army," Sieffel said. "All of the officers' wives are having difficulties finding local help."

Averie felt another flutter of disquiet. It made sense, of course. *She* would not want to be cooking and cleaning for anyone who came marching through Port Elise, no matter how much money was offered.

Lady Selkirk laid down her fork. "They'll come around soon enough when they see the best jobs are to be had in Aebrian households," she said. "Averie, you should rest for an hour before your father and your fiancé return home." She eyed Averie's outfit with disfavor. "And you might see about finding more appropriate clothing."

"I'm not tired," Averie said. "And I like this dress. You may lie down if you like. I'm going to sit outside."

And before anyone could tell her why she shouldn't, Averie slipped out of her chair and hurried through a doorway that led from the *maroya* into the courtyard. It was much warmer outside than it was inside, but once she had settled onto a shaded bench, she realized that she did not particularly mind the heat. The dance of spray in the fountain made a cool and restful sound. She found her eyes closing and her thoughts starting to scatter, and eventually she drifted off to sleep.

When she woke, she was covered in perspiration and momentarily disoriented. Where was this hot and green place? Why could she hear the sound of falling water? She sat up and shook her head, slowly realizing that she was in a courtyard garden of her new home in Chesza. A rumble of noises from behind her must have been what woke her—footsteps, male voices, the high, excited sound of a woman's laugh.

Her father and Morgan must be home! And Lady Selkirk was awake.

Averie jumped up and ran into the house to find the others gathered in the *maroya*. "Father! Morgan! I'm so glad to see you!" she exclaimed and flung herself right at Morgan. He caught her up in a hard hug, laughing. She felt the buttons of his navy jacket press into her chest.

"Look at you! Gone native already!" he replied, kissing her cheek. He set her on her feet but kept his arm around her shoulders, and she took a moment to bury her face against his chest. Morgan was so tall and so reassuringly solid. She just liked to stand next to him and feel beloved and safe.

"I requested that she wear more suitable attire, but

she has made the heat an excuse for extremely lax behavior. And we have only just arrived," Lady Selkirk said in a pettish voice.

"The men complain of the weather, too, and we have allowed them to modify their uniforms," her father said. "Officers must keep to certain standards, of course."

Averie shook herself free and smiled up at Morgan. He smiled back. His wide, full face was tanned from the Chiarrin sun; his sandy hair had been baked several shades lighter. But his dark blue eyes were just the same, and his smile had not changed at all. "I have missed you so much," she said. "It's been four months since you left!"

He captured her hand, kissed it, and let it fall. "I'm sure I have missed you more."

"I understand you made the trip with no trouble," her father remarked, and Averie turned to give him a less effusive hug. She loved her father, of course, he just didn't have much time for or interest in displays of affection.

"By the end, we were both bored, but otherwise it was an easy journey," she said. "I've had coach rides from Port Elise to Weymire Estate where more things went wrong."

"Well, we're very glad to have you here," he said.

"When can I see the city? Is it safe for me to go out alone? Or can Morgan come with me someday soon?"

"It's certainly not safe for you to wander about on

your own," Morgan said. "But I don't know how quickly I will have a day free to squire you around."

Sieffel entered the *maroya* just then and unfolded four small tables. Grace was right behind him with trays of food. Averie climbed into one of the tall chairs and studied her plate while the others settled into place. The main dish tonight appeared to be some kind of steak, covered in brown sauce and offering a wonderful aroma.

"I cannot imagine what that might be," Lady Selkirk said uneasily.

Averie's father glanced down incuriously. "Hodee, probably. Tastes a little like beef. The animals actually look more like goats. You find them everywhere in Chiarrin."

"I wonder if I shall like it," Lady Selkirk answered in a hollow voice.

"I have come to like hodee almost any way it is prepared," Morgan said with a laugh. "You have to. It is almost the only meat available in this part of the world. Well, there's fish, of course, though the Chiarrizi don't eat it as much as we do."

"Fish," Lady Selkirk said hopefully. "Perhaps we could have that tomorrow?"

Grace brought in the rest of their platters, and Averie instantly tried the hodee. She didn't think it tasted at all like beef, but she liked it. It had a smooth texture and a strong, salty flavor. "I think it's delicious," she said.

Lady Selkirk gave her a brooding look. "You would say that even if you didn't, just because you are so determined to like Chiarrin."

Averie laughed. "And is that so bad?"

Morgan smiled at her. "Averie is willing to be enthusiastic about everything. That is one of the things I love about her."

"And it is one of the things that will make you want to throttle her when you cannot get her to drop some subject in which you have absolutely no interest," her father said with humor.

Morgan toasted her with his water glass. "An officer's wife needs energy, endurance, and curiosity, and Averie has plenty of all three," he said.

For a moment, Averie felt her smile waver. Lieutenant Du'kai had said much the same thing. She must be the easiest person in the world to read. She shook off the thought and toasted Morgan in return. "And I intend to be the best officer's wife ever," she said.

Lady Selkirk pushed her food around. "I don't understand why we can't have a proper dining room table," she said. "I feel like this tray will tip over at any moment."

"I believe these individual tables are traditional," Averie's father replied. "Most Chiarrizi live in very small houses and they don't have room for much permanent furniture. So they stack the chairs against the wall and fold the tables away till mealtime."

"They must not do much entertaining," Lady Selkirk said. "Think how inefficient to have to set up tables for fifty or a hundred guests!"

"As to that, I don't know that the Chiarrizi ever arrange dinner parties such as we do back in Port Elise," Averie's father replied. "They tend to hold outdoor evening events. No need for tables then, either."

Lady Selkirk merely sniffed.

"So?" Averie said insistently. "When can I see the city?"

Morgan and her father exchanged glances. "I suppose if she just stays in the western part of town," Morgan said, "Sieffel can go with her. She'd enjoy the market."

"A market? Can I buy things?" she demanded. "But how will I— Heavens! I don't suppose any of them speak Aebrian, do they? How will I talk to them?"

"Most Chiarrizi are fluent in Weskish," her father said.

"They probably know it better than Averie, who rarely paid attention at her lessons," Lady Selkirk said.

"I think I speak it quite well," Averie said, switching to Weskish, though Lady Selkirk immediately criticized her accent. "So when can I go? Tomorrow?"

Her father answered in Aebrian. "If you like. There really should be little risk if you're about in the middle of the day."

"Why should there be any risk at all?" Lady Selkirk asked anxiously.

"I thought it was perfectly safe in Chesza!" Averie exclaimed.

"It was safe, or so we thought until a few days ago," Morgan said soberly. "There have been . . . incidents. Unrest among the locals, particularly in the eastern quadrant. Nothing too serious, and of course we've tightened security."

"Don't know how they got their hands on the gunpowder," her father said.

"Gunpowder!" Lady Selkirk exclaimed. "In the hands of Chiarizzi soldiers!"

Morgan laughed. "Well, you can hardly call them soldiers," he said. "They have no notion of warfare and rather unsophisticated weaponry. But they have proved surprisingly fierce in the northern parts. We have not secured any land north of the Maekath Mountains, and in recent weeks there have been incursions into southern territory we thought we held."

"This is most distressing," Lady Selkirk said. "Perhaps Averie and I should return home on the next ship."

"Nonsense," General Winston said. "Chesza is completely fortified, and the southerners have not been eager to fight. It is just a handful of rebels who are giving us trouble, but we'll have taken care of them before the winter rains."

Averie felt most peculiar listening to talk of war and occupation. She kept remembering Lieutenant Du'kai's bitterness at the presence of Aebrian soldiers in Xan'tai. Clearly the Chiarrizi didn't like Aebrian troops any more than the Xantish did.

So why were they here in Chesza? It was hard to phrase the question just right.

"I know so little about Chiarrin," Averie said tentatively. "Why did we decide—why did Aeberelle decide—to take it over?"

Her father looked briefly pleased that she was interested. "Strategic positioning, mostly," he said. "Best port between here and the southern continents, so it's the perfect place to establish trading houses and provide docking for warships."

"And Weskolia has been eyeing it for years," Morgan added. "The Weskish began trading with the Chiarrizi at least a decade ago. We don't want them to gain a foothold in this corner of the world. It's important that we establish ourselves here first."

Averie wrinkled her forehead. "But did the Chiarrizi want us to come here?"

The men laughed. "I suppose not," Morgan said. "But in a few years they'll be hoping we never leave."

"Turn their economy right around," her father said. "Open up Chesza to trade with Khovstu and the southern continents. In five years, Chesza will be the second busiest port in the world, after Port Elise. You mark my words."

"What do they have to sell?" Lady Selkirk asked.

But Averie remembered Lieutenant Du'kai's conversation. "Emeralds."

Morgan nodded. "That's right. And some woods that are exceptionally fine. Bumain, too, unless I miss my guess. It travels well, and it's very hearty."

"But I suppose they could have exported bumain even if the Aebrian army hadn't landed in port," Averie said. "I just keep thinking—if some of the natives are still fighting the army—well, they really must not want us here."

Averie's father shrugged. "That's progress," he said. "A lot of people don't like it until they've progressed."

Averie thought about saying that her father might not like it if a foreign army *progressed* over Port Elise, but she didn't want to annoy him, not on her very first night. And she didn't want him to rescind permission for her to see the market in the morning. She was sure it would be very exciting.

After dinner, Lady Selkirk retired to her room, the men discussed army business, and Averie returned to the courtyard. She gave Morgan a meaningful glance as she slipped out the door, and he nodded. He would join her as soon as he was free.

While she waited, Averie perched on the thin edge of the stone fountain, trailing her fingers in the water. The sun had only been down about an hour and the water was still warm. When she cupped her hand and sipped from the basin, she thought the water tasted of stone and moss. She drank again.

The door opened and shut, and Morgan's bulky shadow moved through the darkness. "Averie? Are you still out here?"

She came to her feet and ran to him, flinging herself against his body with some force. He caught her close and kissed her hungrily, with much more passion than he had shown in the *maroya* while her father watched. *This* was what she had missed, these long four months of their separation. The feel of his heavy mouth on hers, his strong arms around her back. If Lady Selkirk knew how many kisses they had stolen after dinner parties and in back stairwells at her father's house—!

"Oh, Morgan, I have missed you so much!" she whispered. "Let us be married right here in Chesza. Then my father can't send me back no matter what happens."

He laughed, briefly hugged her so tightly that she could not breathe, and relaxed his hold. "You don't want to be married in such a slipshod way," he said, drawing her over to a bench. They both sat, and she nestled against him. "You want to have a grand wedding in Port Elise."

"No, I don't," she said. "That's what Lady Selkirk wants. If I had my way, I'd have a little ceremony at

Weymire Estate with only the servants present."

He peered at her in the dark. "Really? I admit, I've always liked the idea of standing in some grand hall in full-dress uniform with half a dozen retired generals in attendance. But I'll get married at Weymire Estate if that's what you want."

"What I *want* is to not have to wait much longer," she said. "Think how romantic to be married in a foreign country!"

He laughed, but there was the slightest edge of irritation in the sound. "Think how impossible it is to find a clerk who can perform the ceremony."

She leaned in to kiss his cheek. "We could be married as the Chiarrizi are," she suggested. "What are their ceremonies like, do you suppose?"

"I don't know, but I imagine the festivities involve hodee and bumain," Morgan said. "Wouldn't you rather have beef and proper Aebrian vegetables?"

She was half teasing, but he was half serious. She had never realized Morgan was so conventional. She sighed and resettled herself against him. "Very well, then, we'll wait," she said. "But how long will you be stationed in Chiarrin? A year? Eighteen months? That seems like a very long time."

He kissed her again quickly. "Yes, but you will be here at least some of that time," he pointed out. "So the waiting will not be as hard."

"Maybe I won't go home in six months after all. I'll stay until you're sent home, and I'll sail back with the army," she said.

"That would be even better."

They sat on the bench another thirty minutes and talked with the ease of long friendship. Averie told him about the journey, making him laugh when she recounted particularly agonizing moments with Lady Selkirk, and he described adventures he had had in Chiarrin. She was disappointed when he said it was time to go in.

"Not so soon! We've scarcely had ten minutes together!" she protested.

"Half an hour at least, and you've been yawning that whole time," he said firmly, standing up and drawing her to her feet. "We will have plenty of time to sit in the moonlight and talk, I promise you. But for now we both need sleep."

"Kiss me again, then," she said, and tilted her face up. He complied with gratifying thoroughness, and then they walked to the door hand in hand. He escorted her through the hallways and paused outside her door to kiss her once more.

"Good night, sweet girl," he whispered in her ear. "I am so very glad you are here."

CHAPTER
FOUR

Averie and Lady Selkirk were still at breakfast when Grace announced guests.

"Visitors? We don't even know anyone here!" Averie said.

Lady Selkirk was nodding with satisfaction. "Excellent. I was hoping some of the other officers' families would introduce themselves right away."

"But I want to go to the market!" Averie wailed. "Father promised."

"You can go to the market any day. This morning you will meet Lady Beulah Worth and her daughter Lana. And you will try to look like that—that—*garment* you are wearing is the height of fashion instead of an embarrassingly inappropriate outfit that you might have put on for no other purpose than to shame me in front of strangers."

That made Averie laugh, which somewhat restored her good humor. Today she had on another of the light-weight sleeveless underdresses, this one a pale green fig-ured with tiny white flowers.

And it turned out that Lady Worth and her daugh-ter, who had been living here nearly a month, had already made some modifications to their wardrobes. Lana was wearing a gown very similar to Averie's, and Lady Worth's more proper triple layers of clothing were so lightweight that at least two were completely transparent.

"Oh, I like you already!" Lana said, the instant she had a chance to survey Averie's outfit. Lana was a small and vivacious girl with masses of black ringlets and spar-kling blue eyes. "It was two weeks before my mother would permit me to dress more sensibly, but I see you have wasted no time."

"I resisted as long as I could, but the heat is really quite unbearable if you don't make allowances for it," Lady Worth remarked. She was taller than her daughter and with similar but less dramatic coloring. Her open, cheerful face looked as if it had been weathered by expo-sure to many unfriendly climates. Averie supposed she had often joined her husband on his military travels.

"Yes, but I will quickly run out of things to wear," Averie said.

"You can buy cloth in the marketplace—the most beautiful fabric," Lana said. "And we have found a seamstress who has made a number of simple dresses for me. This is one of them—do you like it?"

"I do! I noticed it as soon as you walked in."

That quickly, the girls were involved in their own discussion, while the older women sat together on the tall seats and began to gossip in low voices. They were all gathered in the *maroya*, but soon Averie suggested that she and Lana move to the courtyard. It was hotter outside than in, so they stayed close to the house, where there was still a little shade. Averie asked, "So what is it like here in Chesza?"

Lana made a face. Her features were small and delicate, and she had the faintest dusting of freckles across her nose. "Sometimes it's quite boring, but I never say so," she said. "Otherwise, my father will never allow me to join him on any campaign again! There isn't much to do, really. There are only a handful of other Aebrian women here, and many of them are married, so I've made hardly any friends."

"Do you see much of the officers?"

"Only if someone is entertaining, and that's happened just three times since I've been here," Lana said, sounding a little aggrieved. "And only one time did anyone think to offer dancing! *That* was fun, since there were so many more men than women."

"How many other Aebrians are here?" Averie asked.

It turned out that ten officers had installed their

families in Chesza, bringing with them an assortment of wives, sisters, daughters, and sons. Not a large group to choose from, Averie thought. "So tell me about the men," she prompted.

In a military family, that meant the young unmarried captains and lieutenants, who were practically adopted by the wives of the commanding officers. Lana dimpled. "Oh, I guess there are about twenty of them," she said, "and Colonel Stode is the favorite, but everyone knows he belongs to you! Carrie Dryser—I can't imagine you'll like her any better than I do—she threw a fit when she learned he was betrothed. He's so handsome!"

"I've always thought so."

"Of the others—everyone likes Captain Martin and Captain Gaele. I have become friendly with Lieutenant Lansdale, but he's hopeless, of course. He has *no* family, and I can't imagine he'll get promoted much past major, even if he's in the army for life."

"Do you know Lieutenant Du'kai?" Averie asked in what she hoped was a casual voice. Though why she wouldn't sound casual she had no idea. She'd scarcely thought of the man since she left him behind on the ship. "He accompanied us from Port Elise, and Lady Selkirk became rather attached to him."

"Ket Du'kai!" Lana exclaimed. "I knew him in Port Elise. That hair! Those eyes! He's even more hopeless than Lieutenant Lansdale, of course, but the most fascinating man. I was so glad when I learned he would be stationed in Chesza."

For a moment, Averie didn't like Lana quite so well. She seemed shallow and forward—and was she actually upon good enough terms with Lieutenant Du'kai that she would call him by his proper name? "Yes, I enjoyed our conversations on the trip here," Averie replied in a somewhat cooler voice.

But Lana was already thinking about someone else. "Now, if you weren't to marry Colonel Stode, you might be interested in meeting Captain Hawksley," she said. "He seems so quiet, and Carrie Dryser is actually rude to him because she thinks he's dull, but I sense a great deal of intensity to him. At any rate, I like him better than old Major Morrier, who really *is* a dead bore."

They talked this way for another few minutes, and Averie found herself liking Lana again. "I wonder if I can persuade my father that we need to host a dinner right away," she said. "Maybe Lady Selkirk will support me. She loves to entertain."

"You should hold a *weekly* dinner party that the officers are required to attend."

Averie giggled. "Then I will certainly need new clothes. I was hoping to get to the market today, but . . ." She gestured instead of finishing her sentence. It was discourteous to say *but then you and your mother arrived*.

Lana squealed and stood up. "Come with us! We were

planning to go once we left your house. It will be so much fun. I can show you everything."

Averie jumped to her feet. "Oh yes, let's go!"

At first Lady Selkirk hesitated, then she insisted Sieffel come along to look after them, but she finally agreed to go. Soon enough they were all seated in the Worths' wagon, threading their way through the streets of Chesza on their way to the market.

"Isn't this awful? Who considers this adequate transportation?" Lady Worth apologized, but Averie didn't mind the hard seats or the jolting ride. The cart's open construction allowed her to take in all the sights as they passed through the city. Once again she noticed the short buildings constructed of warm reddish mud. This time she noticed the plant life, too—mostly spare trees with high, spindly branches, interspersed with low-lying bushes that flaunted amazingly bright flowers. Here and there would be a spray of grass or a rope of some dark vine. Nothing like the lush vegetation of Aeberelle.

Averie oriented herself by the placement of Mualota Fountain, which she could see to their right during their whole slow journey. If the fountain was at the center of the city, they were surely on the western side of Chesza.

The farther they traveled from the governor's house, the more people they saw on the streets. Most were on foot; Averie saw only a few on horseback or in carts. She studied them, trying not to stare. Both men and women seemed to be dressed in colorful lightweight clothing of a flowing design, clasped at the shoulders and falling loosely past their knees. The garments looked both comfortable and cool, even cooler than Averie's underdress. Most of the Chiarrizi also wore bright scarves tied around their heads and shoes that looked like woven leather painted or embroidered with vivid designs. The footwear showed off their ankles and toes and looked *much* less hot than the closed pumps Averie was wearing. She wondered if any were for sale in the market.

She watched faces as closely as she watched clothing, searching for a common look. She found a variety of skin tones, from a deep brown to a pale tan, though in general she would have said the Chiarrizi were darker than the Aebrians and lighter than the Xantish. The ones she saw mostly had broad faces—generous cheekbones, full mouths, wide-set eyes. Hair color tended to stay on the blonder side of brown, though she didn't see anyone whose hair was as fair as her own, and no one with curls as dark as Lieutenant Du'kai's. More than once she spotted someone with a much whiter complexion or a thinner face, hallmarks of a Weskish ancestry.

"They're very colorful, aren't they?" Lana leaned over to say in her ear. "I've bought a few of the scarves, but my mother won't let me wear them. I suppose I'll take them back with me to Port Elise and make them into pillowcases."

"I want some," Averie said instantly. "And I *will* wear them. Maybe at one of our dinner parties." Both girls laughed.

The market, when they arrived, was larger than Averie had expected, for it covered several acres and was densely packed with people. It seemed to consist of hundreds of carts, arranged in absolutely no fashion whatsoever. Apparently people drove to this open square, unhitched their horses where they found an empty spot, and began selling their merchandise from the backs of their rigs. Visitors just wandered through the crazy quilt of commerce and hoped to discover something that they wanted.

Sieffel had already disembarked and was helping Lady Selkirk out of the wagon. Lady Worth was giving the driver instructions about how soon to come back for them. Lana and Averie did not wait for assistance—they just gathered their skirts up and jumped over the low sides of the cart. It was only then Averie had a terrible realization.

"I don't have any money! No Chiarrizi money, anyway."

"They'll take Aebrian coins," Lana assured her.

"Don't you girls think you're going to run through the market and leave us behind," Lady Worth said. "I want you in my sight the entire time."

"You walk too slowly," Lana said.

"If you disappear, I'll never bring you back here," Lady Worth said calmly. "Then you'll be wishing I was walking slowly right behind you."

Lana made a face, but she sighed and nodded. Then she grabbed Averie's arm. "Come on, let's see if we can find Jalessa's cart," Lana said. "She's here most days."

"Who's Jalessa?" Averie asked as she and Lana began winding their way through the maze. The closely packed carts and pedestrians made the temperature seem even higher. Averie took a long breath and released it, just surrendering herself to the heat.

"She and her grandmother sell fabrics. She's the one who recommended our seamstress, too." Lana glanced over her shoulder to make sure her mother was still in sight and then she sighed again. "At this pace, we'll never find her."

But Averie was in no rush. It was all new to her, and she wanted to view the merchandise at every wagon. One vendor was selling wikberries, and Averie and Lana bought some and consumed them on the spot. Some vendors were offering small hand tools; others were showing pans and dishware. One old woman sat in her wagon, holding up a pair of woven leather shoes and chanting out an incomprehensible invitation.

"I want some of those," Averie said, and approached the cart, even though Lana exclaimed, "You don't really mean it!" The old woman looked suspicious when Averie spoke in polite Weskish. "How much? For shoes that fit my feet?"

The woman replied with a frown and a stream of words that did not sound particularly welcoming. "Maybe she doesn't speak Weskish," Lana guessed.

"Or she doesn't like Aebrians," Averie replied, and tried again. "Are these for sale? Could I try some on? How much do they cost?"

Again, the woman's answer was unfriendly and impossible to understand. "Maybe someone else will be selling shoes," Lana said. "Let's move on."

A woman's voice spoke behind them in melodic and strangely accented Weskish. "She is telling you her goods are of the highest quality and that she must measure your feet," the stranger said. "But she hesitates because she has made shoes for Aebrian customers before and then they failed to return and finalize the purchase."

Lana had spun around at the first words. Averie turned more slowly. They had been joined by a Chiarrizi woman who looked to be about their own age or a little older. Her face was round and serene, a golden tan in color; her brown hair was mostly covered by a multicolored headscarf. She was not exactly smiling, but she looked amused.

"Jalessa!" Lana exclaimed. "We were actually looking for you. This is Averie. She just arrived in Chesza yesterday, and she needs new clothing. Her father is General Winston, so she must set the fashion for all of us."

Jalessa did not bow or offer her hand. She merely looked straight at Averie and nodded once. Her eyes were a complex color, brown and gray and green. "Good morning, Averie," she said.

"Good morning, Jalessa," Averie replied, wondering if there should be titles involved and thinking she didn't want to ask. "So you're telling me this woman won't sell me any shoes?"

"I think she would be willing to make you a pair if you paid her today and promised to come back in a week," Jalessa said.

"I would be happy to do so! Can you translate for me?"

"You will have to take your own shoes off so she can measure your feet."

Lady Selkirk most certainly wouldn't like that. "Gladly," Averie said, and kicked off her pumps right there. The packed dirt of the market was hot against her soles.

When Lady Selkirk arrived two minutes later to find the old woman kneeling in the dirt to examine Averie's bare feet, her chaperone nearly choked in her haste to express her horror and dismay. "Averie! *Averie!* You— Step away, you careless girl, you're going to catch all manner of diseases!"

Averie wondered if it was the dirt or the old woman

who was supposed to be rife with infection, but at any rate, she held perfectly still. "She's fitting me for shoes," she replied calmly. "I've already paid for them."

Lady Selkirk huffed some more, but as Averie had expected, the argument quieted her. Lady Selkirk hated to waste money. And Lady Worth did not look scandalized at all.

"I have been eyeing those sandals the natives wear," the other woman said. "They look comfortable, don't they? Averie, you'll have to tell me how you like them."

"Jalessa says they won't be ready for a week. We'll have to come back."

"I knew it was a mistake to come to this . . . this *market*," Lady Selkirk said darkly, but no one else agreed.

When the old woman was finished, Averie stepped back into her own pumps, which felt hot and tight. She glanced at Jalessa. "How do I thank her? And how do I promise that I'll return?"

"Tell her, *mua dei, mua sova*," Jalessa instructed. "She will hear that as 'my thanks, my friend.'"

"*Sova* means friend?" Averie asked.

"It does."

"So I could call Lana *sova*? Is the word the same for men and for women?"

"Yes. Our language is much simpler than Weskish."

"It would almost have to be," Averie said. Lana

laughed, and Jalessa smiled. Averie nodded at the old woman, who had risen to her feet and was watching her closely. *"Mua dei, mua sova,"* she said carefully. The old lady responded with another of her rants, and Averie looked at Jalessa for translation.

"She is merely telling you again about the high quality of her workmanship. As long as you stand here, she will think you are still reconsidering your purchase, and she will continue convincing you of the worth of her merchandise."

"So how do I leave without being rude?"

"You nod and move on."

Averie did so, and their whole party stepped slowly forward. "That was fun," Lana said. "Can I come with you when you fetch them?"

"Of course you can, *mua sova.*"

They both laughed, but Lana turned instantly to Jalessa. "Where's your wagon today? I've been telling Averie about your fabrics, and she wants to buy some."

"Not far. Follow me."

They passed another ten or fifteen carts—all filled with the most inviting merchandise that they didn't stop to examine—before they came to Jalessa's. Sitting in the back of the wagon was Jalessa's grandmother, who looked enough like the shoe seller that Averie wouldn't have been able to tell them apart if they stood side by side. They both had round, wrinkled faces and intense expressions; they were both outfitted in dark purple clothing and headscarves.

Jalessa greeted her grandmother with a flurry of that liquid language, and the older women responded in words that sounded just as hostile as those of the sandal merchant. Maybe the Chiarrizi elders always sounded angry, Averie thought. Still, the old woman moved with ease through the crammed boxes of the cart to start pulling out bright lengths of fabric and hand them out to Jalessa.

Lana and Averie crowded closer, exclaiming over the rich colors and the smooth weave of the cloth. Lana unrolled a bolt of midnight blue shot through with random white patterns and held it up to her chin. "This is lovely. Do you like it?"

"Dark. Too hot," Averie said.

"I would only wear it at night. At your party."

Averie laughed. "Then I think it's very nice! It makes your eyes look huge."

Jalessa held up a bolt of saturated sky blue. "You're fairer, even though your eyes are brown. You would wear something like this."

Averie flung an end of the fabric over her shoulder and turned a questioning look on Lana. "Oh yes," the other girl said. "It makes your hair very yellow."

Averie turned to show Lady Selkirk, because her chaperone had a good eye for color, but the older women had stepped to another cart, where a vendor was selling loose emeralds. Sieffel stood about halfway between the two parties, keeping an eye on both.

"What about something pink? Or rose-colored?" Averie asked.

"I like that royal purple," Lana said.

But Jalessa was shaking her head. "Oh no. You could not wear purple."

"Why not?" Lana asked.

"It is the color of death," Jalessa said.

Both girls stared at her, then glanced up at Jalessa's grandmother. Was the old woman dying? Was the shoe seller? How horrible!

Jalessa shook her head again, smiling slightly. "No, it means their husbands are dead. They are widows."

"So they wear purple all the time?" Lana said. "*Every* day?"

"A widow may wear other colors for her *tallah*—the clothing on her body," Jalessa said, sweeping a hand down to indicate her own flowing garment. "But she always wears purple in her headscarf. Anyone who meets her will realize that she has lost her husband and will know better than to ask after him."

Averie was intrigued. "Do all the colors mean something?" she asked.

"Yes. A girl wears white until the time of her first bleeding, and then she puts on blue of any shade. A girl who plans to marry wears blue entwined with green so that other young men know she is already spoken for. Once she is married, her headscarf is all green. If she has children, she begins to braid other colors into her head-scarf—gold for her boys, blue for her girls. Once they are grown and married, she takes the colors out again, and she wears green again until her husband dies."

"So all you have to do is look at a woman's head and you know a great deal about her life," Averie mused. She thought this was somewhat similar to the Xantish custom that Lieutenant Du'kai had described, of intro-ducing yourself by listing all the pertinent facts of your history. More subtle, of course.

"What happens if she marries again once her husband is dead?" Lana asked.

"She will wear a green headscarf again, but it will be edged with purple."

"What if her husband is unkind and she leaves him?" Averie asked.

Jalessa smiled. "She will want everyone to know how she was mistreated. So she wears white again, this time edged with black. Black always signifies danger or trouble or cruelty. Black markers are left on mountain passes that have fallen in or by swamps that have tricked a man into drowning."

"And men?" Lana asked. "Do they wear colors that mean something, too?"

Jalessa nodded. "Yes. The same colors for the same reasons, though boys wear white until they turn fifteen, at which time they wear gold."

"What about red?" Averie asked. "I saw people wearing red this morning."

"Red means celebration. You would wear red on your wedding day, or when you grew suddenly rich, or when your sick mother miraculously recovered." Jalessa's smile grew broader. "There are wives who wear headscarves edged in red for their entire lives as a symbol of how much they love their husbands."

Averie laughed. "Then I will be wearing red my whole life, I'm sure!"

"You are married?" Jalessa asked.

Averie shook her head. "No, I am . . ." She paused to try to remember. "I am wearing a blue headscarf twined with green," she said, a question in her voice.

"You are betrothed."

"Yes! And if I could convince Morgan, I would be wearing a full green headscarf before I left Chiarrin."

Lana was instantly diverted. "Wouldn't that be wonderful!" she exclaimed. "To be married in Chesza! Think what stories you could tell."

Averie sighed. "He wants to be married in Port Elise. So I suppose we'll wait."

"I wouldn't be so sure," Lana said wickedly. "If you meet him out in the courtyard often enough at night, he might start thinking how very nice it would be to be married right away."

Averie laughed, for she had had the same thought. "Well, I've only been here a day. I'll see what I can do to change his mind. Maybe I'll buy some scarlet just in case." A thought occurred to her; she turned to assess the headscarf that Jalessa wore.

It was an aquamarine color that Averie decided was intended to be blue, although, ominously, it was edged in black. A young unmarried woman—in danger? Averie felt her stomach tighten in what might be apprehension or sympathy. She hesitated before asking the question, not sure if it was impolite. Or if it might bring an answer too painful to hear.

"Your own scarf," she said quietly. "You're wearing black. Are you sick?"

Something flickered in Jalessa's eyes, but the expression on the broad face remained serene. "It means someone I love is at risk," she said. She did not elaborate, and Averie felt fairly certain it would be rude to ask for more details.

"Well, I'm sorry to hear it," Averie said. "And I hope that person is soon out of danger, and you can wear all blue again."

Now Jalessa smiled. "Thank you, Averie. That is most kind."

"I want to buy something," Lana said plaintively. "But

I'm so confused about the colors! Do I have to wear blue all the time? Because I really liked that dark green with the flowers worked into the weave."

"You may wear anything you like for your *tallah*," Jalessa responded, seeming just as pleased to change the subject. "Except for purple or black. Those colors are never worn except to express their meanings. Otherwise, it is only in the headscarves that the colors have any significance. So choose what you like."

They spent a happy twenty minutes sorting through fabric. By the time they were done, Averie had purchased enough cloth in three different colors to make at least four dresses, and Lana had bought even more. Jalessa carefully rolled and tied each bundle of material before handing it over.

"Thank you for your business," the Chiarizzi woman said formally. "I hope you return to my wagon to make more purchases in the future."

"Well, I have to come back next week to pick up my sandals," Averie pointed out. "I'll find your cart and look some more. I think I need headscarves."

"Will your father really allow you to wear one?" Lana asked, a little shocked, as they drifted off to join the older women.

"He will if I don't tell him what it signifies," Averie laughed. "I'll just say it's something that will protect me from the heat."

"With your new shoes and your headscarves, you'll look just like a Chiarrizi girl!"

"I'm falling in love with this country already."

They found Lady Selkirk and Lady Worth both wearing new jewelry—rings and bracelets set with emeralds—and immediately felt less guilty about their own extravagant purchases. Averie wanted to continue shopping, but Lady Selkirk was hot and hungry, and even Averie had to admit she was beginning to wilt in the heat.

"Time to go home," Lady Selkirk said firmly, and they turned back to find their wagon. Sieffel looked faintly relieved to have the outing finished, though Averie thought it had been one of the most pleasant excursions of her life.

CHAPTER
FIVE

Lana and Averie were best friends within a week. The Worths lived less than a mile from the Winstons' house. Back on Weymire Estate, Averie could walk that distance in fifteen minutes, but here in Chesza she was not allowed out in the city by herself. Still, Sieffel didn't seem to mind escorting her to the Worths' fairly often. So every day for the next seven, Averie went to see Lana or Lana came to see her.

The rest of the Aebrian social set also dropped by. Averie did not like Carrie Dryser any better than Lana had predicted—she had a narrow-eyed and scheming look to her, though she was rather pretty. Carrie's mother also wore a calculating expression, and she glanced around the *maroya* as if trying to assess how much its furniture and knickknacks would fetch on the open market. The other officers' wives reminded Averie more of Lady Worth: they tended to be cheerful, well-seasoned women who had seen a lot of the world and were not easily nonplussed. Averie mostly liked them, but she thought she would have been bored indeed if Lana hadn't been nearby.

A few of the younger officers also presented themselves in that first week. They were all of a type she had been familiar with since childhood—well mannered, well bred, high-spirited, and chivalrous—and she was entirely at ease with them.

"I see Lady Selkirk was right. You've become a shocking flirt since I've been out of the country," Morgan told her one night after their dinner guests had departed. They had entertained two majors and a lieutenant, who had kept Averie laughing all through the meal with their hardly credible tales of life in Xan'tai.

Averie laughed again, remembering. "If I ever get a chance, I'm going to ask Lieutenant Du'kai the truth of it," she said. She glanced up at Morgan. They were sitting in the courtyard to enjoy the relative cool of evening, which had become their practice almost every night. "You don't mind, do you? That they flirt with me a little?"

He squeezed her arm. "Not at all! I am glad to see you so comfortable with the young officers. You will be spending the rest of your life with men very like them, after all. It is good to see that they enjoy your company."

"Well, I'm the general's daughter," she said. "They

think I'll put in a good word for them with my father."

"You seem to be enjoying yourself in Chesza."

"I truly am. I wish I could see more of the city, so when you have free time—"

"Maybe in a few days."

"And Lana and I are going back to the market tomorrow for my shoes."

"Oh yes! The infamous sandals! Lady Selkirk has denounced them so often that I admit to a burning curiosity to actually see them."

"I can't see why she's making such a fuss. So my toes will be bare. Who cares?"

"I'm sure your toes, like the rest of you, are quite enchanting," Morgan said seriously. "I am impatient to get a look."

Averie was impatient, too, and the first thing she thought when she woke up the next morning was that it was time to go back to the market. She put on her pale green underdress, braided her hair, and spent a good twenty minutes trying to get a headscarf in place. She had been practicing all week with twisted lengths of green and blue fabric, but the result was never perfect. If Jalessa was at the market today, maybe she could explain what Averie was doing wrong.

Today the older women did not accompany them, but Sieffel and one of the Worth servants did. When they arrived at the market, Averie and Lana scrambled from the wagon and went hurrying through the haphazard aisles of carts. Lana would have dawdled, but Averie wanted to find her shoes. At first, it seemed hopeless to try to locate one specific cart in all this untidy convocation, but finally they spotted the old cobbler, standing in the back of her wagon.

She obviously recognized Averie right away, for she leaned down into the wagon to retrieve the sandals. As she handed them to Averie, she offered a stern instruction.

"What did she say?" Lana whispered.

Averie braced her body against the cart and stepped out of her pumps. "How should I know? Ow, the ground is hot." She slid her feet into the sandals and closed the buckles. "Lana! You would not believe how comfortable these are!" She did a little dance, a skip, and a pivot, and the shoes didn't slip or pinch. "What do you suppose they're made of? They feel smoother than leather."

"Hodee, maybe? Everything else seems to be."

Averie lifted her skirts to peer down at them. "Oh, look, she's embroidered green and white flowers all along the straps!"

"You can see your toes," Lana said. "Not to mention your ankles. Lady Selkirk will never let you wear those in public."

"Just you wait and see." Averie turned to the shoe seller, who was watching them closely. Averie summoned a bright smile and nodded her head emphatically. "*Mua dei, mua sova,*" she said carefully, and the old woman smiled back.

"Let's keep shopping," Lana said.

Averie gathered up her discarded pumps, and they strolled forward, Sieffel and the Worth servant a few steps behind. Really, these were the most comfortable shoes Averie had ever owned. She wondered if she could get them in different colors. Wouldn't it be adorable to have a pair of scarlet sandals to wear with a scarlet dress if she and Morgan actually did decide to get married in Chesza?

They had made it past only three more carts before Lana touched her arm. "There's Jalessa. She looks like she's shopping, too," she said, and the girls hurried over.

Jalessa's broad face broke into a smile when she saw them. "Good morning, Averie. Good morning, Lana," she said in Weskish. "I see Averie is wearing her head-scarf, with just the right colors."

Averie sighed and replied in the same language. "I can't get it just right, though. It gets all bunched up when I know it's supposed to lie flat."

"Come back to my cart and I will show you the proper way to tie it."

But first Averie extended one foot. "Did you see my shoes? I like them so much!"

"Soon you will adopt all our Chiarrizi customs," Jalessa said.

"Well, I wish I knew more about them. I feel like I've been trapped inside the house, hardly getting a chance to see anything."

Jalessa was leading the way through the maze of wagons, but she glanced over her shoulder. "Your families do not like you to be out on the streets without a guard?"

Lana made a face. "They say it's not safe."

"They're right," Jalessa said softly. "A city in wartime is never safe."

She faced forward again and passed a few more carts, but Averie felt momentarily breathless. *A city in wartime.* It was not a phrase it had occurred to her to apply to sunny, exotic Chesza.

She hadn't thought of how to answer that by the time they arrived at Jalessa's wagon. "Where's your grandmother?" Averie asked.

"She developed a cough last week, and I sent her to my sister, who lives near the Maekath Mountains. She needs rest, and here in the city, she is always working."

Averie glanced again at Jalessa's headscarf—the same aquamarine plaited with black—and wondered if the sick relative she had mentioned was her grandmother. "So who do you live with when your grandmother is not here?" she asked. "Do you have other family in Chesza?"

"No. I live alone in my own place."

"Really? A young woman like you?" Lana exclaimed. "That would never be allowed in Port Elise!"

Jalessa smiled. "I am not considered particularly young," she said.

Averie wanted to ask more questions, but Jalessa had pulled out a small mirror and handed it to Lana. "Can you hold this while Averie learns how to wrap her head-scarf? Averie, let me show you how it is done."

Indeed, the whole process was quite simple once Jalessa demonstrated the proper way to fold, twist, and tie the cloth. Averie liked the way the blended fabrics lay sleekly against her head, covering her hair, making her cheek-bones look sharp and her eyes a darker shade of brown.

"I want to learn, too," Lana decided, so Averie held the mirror for her. Jalessa repeated the lesson with a dark blue cloth Lana had chosen. "I rather like the way I look," Lana said, watching her reflection. "Do you sup-pose I could wear this at that dinner party you're going to have? Do you suppose it would create a scandal?"

"Not if people are too busy looking at my shoes," Averie said, and they both laughed. Then Averie turned back toward Jalessa. "Can we see more fabric? Last week you had a very pale yellow—I was thinking that would make a pretty dress."

"Yes, I remember," Jalessa said, climbing into the wagon. "It will take me a moment to find it. I'm sure it is at the very bottom of the pile."

She began pulling out bolts of fabric, two at a time, and tossing them to the other side of the cart. Rose pink and midnight blue. Saffron and delicate lime green. Silver and sienna. Averie toyed with her headscarf and watched the accumulation of treasure.

"Wait . . . I believe it is down here," Jalessa muttered, shaking out a length of scarlet fabric with one hand and a length of purple with the other. "Now if only I—"

The world exploded around them. Jalessa's cart fragmented into bits of plank and color; scraps of metal and wood and unidentifiable debris rained down. There was a hissing sizzle and then another booming explosion, so loud that it momentarily drowned out the screams and cries of panic. Averie felt herself knocked to the hard ground, and at first she thought she'd been hit by another shell, but then she realized Sieffel was on top of her, covering her body with his big one. Lana was beside them in the dirt, shrieking, hiding her head beneath her hands. There was another explosion, and then another. And then suddenly there was only silence and the sound of wailing grief.

Sieffel rolled off Averie, his hand pressed to his head, and she realized he'd been wounded. He groaned but he was moving, he was breathing, and so Averie forgot about him for the moment. Lana! The other girl lay motionless, her hands still folded over the rich blue of her headscarf. Averie pushed herself to her knees and crawled over. Her touch caused Lana to cry out and roll to her back, dropping her arms to cradle them around her chest. Her face was streaked with dirt, but otherwise she seemed unmarked.

"Are you all right?" Averie demanded. "Lana, can you hear me?"

"What happened?" Lana cried. "It was so loud! And then everything just . . . came apart. I saw somebody's head slice away from his body. . . ."

"A mortar shell of some kind," Averie said grimly. "My father said that the Chiarrizi had gotten hold of gunpowder. I suppose they fired it into the market."

"But why?" Lana whispered, her hands coming up to cover her cheeks.

"To kill people," Averie replied. "I don't know why."

Lana looked around wildly, not moving from her prone position. "Are they still here? Averie, how will we get home? Are we going to be killed?"

Sieffel tried to stagger to his feet. "I'll go find the wagon," he said hoarsely.

"Sit down," Averie told him sharply, and he collapsed to the ground again, gasping for breath. "I think we should wait for the soldiers. They'll be here soon."

"How do you know?" Lana asked in a fearful voice.

Because the sound of detonations would have carried for miles through the heavy air. Because her father and Morgan had talked about stepping up horse patrols through the city. Because they were already worried that Chesza was not safe, and they were determined to force order onto a rebellious city. "Because my father is general here, and his men will come find me," she said softly.

Indeed, almost as she said the words, she could hear a small thunder of horses' hooves as soldiers came galloping up. Someone was shouting out crisp commands, making sense out of the chaos. Aebrian troops were on hand; all would be well.

Averie had barely registered the thought when a small whimper caught her attention and she looked up from Lana's face. Jalessa! What had happened to her? She had been in the cart, which was now smashed to pieces. Was that a hand extending beyond the wreckage? Was Jalessa trapped in the rubble? Could she still be alive?

"Averie!" Lana cried as Averie crawled over toward the destroyed wagon and began using her shoulder to try to push it aside. It came apart in a shower of splinters, which caused Lana to shriek again, but Averie didn't care.

There was the Chiarrizi girl, lying bloody and still in a nest of ruined fabric and a welter of shattered lumber.

"Jalessa," Averie breathed, and put her hand against the other woman's cheek.

Cool to the touch and sticky with blood, but the eyelids fluttered and a sigh of breath escaped the lax mouth. "Averie," Jalessa whispered back.

Averie pressed closer, galvanized by relief and determination. "Thank goodness you're alive!" she exclaimed in Weskish. "Where are you hurt? Can you tell?"

"I hurt . . . everywhere," Jalessa said with great difficulty. "But you! You are not injured, are you? And Lana?"

"Frightened but unharmed," Averie said. She was peeling off Jalessa's headscarf and folding down the neckline of her *tallah*. There was blood, but none of the wounds appeared to be extensive. But Jalessa's eyes seemed pale and unfocused; Averie guessed a concussion at the very least. "Can you breathe? You might have broken a rib."

"I don't think so," Jalessa replied. "But my head . . . it hurts—"

"Averie!" Lana called. "Soldiers!"

"Go get help!" Averie responded over her shoulder. "Tell them General Winston's daughter is here. And we need assistance!"

Averie remained bent over Jalessa while Lana stumbled off. Out of the corner of her eye, Averie saw the Worths' servant taking Lana's arm. Sieffel came shakily to his feet and stood close to Averie as if to guard her from further attack.

But most of Averie's attention was on Jalessa. The Chiarrizi woman was struggling for breath and obviously in intense pain. "Don't faint," Averie muttered, patting her hands against Jalessa's cheek. "Stay awake. Help is coming."

Jalessa did not try to reply, she just kept her unsteady gaze on Averie's face and took those hard, difficult breaths. A gash down Jalessa's left arm started to seep blood, so Averie employed one of the ruined lengths of fabric to bind it. She should have used black for danger, she thought, but she worried that the dye might seep into the wound, so she chose white instead.

"Stay awake. Good. You're being so brave," Averie said, continuing a running monologue just to anchor Jalessa's attention. "Help will be here very soon."

Indeed, moments later she heard Lana's voice call, "She's right over there," and the sound of booted feet running in her direction. She found herself enveloped by six Aebrian officers in their dark blue uniforms. They formed a circle around Averie and the downed wagon, their rifles at the ready. One man dropped to his knees beside her.

"Lieutenant Du'kai!" she exclaimed. "Thank goodness you're here!"

His dark face was a study in concern. He put a hand to her shoulder as if to reassure himself that she was alive. "Lady Averie, are you hurt? We have brought the cart around—it is just a few yards away. I can help you if you cannot walk."

She shook her head. "No, I'm fine. *She's* the one who's hurt. Can you carry her?"

He glanced at Jalessa as if he had not noticed her when he first strode up. "Carry . . . who is she?"

"She's a local merchant. We were buying fabric from

her when the blast came— Oh, Lieutenant, what caused all those explosions? They went on and on."

"Mortar shells," he said briefly. "Thrown from a crude catapult. We found the contraption, but the men who operated it were long gone."

"Why would they—?"

"Lady Averie, we don't have time to discuss what happened," he said firmly, coming to his feet and tugging her up with him. "We must get you safely home. Now."

His face showed astonishment when she jerked away and dropped back to the ground, tucking her hands under Jalessa's shoulders. "I'm not leaving without her."

"You want to take her back to your father's house?"

"Yes. I *will* take her. So you help me bring her, or I'm not leaving."

Morgan would have argued. Her father would have grabbed her arm and yanked her away from the scene, not caring how much fuss she made. But Lieutenant Du'kai merely nodded, said, "Very well," and bent to scoop up the Chiarrizi girl in his arms. Averie found herself filled with a fleeting admiration. He had determined that swift action was the most important consideration, and he was willing to do whatever was necessary to get her to safety. He must be strong, too, she thought, as she snatched up a few of the nearest bolts of fabric and came to her feet. Jalessa was a solid girl, and Lieutenant Du'kai had lifted her as if she weighed nothing at all.

"Lady Averie, let me carry those for you," Sieffel offered.

"No, no, you can hardly stand! Do you want to lean on my shoulder?" she replied, following after Lieutenant Du'kai.

"I do not," he replied, with stern pride. Nonetheless, she spared half her attention for him and half for Lieutenant Du'kai as they picked their way through the shattered remains of the marketplace. They arrived in short order at the Worths' cart, where Lana was already in place with her servant and driver. Another cadre of soldiers, still on horseback, stood guard around the wagon. Averie tossed the fabric in, made sure Sieffel could handle the climb over the side, and then scrambled in herself. Lieutenant Du'kai laid Jalessa on the bed of the wagon, then vaulted in beside her.

"Tell Major Morrier I am taking Lady Averie home," he ordered one of his men. Then, lifting his voice to carry to the driver and the mounted men, "Move out!"

The wagon began rolling. Lana sat in a small heap on one bench, softly crying while the Worth servant tried to comfort her. But Averie clutched the side of the wagon and attempted to see past the horses of her escort. Whole sections of the market appeared to have survived, and merchants were grimly repacking their merchandise in their untouched carts. A few yards away there would be a flattened circle of destruction, carts demolished, bodies sprawled on the ground. Averie caught glimpses of colorfully dressed Chiarrizi sorting through the debris, calling out to each other, sitting on the ground and weeping as hopelessly as Lana. Aebrian soldiers threaded their way through the whole scene on foot and on horseback, restoring order, evaluating the extent of the damage.

She drew her attention back inside the cart, checking on Jalessa, who must surely be suffering as the wheels jounced over stones and ruts. No—the Chiarrizi girl had fainted. Her breathing was still heavy, but a little less harsh; there was nothing Averie could do for her until they got back to the house.

Why had this happened?

Averie looked up to ask Lieutenant Du'kai the question, and found him soberly studying her. There was no smile at all in his deep brown eyes.

"You said you found catapults for the mortar shells," she said in a quiet voice. "Why did they fire on the marketplace? Who did it?"

"Bands of rebel Chiarrizi have been gaining strength in the past few weeks," he answered immediately. Something she knew neither her father nor Morgan would have done. "We assume this is one of those groups."

"But why attack the marketplace?" she insisted.

He watched her steadily. "To kill Aebrians."

Averie recoiled. "But—there are only a few Aebrian

families in Chesza! The market is filled with Chiarrizi!"

He nodded. "But Aebrians can be found at the marketplace every day. The chances were good that an Aebrian would be killed or injured by the explosions—or at least frightened. Maybe frightened enough to leave."

"Leave the market?"

"Leave Chiarrin. Taking the whole army along."

She felt stunned and then stupid. "They want us gone. These rebels hate us and want us to go." She looked at him. "And the numbers of rebels are growing."

He nodded. "Yes."

"My father hasn't talked of this."

"Your father thinks the attacks are isolated and unimportant and disorganized. He may change his mind after today."

"Not my father. Opposition only makes him more determined."

"Then I foresee a bloody stretch ahead of us."

She swallowed hard. "Did—did anyone die? That you saw?"

He watched her steadily. "My men and I were moving fast, trying to get to you, so I can't answer definitely. But we saw no Aebrians among the casualties."

"That's not what I asked," she said in a cold voice.

His eyes narrowed. "There looked to be some Chiarrizi down," he said. "I don't know if they were dead."

She flinched and looked away and did not answer. She could not understand it. Could not understand hating someone so much that you would risk the lives of your friends to harm your enemy.

From the corner of her eye, she saw Lieutenant Du'kai gesture. "Who is this woman? The one you wished to save?"

"Her name is Jalessa," Averie said in a listless voice. "I met her last week. She helped me buy my shoes—" She stopped, took a deep breath, and went on. "She lives by herself in the city. I couldn't just leave her there. Who would care for her? Would anyone even have helped her out of the street? She could have just been lying there till she died."

"Do you think to nurse her at your father's house?"

She looked back at him with the ghost of a smile. "You think my father will not like the idea?"

A very small answering smile appeared on his face. "You know him better than I do, Lady Averie."

"At first he will be annoyed, but he will not think it important enough to argue with me. Lady Selkirk will be shocked, but everything I do is shocking to Lady Selkirk."

"And Colonel Stode?"

She actually didn't know what Morgan might think about this particular twist. "I hope he will be pleased when he hears my plan."

"What plan is that?"

Averie briefly touched the back of her hand to Jalessa's cool cheek. "First, I will make sure she is healed," she said softly. "Then, I will see if she wants to come work for me." She glanced briefly at Lieutenant Du'kai, then back at Jalessa again. "My father always believes you should have native servants when you are in a foreign land. He says that is the only way to truly understand an unfamiliar culture."

"Many of the Aebrians in Xan'tai employee Xantish as servants," Lieutenant Du'kai agreed, but there was no inflection at all in his voice.

So she challenged him. "You think it is a terrible idea. You would never take a position in an Aebrian household."

"I have taken a position in a Aebrian army," he countered. "It's much the same thing."

She didn't want to argue, so she returned her attention to Jalessa. "She might not want to stay, of course. But I thought I would ask her. Once she is well, that is. I will make sure she is healed before I send her back into the world."

It was impossible to read the expression on Ket Du'kai's face, but Averie had the impression something she said had surprised him, or intrigued him, or forced him to make a reassessment. But all he said was, "I am sure she will appreciate your care."

"If she survives to learn of it," Averie replied in a whisper.

"I don't think her injuries are that severe," he replied.

"Surely she will recover quickly." He glanced at Lana. "But your friend seems very distraught."

Averie nodded and scooted across the swaying cart to Lana's side. She pushed past the hovering servant to take Lana in her arms. "Lana. It's all right. We're safe."

Lana continued sobbing against her shoulder. At some point, Lana had pulled off her blue headscarf; her black hair was all tangled. "Oh, Averie, it was so awful! That man—his *head* came off! I have never seen anything like— Why did that *happen?*"

Averie hugged her closer. "I think this is what it's like to live in a city in wartime," she said, repeating Jalessa's earlier words. "Not very safe and not very pretty."

"I want to go home," Lana wept.

"We are going home."

"Home to Port Elise."

Averie grew very still. She hadn't thought about it, in the few minutes she'd had time to think since the first shell exploded, but *she* didn't want to go home. She had been in Chiarrin only a week, but it already held a great appeal for her. She wanted to understand it. She wanted to immerse herself in it. She wanted to absorb its colors and its heat and its rituals. Her father might want her safe back in Port Elise, but Averie did not want to go.

She was not going to leave Chesza behind.

CHAPTER
SIX

As soon as the cart arrived at the front door, Lady Selkirk and Grace came running out.

"What happened? Are you all right?" Lady Selkirk demanded. She looked truly alarmed. "We heard these terrible sounds, these explosions, and Grace said they came from the direction of the marketplace. Then we saw mounted troops go rushing past, and—Averie! You're covered with dirt and *blood*! What happened to you?"

"I'm fine," Averie said, giving Lana a last hug and climbing down from the cart. She turned to help Sieffel out, thanking him warmly for risking himself to guard her. He looked a little more solid on his feet now, but he leaned on Grace as she led him into the house. Averie turned back to Lady Selkirk. "Lieutenant Du'kai says rebel Chiarrizi attacked the marketplace," she said.

Lady Selkirk looked even more upset. "Rebel Chiarrizi! Attacked—attacked *how*? Oh, Lieutenant Du'kai, thank goodness you were on hand to save Averie."

"He saved all of us," Averie said, but she had already lost Lady Selkirk's attention. Lieutenant Du'kai had swung down from the wagon, then lifted Jalessa out.

"What—? Who—? Averie Agatha Winston, who is that?" Lady Selkirk said. All the worry had left her voice to be miraculously replaced by cold suspicion and icy hauteur.

"It's Jalessa. We bought fabric from her last week, remember? She got hurt, and she has no one to care for her. I'm taking her in."

"Oh, no, you most certainly are not."

Averie simply walked past the older woman and held the door open for Lieutenant Du'kai. "Go in and turn through the *maroya* to your left," she told him. "We'll take her to my room."

"Averie! You will not take that—that—*person* into your bedroom! *Averie!*"

Lady Selkirk's rant grew fainter as Averie and Lieutenant Du'kai stepped inside and followed the angles of the hexagon to the wing housing the family bedrooms. Averie was impressed again that he didn't waste time arguing. He merely walked behind Averie until they came to her room, and he followed her through the door. Then he hesitated.

"Where should I—?"

"Put her on my bed, of course."

"Lady Averie, I'm sure that Lady Selkirk—"

"On the bed," Averie said impatiently. "You can't very well lay her on the floor."

"But if she starts bleeding—"

"Then we will wash the covers. Lay her down."

He did so, being careful not to jar Jalessa's head. Averie was already at the boxy dresser, looking for a clean towel. She said, "Could you send Grace to me, if Sieffel doesn't need her? And tell Lana I'll come see her later."

He took that as the dismissal it was, and gave her a slight bow. "I will. Be careful, Lady Averie."

That made her pause on her way to the bathing room. "I think you're in more danger than I am, if rebel Chiarrizi are really trying to kill Aebrian troops."

Again he gave her that faint smile. "I am more used to dealing with danger than you are, I think. And you are more careless than I am."

She laughed. "Well, that's probably true. Will you come back sometime and see how my patient is doing?"

"If I can," he said. "Although I am more interested in your well-being than hers."

She smiled a little. There was so much to do. She had to get Jalessa stripped down and cleaned up, had to try to make the Chiarrizi girl comfortable. And yet she was standing here, twisting the towel around her hands, talking diffidently with Lieutenant Du'kai. Almost flirting.

"I had thought I would see you before this," she said. "Most of the other officers have come by in the past week. Then I thought maybe you had been stationed up by the Maekath Mountains."

"I have had assignments in Chesza that have kept me busy. And I knew you were well—all the other officers came back with tales of the general's lively daughter."

"Lively. Was that their word, or yours?"

He grinned. "I believe Captain Martin called you captivating, and Captain Gaele said you were—let's see—'a merry little thing.'"

She laughed again. "Lana thinks we should have a dinner party for all the officers and their families. Would you come?"

"I would certainly come if you invited me."

"Then I shall make my father let me plan one." She glanced at the bed, where Jalessa lay unmoving, and all her gaiety died. "Or . . . I will . . . once this is all sorted out."

Lieutenant Du'kai bowed again. "You're busy here. I'll see to Lady Lana."

"It was good to see you again, Lieutenant," Averie said.

"Very good to see you, Lady Averie." He bowed one more time and was gone.

Averie hurriedly soaked the towel and returned to the bed to begin tending to Jalessa. Grace stepped inside the room and shut the door, but not before Averie heard Lady Selkirk's voice, raised in a continuing tirade.

Averie glanced over at Grace, who was carrying a basket full of medical supplies. "You aren't afraid of Lady Selkirk, are you?" she asked with a slight smile.

Grace shook her head. "No, my lady. The general told me I was to assist you in any way you liked. And I think we should help this poor girl."

"How's Sieffel?"

"He'll be fine once he's rested. He's a tough old man. Been hurt worse than this."

Averie surveyed their patient. "I hope you're better at nursing than I am. I've had a little experience, because someone was always falling sick at Weymire Estate, but I confess we always called a doctor in for cases this serious."

Grace set the basket on the bed and settled on the mattress across from Averie. "I've traveled with your father to places more wild than Chesza," she said quietly. "I can manage almost as well as any doctor."

Between them they did a fairly good job, Averie thought later, as they undressed Jalessa, cleaned and bound the many small wounds, and slipped one of Averie's fresh nightshirts over her head. Jalessa woke, disoriented and frightened, and appeared not to understand when Averie spoke in Weskish to try to reassure her. Instead, she kept asking them urgent questions in her own language. Finally, Averie just said *sova* over and over again. *Friend.*

That seemed to register enough to calm the Chiarrizi girl, and she subsided and closed her eyes.

"Do you think she ought to sleep?" Averie asked in some concern. "If she's had a blow to the head, as I think she has—"

"I think we should let her rest for now," Grace said. "We'll wake her up in an hour or two and see how she is. But *you*, my lady. You need to wipe your face and perhaps take a rest yourself. I can make up the bed down the hall in the empty room."

"I'm not tired," Averie said.

"Well, you'll be sleeping there tonight anyway."

"No, I won't. I'll sleep in here, in case Jalessa needs me."

Grace looked doubtful. "I expect your father will have a different opinion about that. Not to mention Lady Selkirk."

"I can deal with both of them."

Grace smiled again. "In any case, you need to wash up and change clothes."

"And I'm hungry," Averie realized. "Give me fifteen minutes, and I'll come to the *maroya*. I'll have something to eat—and see if I can calm down Lady Selkirk."

It was easier to achieve the first part of this plan than the second. Cleaned, changed, and munching on wikberries and hodee cheese, Averie spent a good quarter hour trying to soothe Lady Selkirk, who was in no mood to be soothed.

"This is just like you!" the chaperone raged. "Remember that time you brought that—that *urchin* home with you! A poacher's son, no doubt, but he'd broken his leg, and you said you had to nurse him *with your own hands*! Then there was that servant girl—what was her name?—the one who got herself in trouble with the blacksmith's son. You told her she could stay on at the estate! You told her you had always wanted to play with a baby! You were fourteen. What did you know about babies and how girls got them? I sent her packing because *I* know trouble when I see it, but you—"

"I gave her money before she left," Averie said, helping herself to another slice of cheese. "I sent her some for the next three years, in fact. But she's married now."

Lady Selkirk goggled so hard it seemed likely her eyes might pop right out of her head. So much for trying to calm her down. "You *what*? You gave her *money*? That terrible girl? Averie, how could you? Have I taught you nothing about the world?"

"You've taught me what *you* wanted me to know," Averie said, unmoved. "But I realized a long time ago that there was a lot more to learn."

"When your father returns tonight, there will be a reckoning," Lady Selkirk promised grimly. "He will not take your antics so lightly. *Nor* will Colonel Stode."

"Morgan will just be happy I'm alive," Averie said.

As it happened, neither of them was completely accurate in her predictions, though they didn't find out until almost midnight. By then, Averie had returned numerous times to check on Jalessa, who seemed much more comfortable. Averie had also sent a note to the Worth house and gotten one back from Lana. *My mother is insisting that I go to bed before the sun has even set,* Lana had written. *Come see me tomorrow.*

Both Lady Selkirk and Averie were too obstinate to follow that same sensible course of action, so they stubbornly stayed awake, awaiting the return of the men. Lady Selkirk dozed in the *maroya,* while Averie sat in the courtyard, listening to the gentle tinkle of the fountain. She was half asleep when she heard voices inside the house. She took a deep breath, shook her head to clear away the drowsiness, and hurried inside.

Morgan saw her first and strode over to catch her in a powerful hug. "When we realized where the explosions were and knew you might be at the market—" he muttered into her hair. "I thought my heart would stop."

She pulled free just enough to kiss him, despite her father and Lady Selkirk standing right there. "I'm fine," she said. "But tell us what happened. Who set off the explosions, and why, and what you've done about it."

"You don't need to know all that," Morgan said.

"Yes, I do," she insisted. "I was right in the middle of it. I deserve to know."

Her father shrugged. "There's a faction that is not

inclined to submit to Aebrian rule," he said in his usual unemotional style. "They have developed crude explosives, but we don't know where they're getting the blasting powder. You can be mighty sure we're keeping our own supplies under a tight guard."

"How many are in this faction?" Averie asked.

Her father shrugged again. "We don't know. Logistics of today's event would indicate at least twenty. Maybe there are a hundred. Maybe there are a thousand, setting up camp somewhere back of the Maekeths. We've sent troops out to investigate."

"We'll find them," Morgan said. He sounded scornful, Averie thought. "Untrained men with few military resources. They can't possibly hide for long."

"Is it safe in Chesza?" Averie asked.

Morgan put his arm around her shoulders. "We've doubled the perimeter patrols, put more troops on the street, and instituted a curfew," he said. "It's safe."

"I swear I am not leaving this house again without an armed guard beside me," Lady Selkirk declared.

Averie's father was nodding. "Not a bad idea. Even if I believe you're safe in Chesza, it sends a message to all the Chiarrizi. We defend our own."

"I'll have a detail assigned to you in the morning," Morgan promised.

"I think the Chiarrizi don't want us here," Averie said.

Her father snorted. "No, but we're here now, and

we're staying," he said in a hard voice. "We have been re-strained so far—we have done as little damage as possible to Chesza and the surrounding countryside. All that will change if they continue to fight us."

"I wish you had been more forceful at the beginning," Lady Selkirk complained.

"We wished for peaceful occupation," the general replied. "It maintains the economic integrity of the country, makes for an easier transition. Fewer dead, less rebuilding that has to be done. It seemed like the right strategy at the time."

"Everyone supported you in that decision, sir," Morgan said respectfully.

The general nodded. "But if it was the wrong one, well, plenty of time to show them what we're capable of."

"You need to show Averie what you're capable of," Lady Selkirk said spitefully. The depth of her anger had made her almost childishly eager to tattle, Averie thought. "Because *I* can't seem to talk sense into her. *I* can't seem to control her."

Now the chaperone had the attention of both men. Morgan dropped his arm and peered at Averie's face.

"What is it this time?" Averie's father asked.

This time! Averie thought indignantly. *As if I am always in some kind of trouble.* "We were at the marketplace—" she began, but Lady Selkirk interrupted.

"General, she brought home a Chiarrizi girl! Some—

some random woman who was hurt in the blast! That woman is *in Averie's bed* right this very minute!"

"Averie! Is this true?" Morgan demanded.

Her father grunted. "Of course it's true. It's the sort of thing she would do in a heartbeat. She was always bringing home strays."

"Well, you can't bring home stray Chiarrizi," Morgan said.

"Well, I've already done it," Averie shot back. She was so disappointed in Morgan's reaction that she was instantly hot with anger. "She's here, and she's staying, at least until she's well enough to leave."

"Averie, you *can't* take in wounded natives just because you feel sorry for them!" Morgan exclaimed. "This is a war! There will be wounded Chiarrizi every day!"

"She got hurt talking to *me*. If I had been standing two feet closer to her, *I'm* the one who would have been hit," Averie said. "She's my friend."

"She's your *friend*?" Morgan's tone was disbelieving. "Can you have had more than three minutes of conversation with her?"

Averie hunched her shoulders. "She was kind to me, so I will be kind to her. Once she's strong again—well, then we'll see."

"We'll see what?" Morgan wanted to know, but her father showed some interest.

"She might be grateful enough to do us some good,"

he said, nodding. "Give us some names, make some introductions."

That wasn't exactly what Averie had meant, but she nodded. "Yes. Or even come work for me."

"Hire on as a servant?" he mused. "I would agree to that."

Lady Selkirk was incensed. "You cannot mean to let— General, you cannot allow that woman to stay in this house!"

He shrugged. "I don't see why not."

"It's indecent," Lady Selkirk gasped.

"Sir, it's very odd," Morgan added.

"But she might be useful, and she's hardly a threat," he replied.

Averie found herself in the rare position of siding with her father. "Thank you, Father," she said, giving him her best smile. She was enough of a general's daughter that she knew when a retreat was in order. "I'll see you all in the morning."

And she escaped before anyone could say anything else. Morgan called her name in a low voice, but she was too angry to acknowledge him. How could he be so heartless? Or was he merely being conventional, like Lady Selkirk, afraid of what the officers and their wives might think when they learned his fiancée had rescued a native woman? She couldn't decide which option offended her most.

Back at her own door, Averie entered quietly. Jalessa was sleeping, but her skin seemed cool and her breath was easy. All good signs. Grace had made up a bed on the floor, and the sight of the pillows and comforters made Averie smile. She had won this battle, or at least this skirmish. She would need rest to see her through the conflicts of the next day.

CHAPTER SEVEN

When Averie opened her eyes in the morning, Jalessa was sitting beside her on the floor, studying her with a calm intentness. The morning sun was slanting in through the gauze curtains, throwing Jalessa's face into bright relief. Her broad features looked peaceful, but her multicolored eyes seemed shadowed.

Averie scrambled to a seated position. "You're awake! Do you feel better?"

Jalessa nodded. "Yes."

"How's your head? Are you having any trouble breathing?"

"I am in some pain, but it is bearable," Jalessa replied. "But mostly I am confused. How did I come to be here? Are we in your father's house? Am I a prisoner?"

Averie was aghast. "No, of course you're not a prisoner!

We were in the market yesterday, and there were explosions. Your cart was destroyed, and you were knocked to the ground. I was afraid to leave you behind. You said your grandmother was gone from the city, and I didn't know if anyone would look after you. So I brought you here."

Jalessa retained her tranquil look, but Averie thought she must be feeling some astonishment. "You carried me to the house of the Aebrian general? To care for me?"

"I hope you don't mind. Perhaps you don't like the Aebrian army any more than the rebels do. Perhaps you'd rather I hadn't brought you here."

Jalessa laid a hand on Averie's forearm. "It was a great kindness," she said gravely. "Not one woman in a thousand would think to take in a stranger who was hurt."

"But you're not a stranger. Not exactly. You notice I didn't go running through the marketplace, checking to see who had survived the blasts."

Now there was a flicker of emotion on Jalessa's face. "How many explosions?" she asked fearfully. "How many hurt? Or dead?"

Averie shook her head. "I don't know yet." She glanced diffidently at the other woman. "I'm sure you must be acquainted with some of the other merchants. I will find out what I can as soon as possible."

There was a short silence, and then Jalessa asked, "So am I free to go?"

"As soon as you feel well enough to walk, you may go out the door. Lady Selkirk will be happy to see you gone, to tell the truth." Averie gave Jalessa another quick appraisal. "But I thought—well—you might be interested in a proposition. An offer."

Jalessa's expression sharpened just a little. "What kind of offer?"

"If you wanted, my father would allow me to hire you as my personal maid."

"A servant."

"Is that an insult to a Chiarrizi?" Averie asked anxiously.

"We don't have servants. It is a word we learned from the Weskish, but we have had a hard time understanding it. The wealthier often employ those with lesser means, but it is a respectful arrangement of benefit to both. From what I understand about the Aebrians and their servants—"

"Yes, it's a very unequal sort of contract," Averie admitted. "And Lady Selkirk is particularly conscious of class distinctions. You might not be able to stand it."

"What would you expect me to do?"

Averie drew her knees up and let the covers fall to her ankles. "Well, I'd want you to help me with my hair and my clothes in the mornings, and help me dress in the evenings if we were having any special events. I'd want you to make sure my dresses were clean and any rips were mended. Grace has been keeping my room tidy, but she would expect you to take over that responsibility. I might want you to run errands from time to time."

"Basically, I would care for you and do your bidding."

"Yes," Averie said, feeling anxious again, because phrased that way it did not sound like a very appealing life. "But you would not be a maid so much as a lady's companion. You would be my friend, I hope. *Sova.* There's so much I want to learn about Chiarrin, and there's so much you could teach me!"

Jalessa did not answer, so Averie continued a bit uncertainly. "I will understand if you do not want to take this position. But I thought—I didn't know—I saved what I could from your wagon, but I'm afraid you lost most of it when the shell exploded. I don't know how much you can afford to lose, how much money you have. I thought you might need a job. This one wouldn't be very hard. And my father pays well."

But Jalessa seemed to have heard only one phrase from this particular speech. "You saved some of my goods from the wagon?" she repeated.

Averie pointed to where the bolts of fabric were piled up in the corner. "Not much. All I could carry."

"That was as great a kindness as saving my life."

"Hardly. We were in a hurry or I would have brought more."

Jalessa nodded and seemed to be thinking. "Tell me more about this position as a maid," she said in her deliberate way. "Would I be expected to live in this house? Would I stay in your room with you?"

"No, you would have a room near the kitchens, where the other servants sleep, but, yes, I would hope you would stay in the house," she said. "If you wouldn't be willing to do that—"

"I would be," Jalessa said. "But I would want to be able to spend the night at my own place now and then."

Averie nodded. "That could be arranged. You would have—oh, three afternoons a week when you could do what you liked. And any other time you needed off, you would just have to let me know."

"Would I be confined to my quarters and yours?"

"No, you could go to any of the common areas, such as the kitchen and the *maroya* and the courtyard," Averie said. "You'd have to stay out of the other bedrooms, of course. No one ever steps into someone else's bedroom uninvited! It's considered improper."

Jalessa looked interested. "Surely you have been in the bedroom of Colonel Stode?"

Averie was mortified to find herself blushing hotly. "Well—well—I *have*, but only briefly, and both of us knew it was wrong," she said.

"But if you are to marry him, aren't you curious if he will be a good match?"

"Oh, of course he will be a good match! His family is not as prominent as mine, and there was a scandal with his father, but his military career and my father's connections—"

"I meant, a match in the way your bodies fit together," Jalessa said calmly. "That's not important to the Aebrians?"

Her face was still red, Averie was sure, and she found herself both shocked and curious. "I suppose it's important, but it's something we don't find out until after the wedding vows are spoken," she said. "Do you mean . . . among the Chiarrizi . . ."

Jalessa nodded. "A man might have fine property and good manners and a bright smile, but if he doesn't please a woman in the bedroom, she is unlikely to marry him."

"But then if she— Once she's— I mean, if she's already had relations with a man and is still unmarried, isn't she considered damaged?" Averie asked.

Jalessa stared as if she didn't understand the word. "Damaged? In what way?"

"In her reputation? In Aeberelle, a man likes to know the woman he's marrying has—is—has saved her body for him," she said. She was floundering. It had never occurred to her that this central tenet of social relations might be set aside as valueless.

Jalessa still seemed mystified. "Why would she want to save her body? Why would he want to save his?"

Averie took refuge in another laugh. "I don't think I can explain it!" she said. "But just trust me when I say, no, I have not spent the night in Morgan's bedroom. Nor am I likely to any time soon. And that's not what we were talking about, anyway."

Jalessa nodded. She seemed faintly amused, though her expression remained so placid it was hard to tell. "You were telling me where I could and couldn't go in this house. I don't think I would feel too confined."

"So what else would you like to know?" Averie said. "What about a salary?"

"How much would you offer?"

"How much money would you generally make in a year selling your goods?"

Jalessa shrugged. "About a hundred and fifty of your gold coins."

"In a *year*? That's all?" Averie demanded.

"It's considered a good income."

"Well, I could pay you twenty gold coins a month," Averie said.

Jalessa's eyes widened a little. "That would be generous."

"And you would eat your meals here, of course, which would save you money as well." Averie came to her knees and bounced on the bedding. "Oh, *do* say you'll consider it, Jalessa. I would love to have you nearby, teaching me about Chiarrin."

"May I have a day to consider it?"

"Of course! Do you want to stay here while you think it over?"

"I'm strong enough to return to my place, I think. Besides, I must go home anyway and pack my things if I am to come live here."

Averie clasped her hands before her. "So you want to leave now—and if you accept my offer, you will be back?"

"Yes. I will return tomorrow morning."

"And if you don't accept my offer, will I see you again? Will you return to the market to sell your goods?"

Jalessa looked amused. "I will. If I don't become your maid, I must earn my living somehow."

Jalessa rose, looking not entirely steady on her feet, and Averie jumped up beside her. "Would you like me to order the wagon for you? How far do you have to go? Oh, and there's your fabric! You won't be able to carry that any distance."

Jalessa glanced again at the cloth lying in a neat pile in the corner. "Yellow and green and blue," she said with a smile. "I see you saved all your favorite colors."

"Well, I remembered that purple and black signify death and danger, and I was trying to be hopeful about your situation," Averie retorted.

"If I return to work for you, we will make these cloths into dresses for you," she said. "If I don't, perhaps you will accept them as payment for your kindness."

"Kindness never needs to be repaid," Averie said.

"Still, there should be some sort of balance between people," Jalessa replied.

"So shall I order the wagon?" Averie asked again.

Jalessa shook her head. "I'm fine. Thank you again for all you've done for me."

Averie trailed after her as Jalessa moved down the hallway. Indeed, after the first few careful steps, Jalessa seemed perfectly steady, and she moved purposefully toward the *maroya*. "Would you like some food before you go? Water to take with you?"

"I will buy food from a vendor and drink water from the fountain," Jalessa said.

"You're eager to go."

"It has been a strange two days," Jalessa admitted. "I want to be home."

By this time they were in the *maroya,* at the main door, and Grace was there, dusting the crowded furniture. "I hope I see you again tomorrow," Averie said wistfully. "Or sometime."

Jalessa smiled. "I think, one way or the other, we will meet each other again. Thank you once more." And she nodded and slipped out into the sunshine.

Averie, feeling lost and disconsolate, turned back toward the dim coolness of the interior. Grace had laid aside her cleaning rag and was unfolding one of the small tables. "How about some breakfast, Lady Averie?" she asked in a motherly voice. "After the excitement you had yesterday, I'm sure you must be hungry."

After eating, Averie spent twenty minutes arguing with Lady Selkirk, two hours visiting with Lana, and the rest of the day drifting around, feeling simultaneously bored and unsettled. She was both pleased and irritated when Morgan arrived for dinner with three other young officers in tow—irritated because the men always stayed late, and that meant there would be no time for her to sit in the courtyard with Morgan after dinner.

Pleased for the same reason. She was still disgruntled with him for his comments yesterday. She was sure he would be dismayed to learn she had gone ahead and offered Jalessa a position.

"You've had quite a time of it, haven't you, Lady Averie?" Captain Gaele asked as they started the main course. He was a big man with a big smile and a deep laugh; it was impossible not to feel jolly when he was nearby. "We heard you were in the thick of trouble yesterday."

"You should have seen the troops jump when they heard the noise!" Captain Martin added. He was shorter, more compact, and more classically handsome than his friend. He was also more reserved, though friendly enough. "Terrible sound. We were sure there would be casualties. What a great good fortune that there weren't."

Averie toyed with the food on her plate. Fish and fried bumain, with some kind of vegetable she didn't think she'd tried yet. "Even among the Chiarrizi?" she asked.

"What?" Captain Gaele said, surprised.

"The Chiarrizi," Averie repeated. "Were any of them killed?"

"Seven, I think," Captain Martin said.

"How dreadful for their families!" Averie said.

Morgan couldn't restrain himself. "It was they who sent the shells into a civilian space," he said, scowling.

"I imagine it's just as hard to lose people you love if they're killed by friends instead of strangers," Averie replied.

No one had an answer for that, though the officers exchanged swift glances. Lady Selkirk sailed into the breach. "I believe Lady Lana was quite shaken by the event," she said. "Was she recovered when you went to visit her, Averie?"

"Mostly. Yesterday she said she wanted to go back to Port Elise, but today she said she wasn't afraid to stay."

"Well, she'll be safe," Averie's father said. "We're assigning five-man details to each of the Aebrian households here in Chesza. Wouldn't be able to spare the men, but a new troopship arrived yesterday, so we've got the numbers."

"Hey, now! That's a post I'd be happy to take!" Captain Gaele exclaimed. "May I be assigned to watch over Lady Averie?"

"Duel you for the honor," Captain Martin said quickly.

Averie smiled. "Perhaps I will set you each a hard task, and whoever accomplishes it first can be my escort."

"I'm afraid captains have more important jobs than squiring young girls around," Morgan said. "It'll be first or second lieutenants on duty at the households."

Averie was annoyed to think he considered her safety unimportant, but her good humor was instantly restored when Captain Gaele said, "Well, you know, there's many a man who will tell you I've been promoted beyond my abilities. I might be better suited as a lieutenant, what do you think?"

Averie toasted him with her water glass. "I think you're chivalrous but ridiculous to think of giving up any rank for *me*," she said. "But I honor you for the thought."

"How do you know he wasn't willing to give up his career for Lady Lana, not you?" Captain Martin asked, and they all laughed.

"Well, I do think you should go by the Worth house to cheer her up," Averie said. "Although she told me she would recover her spirits quickly if I had a party."

Lady Selkirk looked up at that. "Indeed, yes! I have been thinking we must entertain now that Averie and I have been here long enough to get our bearings."

Averie's father nodded. "Fine with me. Plan what you like."

"An evening event would be best," Lady Selkirk said.

"Oh, can we have it outside?" Averie asked.

"Music and drinks in the courtyard," Captain Martin told her. "That's how the governor entertained, so I've been told."

"I don't think we need to follow the example of Chiarrizi civil servants," Lady Selkirk said coldly.

"Might be fun, though," Captain Gaele said, smiling widely. "Serve Chiarrizi appetizers, let the ladies wear some of those Chiarrizi fabrics you've been buying in the marketplace. Sort of a welcome to Chesza."

Lady Selkirk took a breath to expound on her abhorrence of Chiarrizi customs, but Averie spoke up quickly. "Encourage everyone to wear Chiarrizi emeralds," she said. Lady Selkirk instantly seemed to think this might be a good idea. "Everyone must come to the party wearing *something* from Chiarrin."

"Or bearing a Chiarrizi gift for the hostess," Captain Gaele suggested.

Averie laughed. "Yes! An excellent idea!"

"I think there might be some merit to this approach," Lady Selkirk said.

"When shall we have it? Next week?" Averie demanded.

"My goodness, we'll certainly need more time than that to organize!"

Averie's father touched his napkin to his lips. "Not

much longer," he said. "We are planning an incursion north of the Maekath Mountains, and we'll be pulling most of the troops with us. Everyone at this table will be gone for ten days or more."

Averie paled a little and glanced at Morgan, who had not mentioned this. But he was nodding, as if he had known all about this expedition. "It will be good to see some action after sitting here in Chesza for weeks," he said. "I always think I'll enjoy the peace, and then I find that the time hangs too heavy on my hands."

Time spent with me, Averie thought indignantly. But the other men were nodding. Captain Martin began to tell a tale about a dull stretch of time he'd spent in Neuri, the capital city of Xan'tai, and the various kinds of trouble he'd gotten himself into. Everyone was soon laughing, although Averie found herself wondering if Lieutenant Du'kai would have enjoyed the story quite so much.

The rest of the meal passed pleasantly enough, and Averie managed to enjoy the conversation. But she left the table early, pleading lingering exhaustion after yesterday's adventure, and returned to her room in a thoughtful mood. Somehow she didn't like *any* of the Aebrian officers so much tonight. She supposed she would feel better about all of them tomorrow. Even Morgan.

CHAPTER
EIGHT

Good news came late the next morning: Jalessa returned, a bundle of belongings in her hands, prepared to take the job as Averie's companion.

Lady Selkirk had been aghast when Averie told her she had made the offer, and she had gone straight to General Winston to complain. He had not only supported Averie, he had said, "You could pay her twenty-five a month, if you like." Averie already had the stack of coins sitting in her room so she could give Jalessa a salary in advance.

Jalessa still seemed pale from the aftereffects of her injury, and she admitted to having a headache. "But I am not dizzy, and I feel stronger every hour," she said.

"We will be careful for a day or two," Averie promised. "But I'm so glad you're here!"

Averie had insisted on following Grace down the hall

to get Jalessa settled in her new quarters. The room was much smaller and more spare than Averie's, but comfortable enough even so, Averie thought. The window looked out over the street, rather than the courtyard, but Jalessa said she preferred that.

"I like to hear the sound of the city at night," she said.

Soon enough they were back in Averie's own light-filled room, sorting through the bundles Jalessa had brought. In addition to her own clothes and personal items, she had carried a selection of fabrics that were much finer and more beautiful than those she sold in the market.

"I only bring out the most expensive fabrics for my best customers," Jalessa said when Averie exclaimed over their rich textures. "I thought you would like them."

"Do you suppose we could make a dress for me in the next week or so?" Averie asked, fingering a length of cloth. It was the color of a summer sky shot with silver threads. "We are going to host a dinner party, and we have decided that everyone should bring or wear something from Chesza. If I had a dress from this fabric—"

"A dress like the Aebrians wear or a *tallah* like the Chiarrizi wear?" Jalessa interrupted.

Averie stared at her, for it hadn't occurred to her to commission anything other than a simple Aebrian frock—modified for the heat of Chiarrin, of course. But she felt the corners of her mouth turn up as the idea took possession of her mind.

"Now, I don't think I could wear something *exactly* like a *tallah*," Averie said, stepping back to consider Jalessa's clothing. As always, Jalessa wore a loose, sleeveless garment attached at both shoulders and falling with very little tailoring a few inches past her knees. The many folds seemed to flow comfortably about her body and probably kept cool air moving against her skin, Averie thought. "We could use the same basic styling as long as the hems reached my ankles, I think. The neckline is certainly high enough, and nobody ever cares if you show your arms. Oh, Jalessa, I like this idea."

"You already have Chiarrizi shoes," the other girl pointed out. "And Chiarrizi headscarves. You almost have a Chiarrizi wardrobe already."

Averie nodded. "But we have to think a little bit like the Aebrians! *We* like everything to be fashionably co-ordinated. So if I am to wear blue and green scarves, then my dress should be blue or green—oh, and perhaps I could have emeralds sewn onto the shoulder clasps. There are green flowers embroidered on my shoes already. Perfect!"

Jalessa seemed amused. "So every detail must match? Even your jewels?"

"*Especially* the jewels! Back in Port Elise I have whole sets of amethysts and sapphires and pearls that I wear

with certain dresses. I have a beautiful topaz necklace that
my father brought back from Xan'tai for me, and it only
goes with one dress I own, so I hardly ever wear it!"

Jalessa gestured at Averie's left hand, nested in a spill
of blue fabric. "If you are only going to wear blue and
green to your party, will you leave off your ruby ring?"

Averie was surprised into a choked laugh. She cradled
her hand against her heart. "My engagement ring! Oh
no, I never take this off." Though she was out of charity
with Morgan at the moment, she certainly wasn't angry
enough to repudiate the ring. "So I will be in blue and
green, with one single spark of red."

"For celebration," Jalessa suggested.

"For celebration, indeed."

Two days later, when Jalessa pronounced herself completely recovered, she and Averie set out for the Chesza
market to shop for emeralds. Their wagon was escorted
by four enlisted men and the shy but soulful Lieutenant
Lansdale, whom Averie suspected was sweet on Lana. All
five dismounted and trailed Averie as she navigated the
twisty aisles of the market. It did not make for the most
spontaneous shopping experience, but, on the whole, she
was glad to have them along. Her memories of her last
visit to the marketplace were quite fresh. She did not
want to live through such an experience again.

Emeralds were sold at quite a few wagons, Averie discovered, and could be purchased in almost any form—cut or uncut, loose, set in silver, set in gold. Eventually Averie selected two silver pins each garnished with three stones. Jalessa bargained with the merchant and got them for a very good price.

On the way back from the market, Averie looked with longing at the great white plume of Mualota Fountain. "I just want to go put my hand in the water," she said. "I'm sure it's the very same water that comes pouring out of my spigots every morning, but it *looks* different."

Jalessa glanced at her. "You haven't visited Mualota Fountain yet?"

It just now occurred to Averie that the word might mean something in Jalessa's language. "Mualota—how does that translate? *Mua*, that's 'my,' isn't it?"

Jalessa nodded. "It means 'my heart.' The heart of the city."

Averie motioned Lieutenant Lansdale over and pointed toward Mualota. "Can we go to the fountain? Is it safe? We wouldn't have to stay long."

Lieutenant Lansdale glanced around at the escort, and Averie could almost read his mind. Five Aebrian soldiers, products of the best military training in the world. How could they come to harm? "I don't see why we couldn't, my lady."

Averie almost bounced on the hard seat of the wagon. "Then let's go! Right now."

The driver obligingly turned the horses toward the left when they came to the next crossroads. Averie gripped the side of the cart and looked around with interest as they passed down the narrow street. The way was lined with a honeycomb of buildings, all made of smooth mud and planed wood, all piled against each other so that there appeared to be one unbroken facade looking outward toward the street. No building had more than two levels, but many were only one story, so there was a charming, idiosyncratic rhythm to the changing skyline. Every building had at least one door and tall, narrow windows. At some doorways, an array of plants offered spots of shade and greenery in the hard summer light, but most were bare and not particularly expressive of personality.

"What are these places?" Averie asked Jalessa.

Jalessa glanced at her with a smile. "Dwellings. Much like the place I live."

"*Houses?* They're tiny!"

"Not houses, not like the one you live in. Behind some doors are only one or two rooms. Behind others you might find eight or ten rooms, all belonging to a single family. Most of the residents of Chesza live in spaces like these."

Averie thought about that. "How big is your place?"

"One room. A little bigger than your bedroom."

"So small!"

"It would be plenty of space if I did not have bolts and bolts of fabric piled up along the walls!" Jalessa retorted.

Averie laughed. "Then you must sell more of it to me."

Another ten minutes they wound through narrow streets, and then they broke free into a clearing nearly as large as the market. The uneven paving of the streets gave way to an intricate mosaic of tiles in shades of baked gold, sienna, and deep red. The whole space was dominated by Mualota Fountain, a roaring, powerful jet of water that towered over its surroundings. Averie leaned out of the cart to see more details.

The fountain was contained in a large circular stone basin made of rough reddish stone. Posed along the perimeter of the fountain, just inside the bubbling bowl of water, was a parade of figures, some human, some animal. They were carved of black marble that showed up very clearly against the rusty background of the basin. They were all covered with a fine spray so that they glistened in the afternoon sun.

The whole clearing was thronged with Chiarrizi in their brightly colored clothing. Most were women, hurrying either to or from the fountain with buckets and jars in hand. Many were children, reaching in to scoop up handfuls of water to drink or to fling at one another in glittering arcs. A few men moved more purposefully through the crowd, pausing at the fountain to slake their thirst or splash water onto their hot faces. Averie saw friends greet one another, pause to talk, exclaim over new items of clothing, point to misbehaving children, laugh at some joke or story. Mualota Fountain was clearly a meeting spot for the whole city.

"This is a happy place," Averie decided.

Jalessa glanced at her. "An interesting way to put it. Yes. I would agree."

"Can I get closer? I want to look at the statues."

Jalessa vaulted with easy grace over the side of the wagon. Averie saw that Lieutenant Lansdale was less than eager to have her follow suit. But he did not stop her when she climbed out of the wagon and dropped onto the tiles beside Jalessa.

The Chiarrizi made way for them as they slowly approached the fountain. Averie hoped it was her imagination that the happiness of the place seemed to dim when the Aebrian girl stepped closer to the heart of the city. When they were near enough, Averie trailed her hand in the water. It was warmer than she had expected, probably heated by its long run from the rivers through the aqueducts. She could not resist. She bent and took a sip from her cupped palm. It should have tasted exactly like the water that poured from the spigots in her room, and yet there seemed to be a wilder flavor to it, of old moss and riverbanks and the granite of the basin itself.

Smiling over at Jalessa, she bent down and splashed herself liberally with water from the basin. Warm or not, that felt good on such a hot day. The soaked cloth clung to her shoulders and bosom. Good thing Lady Selkirk was not near enough to see.

Shaking her hands dry, Averie began to pace slowly around the circle, studying each small black statue in turn. One was a woman whose sculpted headscarves streamed behind her as if in a heavy wind. One was a small goatlike animal that Averie assumed was a hodee. One was a creature that looked more like a wolf or a dog; its front foreleg was missing, but it appeared to be caught in the middle of a healthy lope even so.

There were two more small animals that looked like they could be livestock or game, a statue of a man, and a statue of a laughing child. These rather ordinary pieces were interspersed with two more disturbing sculptures. One was of a large fish, twisting its body in a spectacular leap out of the water; its left eye appeared to have been gouged from its head by a fisherman's ill-placed lure. The other was some kind of predatory bird, its wings spread for flight even though an arrow pierced it through the breast. Somewhat troubled, Averie paused in front of the bird sculpture and surveyed the whole fountain.

When Jalessa came up behind her, Averie turned and demanded, "Why do three of these statues show creatures that have been maimed?"

"They are the familiar gods of Chiarrin," Jalessa replied. "*Doena—*"

"What?"

Jalessa pointed at the three-legged wolf. "*Doena.* He rules the land. *Kayla*—I suppose you would call it a fish. He rules the seas. *Seena—*"

"The bird?"

"She rules the air. They are among us on a daily basis. They are our omens, our talismans, and our guardians."

"But why are they . . . hurt? Broken?" As soon as she said the word, Averie remembered what Lieutenant Du'kai had told her—that the Weskish called Chesza "City of Broken Gods." Now she would learn why.

"They are fierce and stubborn gods," Jalessa said in a soft voice. "*Doena* is caught in a hunter's trap, but rather than allow himself to be killed and skinned for his pelt, he gnaws off his own leg. *Kayla* tears himself free from the hook, losing his eye but gaining his freedom. *Seena* is crippled, but she manages to fly away to safety."

"But an arrow placed just like that—she'll die," Averie objected.

Jalessa smiled a little. "She has not died yet. And she has been crippled a very long time."

Averie took a deep breath. "I think you have rather frightening gods in Chiarrin."

"I know only a little about the gods in other countries,

but none of them sound mild to me," Jalessa answered.

Averie didn't know much about gods in other countries, either. In Aeberelle, religion had fallen out of fashion, and she had never been inside a house of worship.
"Perhaps not. But your gods . . . well, they don't seem
very *comfortable*."

Jalessa shrugged. "When your own burdens are heavy
and your own losses great, you tend to remember that
seena can fly with an arrow through her breast or *doena*
has the courage to bite through his own flesh," she said
softly. "And it gives you strength. That is comfort of a
sort."

Described that way, the broken gods of Chiarrin
seemed easier to admire, Averie thought. "So does everyone have a favorite god? Can you choose the one you
pray to?"

"Everyone chooses. *Seena* is the most popular among
women, *doena* among men. Although many people of
Chesza pray to *kayla*, for they are so close to water."

"Which is your god?" Averie asked.

Jalessa reached up a hand to stroke the wet feathers
of the bird-god's head. *"Seena,"* she said. "For she is
wounded to the heart and will not die."

Averie shivered a little, despite the heat. Jalessa's voice
was so sober, her words so sad. Had Jalessa too been
wounded to the heart? "Where do you go to pray?" she
asked. She hadn't noticed any shrines or temples on their

way across the city. Then again, she hadn't known to be looking for symbols of crippled beasts fleeing from cruel hunters.

"Here. Or the temple. Or my room, where I have a small statue of the goddess. Most people keep such statues, or carry small charms shaped like one of the gods."

"Where do you get such charms?" Averie asked instantly.

Jalessa turned to give her a long, measuring look. "Why? Do you want one for yourself? You have no need of protection from the Chiarrizi gods. You have plenty of protection from Aebrian soldiers."

"I just wondered," Averie said. "Someday I will go back to Port Elise and eventually all my memories of Chiarrin will fade. I want to have things that will make me remember this place forever."

"I would have thought emeralds would be sufficient."

That was clear enough. The gods were off-limits to Aebrians. So Averie said, "They certainly will be. They are beautiful emeralds indeed."

Lieutenant Lansdale, who had followed them around the fountain but had stayed a respectful distance behind, took this moment to approach. "Lady Averie. Have you seen what you came here to see? I think it is time to return to your father's house."

"Indeed it is," she said, and followed the lieutenant back to the wagon. Within a few moments, they were on their way again. It was so hot that Averie's dress had completely dried while they were still some distance from the house. No traces of the fountain water remained, except as vivid images in her mind.

Averie had expected Lady Selkirk to be angry that she had made the trek to Mualota, but, in fact, Morgan and her father were the ones who were really furious. Her father actually showed his temper. "You went *where*?" he demanded. "To the fountain? Haven't you been paying attention? Don't you realize that the city is dangerous? Don't you understand that you were given a guard for a reason?" Morgan just sat there, white-faced and tense, his hands closed into fists.

Averie apologized and promised that, in the future, she would ask someone's permission before she traveled beyond the acceptable boundaries of her house, Lana's house, and the market. Privately she wondered why she had been given a military escort at all if she was never going to be allowed to go anywhere, but she knew better than to say so aloud.

The shouting and the appeasing took place over dinner and effectively killed the conversation. Averie was just as happy when the meal was over and she could escape outside and enjoy the cooler air of evening. She sat on her favorite bench and listened to the light patter of water, thinking how small and insignificant her own fountain seemed now that she had been to Mualota. No carved statues stood beneath the spray in *this* particular basin; perhaps the governor had not been a religious man.

She had been outside nearly an hour when Morgan came to join her. He was still angry; he moved stiffly, and his face, hard to see in the darkness, seemed set in disapproval. Nonetheless, he sat beside her and settled his arm around her shoulders.

"I really am sorry," she said in a tentative voice when he didn't speak right away. "I didn't mean to upset everyone."

"Any more tricks like that, and your father will send you back to Port Elise," Morgan said sternly.

Averie pulled away. "It wasn't a *trick*," she said hotly. "It was just stupidity. I didn't think."

"Well, and Lieutenant Lansdale didn't think either," Morgan said, his voice still dark. "*He* won't be on your escort duty after today."

Now Averie did feel bad. "Oh, no, I hate for him to get in trouble because of me!"

Morgan gave her a cold look. "He made an error in judgment."

"You're not sending *him* back to Port Elise, are you?"

"He'll be reassigned. Someone else will take his shift."

He spoke in such a remote voice that Averie completely lost her temper. "Well, I *am* sorry, and I *wish* you would believe me, but if you keep treating me in this hateful way I'd rather not have any conversation with you at all," she said, jumping to her feet.

Morgan stood just as quickly and put a hand on her arm. "I don't mean to be hateful," he said quietly. "But the thought of losing you . . . you're so careless."

"I'm just curious. I wanted to see. Morgan, I did not come all the way from Port Elise just to sit in a house and do nothing! There must be some parts of Chesza that are open to me! Tell me where they are, and those will be the places I go."

He looked uncertain, but at least that was an improvement from looking angry. "I will talk to your father. For now, please confine yourself to the Aebrian residences and the market. And never leave the house without soldiers at your back. Promise me."

She lifted her arms and he stepped closer, taking her into an embrace. "I will promise," she whispered, "if you will kiss me."

He did kiss her, then, and not one of those absent-minded and perfunctory kisses that she had come to expect when he was busy or worried. This kiss took her all the way back to their stolen moments in Port Elise, when they had not been able to keep their hands off each other even though there was the constant risk of being caught by passing servants or a zealous chaperone. This was a kiss that left her ribs bruised and her mouth tender, and Averie was smiling when she finally drew away.

"See, you do love me," she whispered.

He pressed his mouth swiftly onto hers. "I didn't know there was ever a doubt of that."

"Of course there wasn't. Kiss me again."

But later, back in her room and brushing out her long hair, Averie thought about that last exchange, and a frown came to her face. When had she begun to doubt the strength of Morgan's affection for her? Or hers for him? She loved him, of course she did; they had had a few misunderstandings, but she was impetuous enough to have misunderstandings with *everyone* sooner or later. What had made her think she needed reassurance?

What had made him think she didn't?

CHAPTER NINE

Most of the next day was spent with Lady Selkirk, reviewing plans for the upcoming party. The first hour was fairly disagreeable, as Lady Selkirk continually recurred to the most interesting topic of the day—"You went to the *fountain*! You could have been killed!"—but even she grew tired of the litany after a while, and the time passed much more pleasantly.

There was no need to discuss who would be invited: all the officers and all the officers' families. So the real questions came down to what kind of food to have and how to decorate. Should they plan a formal dinner or offer only light refreshments? How should they set up the courtyard? Could they hire Chiarrizi musicians for the evening?

"*That* I will not permit," Lady Worth decided. "Who knows what kind of barbaric music these people might produce? We will have good Aebrian players, or we will have silence."

Averie sighed but gave in. She was fairly certain that her father and Morgan would not be in favor of Chiarrizi musicians either.

She spent the rest of the day engaged in the pleasurable task of helping Jalessa design her dress for the party. They were in Averie's room, measuring and cutting fabric, when Lana arrived. "Grace told me I could find you back here," the other girl said, settling down on the bed as casually as if it were her own. "Good to see you, Jalessa! How do you like working for the Aebrians so far?"

"It has been only a few days, but I like it well enough. Averie is very thoughtful."

"Yes, but keep away from Lady Selkirk," Lana said.

"That's not hard to do, since Lady Selkirk likes to pretend Jalessa doesn't exist," Averie retorted.

Lana took a moment to survey the oceans and valleys of materials arrayed on the floor. "What are you doing? Making a tent?"

Averie snorted. "I hope it looks better than a tent! Jalessa is making a dress for me. Can you keep a secret?"

"Maybe," Lana said doubtfully.

"At our party next week, I'm going to wear a dress cut in the Chiarrizi style."

Lana's eyes grew big. "Short like that? Lady Selkirk will never allow it!"

"Longer," Averie conceded. "But draped." She fluttered her hands from her ribs to her knees. "Flowing from the shoulders. Made of Chiarrizi fabric."

"And these are your colors? Blue and green? Do you have emeralds to match? Oh, Averie, this will be lovely!"

"And a matching headscarf."

"No! You're not wearing a headscarf to the party! Lady Selkirk will have a fit."

"I won't tell her. And you can't tell your mother or anyone else what I'm wearing. Promise?"

"I won't breathe a word," Lana said.

Averie grinned. "Now, aren't you glad you've decided not to go back to Port Elise?"

"Maybe," Lana shot back. "But I think *you'll* be on the next boat back as soon as Lady Selkirk sees your outfit, and they might decide to send me with you."

Now Averie laughed. "Everyone's already mad enough to want to see me gone," she said cheerfully. "This might be enough to get me sent away for good."

Lana settled more comfortably on the bed. "Why? What have you done now?"

"Jalessa and I went to the Mualota Fountain yesterday, and apparently everyone thought I was risking my life," Averie said. "And I'm not sorry at all, because really it was quite amazing, except that Lieutenant Lansdale got punished for allowing me to go. They've taken him off my escort detail and banished him somewhere."

"Banished him to me!" Lana said gaily. "And you know I think he's just adorable—ineligible, of course, but so sweet. So I'm happy you misbehaved yesterday. But who's become your official escort?"

"I don't know yet. I haven't left the house today. I plan to go to the market tomorrow, though, and look for decorations. I suppose I'll find out then."

And in fact, the next morning when Averie ordered the wagon and scanned the faces of her escort, she was delighted to see a familiar face.

"Lieutenant Du'kai!" she exclaimed. "Oh, tell me this was an assignment that you didn't plead to be excused from!"

He smiled at her merry greeting and took her hand to help her into the wagon. But she stood there a moment beside him, wanting a chance to talk. Jalessa required no assistance, just lightly sprang over the side and settled herself, patiently waiting.

Lieutenant Du'kai dropped Averie's hand, but continued to smile at her. "You seem to have recovered from your adventure well enough," he said. "I see you have not lost your enthusiasm for Chesza's market, at any rate."

"I have not lost my enthusiasm for Chiarrin at all," she replied. "But you did not answer my question."

His smile widened. "No, indeed, Lady Averie, I did

not feel the slightest dismay at being named to your guard. In fact, I was pleased by the assignment."

"We are having a party next week," she said. "Will you come?"

"Of course. I have not been to nearly enough parties in my life."

She laughed and allowed him to hand her into the wagon. "And this one will be special, I think," she said. "Let me tell you about it as we go to the market."

He brought his horse alongside the wagon and listened most courteously as they made their way through the city. She would have spoken in Weskish for Jalessa's benefit, but the Chiarrizi girl had settled on the other side of the wagon, and really, it was easier to have the conversation in her native tongue.

"Lady Selkirk won't let me hire Chiarrizi players, though," Averie said, finishing up the recital on a regretful note. "So I don't know that we'll have any music."

"Oh, that's easily solved," Lieutenant Du'kai answered. "Some of the fellows from the regiment have brought their instruments from home. We had a few songs after mess the other day—I thought they were quite good."

"Excellent! Could you ask them if we could hire them for the night?"

He laughed. "I don't even have to ask. If it means they're off duty for an evening and have a chance to mingle with pretty girls, they will most certainly be agreeable."

"But ask them anyway. Just to be sure."

"Lady Averie, I live to serve."

So that was a most enjoyable and productive conversation, and the trip to the market proved just as fruitful. Averie bought tall potted trees and brightly embroidered streamers to hang from their highest limbs; colorful glass globes to set over burning tapers; and hammered copper braziers and bricks of incense to burn in them. Averie's favorite purchase was a set of silver chiming balls that were meant to be dropped in the fountain.

"I think I will want to keep these long after the party is over!" Averie exclaimed to Jalessa in Weskish.

Jalessa smiled. "Many people feel the same."

"I am certain this will be the most delightful party ever."

"I am looking forward to it," Lieutenant Du'kai answered.

There were no frightening incidents at the market this day, and Averie did not allow herself to be tempted into making any side excursions on the way home. She did glance with some longing at the distant plume of Mualota Fountain, but Lieutenant Du'kai saw the direction of her gaze.

"Do not even ask me to escort you there," he said in a firm voice. "I am charged with proving I am a better man than poor Jamie Lansdale, and I am determined to do so."

Averie laughed. They were speaking in Aebrian again, for Jalessa was once more sitting on the other side of the wagon. "And what if I defied you?" she asked. "Jumped down and went running through the streets as fast as I could? You are always so proper—I cannot picture you snatching me up and throwing me back into the wagon."

He laughed as well, but there was something in his eyes that gave her pause. "I think you misread me to some extent, Lady Averie. I am a soldier. I am capable of a certain ruthlessness when the situation requires."

She arched her eyebrows. "I had better not test you, I suppose."

"Are you in the habit of testing people?" he asked softly.

That made her blink. She was going to give him an automatic *no*, and then she thought about it. "Sometimes," she admitted. "I like to know how people will react."

He was still watching her rather closely. "And how do you react when people test *you*?" he said.

An even more baffling question. She nibbled at her lower lip and reviewed some of her past history. "I suppose it depends on the situation," she said slowly. "If they are trying to see how well they can control me, I react very badly. If they want to see how good I can be, I think I behave rather well."

He laughed almost soundlessly. "There is not much pretense with you, is there, Lady Averie?"

No, but that wasn't what she chose to answer. "I wish you would call me Averie," she said in a complaining voice.

"I do not believe our circumstances allow for such familiarity."

"I would call you Ket," she offered. "Unless you wouldn't like that."

"Of course I like the sound of my own name pronounced by a pretty woman," he said in his usual gallant way. "But it would be most inappropriate." He smiled. "Testing Lady Selkirk too far," he added.

"Well, she needn't know," Averie said. "We would only be so casual with each other when no one else was around to hear."

Now his expression was rueful. "There is always someone around to hear."

True; they were accompanied by four soldiers and Jalessa, though Averie didn't think any of them were likely to carry tales to Lady Selkirk. But she received the message well enough. Ket Du'kai was not comfortable extending their friendship so far.

"Then, Lieutenant Du'kai, please escort me home. I believe I am all finished with my shopping for the day."

In the morning, Jalessa was gone on one of her holidays. Averie missed her quiet voice and good-humored company, particularly as compared with Lady Selkirk, who seemed particularly strident this day. In the afternoon, Averie escaped to Lana's. They spent a long time discussing what Lana should wear to the dinner, which of the officers they most wished to dance with, what would have to transpire to make Jamie Lansdale a respectable match, what made Captain Gaele so appealing, and whether or not they missed their friends back in Port Elise. Lana did; Averie did, too, but not nearly so much. She was still enraptured by Chesza, and it took up all her time.

"And you have Colonel Stode to bear you company," Lana pointed out. "You would not be nearly so content if he were not here."

"You could be right, but he has been infuriating half the time, so more than once I have wished him back in Port Elise," Averie said frankly.

Lana looked up quickly. "Oh, no, you can't mean it! What has he done?"

Averie shrugged. It was so hard to put into words. "Little things. Careless things. Perhaps it's just that he seems too busy to pay me much attention, and I resent it."

"My father says that a soldier's wife can't expect a man to be full of poetry and romance," Lana said wisely. Major General Worth was second in command in Chesza and had no doubt been in the army as long as Averie's father. "My mother always adds, 'Yes, your father told me exactly once that he loved me, and I've had to take it on faith all these years that he still means it.' I think that's just how military men *are*. They're efficient. They do a task and move on."

"Well, I'm not quite ready to have Morgan *move on* from the stage of wooing me, and I shall let him know that if I ever think he has slipped too far," Averie said.

Lana laughed. "And I think Lieutenant Lansdale would be quite willing to lavish affection on a girl for years and *years* if he thought she would love him in return," she said. "But what of Captain Martin? Efficient as Colonel Stode, don't you think? Court you and then be done with the task when he thought it was fully achieved."

Averie grinned, and they returned to their giggling game of sizing up the men of their circle for their romantic possibilities and their marriage potential. Strangely, Lieutenant Du'kai's name did not come up once. Perhaps Lana did not wonder about him at all. Averie did not like to admit it, but she knew she wondered about him too much.

CHAPTER TEN

Finally, finally, the day of the party arrived. Averie and Lady Selkirk spent the day overseeing Sieffel as he decorated the courtyard; they checked on Grace and a borrowed cook as they prepared Chiarrin food. Averie's father and Morgan came home early enough to admire the decorations, eat dinner, and change into their formal uniforms. The first guests would arrive shortly after sundown, as soon as the air began to cool.

"I want you in the *maroya* with me within the half hour," Lady Selkirk told Averie as the women retired to dress. "No dawdling! You will stand with me and your father and Colonel Stode to welcome visitors to our house."

"Of course I will," Averie said, though she had no intention of doing so. The house must be full of guests before she made an appearance, or Lady Selkirk would send her back to her room to change.

Therefore, she met Jalessa in her chambers, locked the door, and proceeded to get ready at a very sedate pace. It was easy to step into the *tallah* and fasten the emerald clasps at the shoulders, but Jalessa had to help her with the headscarves. Once Averie had buckled on her new shoes, she turned to face the mirror set into the wall.

She caught her breath and stared. She absolutely would not have been able to pick herself out of a crowd. The scarves, tied to completely cover her hair, laid a bright border around her face and gave her cheeks an unfamiliar contour. The loose folds of the *tallah* felt very different on her body from the close panels of an Aebrian ball gown. She felt as if she would take bigger steps, deeper breaths, as if she would move with an unaccustomed grace and freedom.

Who knew how a person might behave if she was attired like this?

"Oh, Jalessa," she murmured. "I don't look anything like myself."

Jalessa smiled over her shoulder. "Is that something to be celebrated or regretted? It is not too late for you to change into something else."

"Oh, no. *This* is what I want to wear."

At that moment, Lady Selkirk's imperious voice came echoing down the hall. "Averie! Hurry up! Captain Gaele and Captain Martin are strolling up the walk, and you are nowhere in sight!"

Averie ignored her and continued watching herself in the mirror. She caught the sound of new arrivals—the Drysers, the Worths, a few more of the unattached officers. From her bedroom window she could see guests begin to spill from the *maroya* into the courtyard. She could hear the pleasure and appreciation in their voices as they discovered the musical balls in the fountain, the scented incense in the air. Still, she waited, practicing a few dance steps in her Chiarrizi sandals. Once she spun entirely around, just to watch the blue and green hems go floating up around her ankles. Oh, she loved this *tallah*.

Finally, half an hour after the first guests arrived, Averie nodded at her reflection and smiled at Jalessa. "It's time for me to make my appearance," she said.

She hurried down the hallway, following the sounds of laughter and conversation. Lady Selkirk was no longer at the front door, so everyone must have already arrived. Indeed, all the guests appeared to be gathered in the courtyard, enjoying the night air and the casual food. There were maybe forty-five people, mostly men, clustered in groups by the fountain and the small refreshment tables. A trio of musicians—young Aebrian enlisted men—sat on stools behind some of the tall plants and played quiet music that fell as restfully over the assembled guests as the sound of chiming water.

Averie took a deep breath and stepped outside. For a moment, no one noticed her, and she tensely waited to be discovered. Then there was a muffled shriek, and Carrie Dryser's high, thin voice rang out. "I don't believe it! That's Averie!"

And then everybody was staring.

For one dreadful moment, Averie thought she had gone too far. She didn't dare look at Lady Selkirk or her father, for she already had a fairly accurate idea of what their faces would show, but the dead silence of the crowd made her fear that everyone else was just as shocked. A proper Aebrian heiress dressed up like a common woman of Chesza? What a hoyden! What a blunder!

And then Carrie spoke again. "I *love* that dress! Averie, where can I get one?" And all the young girls were descending on her, oohing over her *tallah,* touching her headscarf, exclaiming at the jewels, the fabrics, the colors. Their mothers were only a step or two behind, asking who had sewn the outfit for her; was it comfortable; was it cool; did the colors mean something, for they had heard hue mattered to the Chiarrizi.

"Averie, you look so beautiful!" Lana exclaimed.

"Turn around once, let me see the back," Lady Worth demanded, so Averie spun. "You know, it's a very practical outfit for this kind of climate, isn't it? Makes me wish I was wearing that instead of what I've got on right now."

Lady Dryser echoed the sentiment, and then for a brief moment the conversation veered toward the discomfort of certain tight undergarments, necessary when a woman reached a certain age but miserable all the same.

"But you wouldn't need anything like that if you were wearing a dress like this," said Major Harmon's wife, Miranda. She was middle-aged, rather large, and clearly feeling the heat in all the folds of her ruffled magenta dress. "Does it have to be made of quite so many colors? Couldn't I get something like this in a nice solid brown?"

Averie bubbled with laughter. "I'm sure you could have it made however you like! Lana knows a seamstress, and there must be others."

"Is that who made your dress?" Carrie Dryser asked.

"It's called a *tallah*, but no," Averie replied. "It was sewn for me by a friend. I'm hoping she'll make me another one."

"Oh, heavens, yes," said Miranda Harmon. "I think you've started a new fashion."

So the daring experiment turned out to be, after all, a rousing success, and Averie glowed with triumph for the rest of the evening. Mindful of her responsibilities as hostess, she made a slow circuit around the fountain, managing to exchange a few words with almost every guest. Lana and Carrie and a few other young women trailed behind her, flirting with the young officers and talking prettily to the older ones.

"So I suppose you're all going to come dressed up

as Chesza girls next time there's a party, hey?" Captain Gaele asked in his jovial way. "Don't know that I'll be able to tell you apart if you all look so much alike."

Carrie laughed and rapped him on the wrist. "What a disgraceful thing to admit! You think we all look so similar? How do you tell us apart *now*, Captain?"

"Lady Lana's a dark-haired girl, and you've got all those curls," he said promptly. "Lady Averie has the long blonde hair. But if that's all covered up with some contraption on your head— Well, a poor soldier like me is going to have a mighty hard time of it."

Carrie batted her eyes. Technically speaking, Captain Martin was a better catch, but Captain Gaele was everyone's favorite, and Carrie was completely shameless in her pursuit of him. "Give me a scarf or a bouquet to carry, and you'll instantly know which one is me," she purred.

He did not respond with the gallantry she clearly hoped for, but laughed out loud. "A most excellent notion! I shall give each of you some token to wear, and I shall write down on a card who has been given what. All I'll need to do is consult my notes to discover if I'm talking to the general's daughter or the Worth girl."

Carrie pouted, but the rest of them laughed. "I don't think it can be that hard to sort us out," Lana said. "But take pity on *us*, if you will! Every man of the Aebrian army dressed in exactly the same uniform, except for a few pieces of frogging on the shoulder that are meant to tell us if he's a first lieutenant or a full colonel! But you don't see us scrambling to keep you straight. We know exactly who you are and what your rank is."

Captain Martin and Lieutenant Lansdale had joined them, and they made a small happy knot of people in the middle of the courtyard. "You keep track of us because you're always aware of our potential in the marriage market," Captain Martin said with good-natured cynicism, provoking a storm of laughter and protests.

"You won't have any potential at all if you continue to make comments like that!" Lana informed him.

He gave her a deep bow. "My apologies. How can I atone?"

"You can see whether our musicians can play anything more lively," said Edna Harmon. She was as heavyset as her mother and just as outspoken, and Averie liked her a great deal. "I wish they'd play something we could dance to."

"Dancing!" The word went up from more than one of the gathered guests. But Averie glanced around and shook her head.

"There's barely enough room for us all to stand together," she said.

"In the *maroya*?" Carrie suggested. "If you push back the furniture?"

"It's just that almost no one else has even thought

to have musicians," Edna explained. "I hate to waste them!"

Averie took another quick look around the courtyard. Lady Selkirk was standing with the other matrons, her back most firmly turned toward Averie. Her father and Morgan had drawn into a tight group with a few of the other senior officers. Their stern expressions and squared shoulders led Averie to think they were discussing matters more weighty than whether or not the party was a success.

"We could help you move the tables," Lieutenant Lansdale offered hopefully.

"I'd love to, but I don't dare be the one to ask," Averie said. "If someone else makes the request of Lady Selkirk—"

That elicited another round of laughter. "My skills of diplomacy are always rated most high," Captain Gaele declared, a statement that earned him some derisive comments from his fellow officers. "I'll go make the request. Lady Lana, won't you come with me? Together I'm sure we can persuade her." He offered her his arm, and they strolled over to the knot of older women.

"The musicians have to be willing as well," Averie said.

Captain Martin bowed again. "Don't give it a thought," he said. "Two of them report to me. They'll sit where they're told and play what they're ordered."

She smiled at him. "Then I suppose the only question left is whether there are enough men who are willing to dance? For in my experience, it is always the women who wish to waltz, and the men who scorn such entertainment."

"Again, leave the problem in my hands," he said. "Gaele and I outrank a number of the men in attendance. If you find anyone too laggardly in soliciting your hand, just let us know, and we will find you partners soon enough."

"I don't know that anyone has ever been *commanded* to dance with me before," Carrie said. "I wonder if I might find such a thing insulting?"

"It won't bother me in the slightest," Edna said. "I just want to dance."

Averie was watching Lana and Captain Gaele make their proposition to Lady Selkirk, who looked at first annoyed, then unwilling, then resigned. From this far away, Averie couldn't hear what anyone was saying, but she guessed that Lady Worth and the others standing nearby must have exclaimed how much fun it would be to set up an impromptu ballroom. Lady Selkirk was never very good at resisting the pressure of public opinion. If her cronies were in favor of dancing, dancing they would have.

Accordingly, about twenty minutes later, the *maroya* had been cleared, the musicians had been recruited, and twelve or fourteen of the younger guests had paired off. Averie, as hostess, was much in demand. She passed from Captain Martin to Lieutenant Lansdale to Captain Hawksley as the music changed, and she had promised two others that she would accept them for the very next set. Morgan had chosen to stay outside with the older officers, and she told herself she did not mind at all. Instead, she concentrated on paying attention to who solicited whom for the first reel, the second cotillion. Lana and Lieutenant Lansdale; well, that was hardly a surprise. Carrie and Captain Martin. Edna and Captain Hawksley. Captain Gaele and a very young girl, Edna's little sister, who by rights shouldn't even be at this party but who appeared to be having more fun than all the rest of them combined. Averie smiled to watch them, thanked her partner when the music ended, and stepped from the makeshift dance floor almost into the arms of Ket Du'kai.

She had not even realized he was at the party.

"Lieutenant!" she exclaimed, unable to hide her pleasure. "When did you arrive?"

He smiled and took her hand. "I have been here since before *you* deigned to join the festivities," he said, gently teasing. "You have been so surrounded by admirers that I haven't had a chance to talk to you till now."

She grimaced and then she laughed. "Admirers and detractors," she said. "I don't think everyone has been entirely won over by my appearance tonight."

"You look charming."

"Lady Selkirk has not said a word to me."

"Then no doubt you have enjoyed the evening immensely."

She laughed even harder at that. "In fact, I have. Have you come to dance? Or are you one of those men who prefers to watch from the sidelines?"

"He dances well enough, but you're promised to me for this set," Captain Gaele said, coming up and grabbing Averie's hand. "And if he protests, I'll have him flogged."

"Oh, I couldn't be responsible for such a dreadful fate befalling such a fine young man," Averie said. In truth she was a little irritated; she had rather looked forward to dancing with the Xantish man. "Forgive me, Lieutenant Du'kai! But it is only to save you pain and humiliation that I give myself to this brutish officer."

"I would risk both for the opportunity to squire you around the room," he said.

"Not a chance," Gaele said, and tugged Averie into his arms as the music started.

It was no great hardship to dance with Rufus Gaele, who whisked her around the dance floor with great energy and kept her laughing the whole time. Still, Averie could not keep herself from peering over his shoulder to learn who Lieutenant Du'kai had found as a partner. Not until the music ended did she catch sight of him rather slowly releasing Carrie Dryser from the embrace demanded by the waltz. Carrie was smiling up at him as if he was the richest prize in the matrimonial race and she had already won him.

Well. Carrie Dryser. Who would have thought the lieutenant had such uninspired taste in women?

"I see you are enjoying yourself even more than you expected to," said a voice in Averie's ear, and she throttled a guilty start to turn and smile at Morgan.

"I don't know. My expectations were fairly high," she demurred.

He was smiling, but she thought she detected a little strain on his handsome face. Was he angry with her, but working to conceal the emotion, or was something else bothering him? "And have they been met this evening?"

"They will be if you dance with me," she responded. She lifted her hands, a mute invitation, and he took her in the proper hold. The musicians offered up a sparkling tune, and they joined the couples already on the floor. Morgan danced much the way Captain Martin did—with perfect technique and flawless civility—not at all like Rufus Gaele, who sometimes actually dragged his partner across the floor. "What about you?" she asked. "Are you enjoying yourself?"

"You and Lady Selkirk have outdone yourselves," he responded.

That was not really an answer. Averie frowned, but before she could inquire more closely, he added, "And your dress is *most* fetching. You created quite a stir, of course, but you have dazzled rather than offended."

"Were you afraid I might have offended some of the proper matrons?" she asked at once. "Would that have made you angry with me tonight?"

He looked down at her gravely. "I love your high spirits and your fearlessness," he said. "I do think they might get you into trouble some day. An officer cannot afford to have his wife flouting convention at every turn. But I know you, Averie. I trust you. You would never go too far." He drew her a little closer than decorum would suggest. "And you do look most beautiful in your Chiarrizi dress."

His final words almost mollified her, but she was so ruffled by the first part of his speech that she couldn't bring herself to answer. He did not even seem to notice that she was displeased with him. "Lady Selkirk may never forgive you, though," he added.

"Lady Selkirk has a long list of things for which she will never forgive me," Averie said in a tight voice. "I'm sure there will be enough distractions in the coming days that she will soon look past this transgression."

"I will not be able to help you distract her, I'm afraid," he said, and he sounded so sober that Averie pulled back to look at him in alarm.

"I know you will be leaving for the Maekaths soon," she said. "But has something happened?"

He pressed his lips together and nodded. "There's been a disturbance up by the mountains," he said. "Your father and I will be riding out in a day or two to take care of it. Worth will command Chesza while we're gone."

How did Aebrian soldiers "take care of" something they considered a "disturbance"? Averie felt a clutch of cold around her heart. "Morgan," she breathed. "What's wrong? Will you be in danger?"

"No, no, we'll have five hundred soldiers with us, and the rebels have never been able to muster more than a handful of men at a time. But they've still got some stores of gunpowder, which they've used to blow up a supply wagon heading toward our outpost in the mountains." He saw her face and hugged her again. "A few men were injured—the job was clumsily done. But we have to assume they've got more. We need to find their reserves, and we need to shut them down."

She was troubled by the notion that he would be venturing into a volatile situation. She was troubled by what he might be required to do to contain it. She wasn't certain how to express either thought. So instead she said, "I have been trying not to think about how much I will miss you. How long will you be gone?"

"It's not clear. Not less than a week, I imagine, and maybe two."

"Two weeks!" She stared at him in dismay. "It's not even three weeks since I arrived! And you're leaving already?"

His smile was sympathetic. "I know. A soldier's wife leads a dreadful life, does she not? If he's stationed at home during a spell of peace, he mopes about the house and complains that life is dull. If he's called up to action, either he leaves his wife behind to fret about him for months at a time, or he brings her along—to do her best in some wretched climate with inferior accommodations and the constant threat of violence. And he's *still* gone half the time! I swear, I don't know why any girl marries any man in uniform." He gathered her more tightly and actually lifted her off her feet to swing her around. He whispered, "And yet, I'm very glad that you have agreed to marry *me*."

"Yes, and I'm so glad to be marrying you," she replied automatically, though part of her was thinking, candidly, that the life he described was not very appealing at all. Whenever she imagined being married to Morgan, they were *together*, and they were either in Port Elise or some romantic foreign capital. "But I don't find Chiarrin to be wretched at all, despite the heat," she added.

He made a derogatory noise. "It's worse than Xan'tai," he said. "Though the food's better."

She disliked the way he cavalierly dismissed the charms of both countries, but the music stopped before she could answer. Morgan offered her a deep bow, so she responded as well as she could. The *tallah* wasn't really designed for sweeping curtsies. A giggle nearby alerted her to Carrie Dryser's presence.

"Oh, Colonel Stode, you're the best dancer here!" the other girl exclaimed. "And so gallant! Averie really is the luckiest girl in Aeberelle."

Clearly, the only civil response to that was a request that Carrie then take a turn with him. Still giggling, Carrie laid her hand in Morgan's and led him rather triumphantly onto the makeshift dance floor.

Averie found herself face-to-face with Ket Du'kai.

"How strange," he murmured. "Moments ago, it was *my* chivalry that Lady Carrie found so delightful. Yet Colonel Stode makes all my efforts appear paltry."

Averie dissolved into laughter, cheering up immediately. "I won't make unkind remarks about her if she is one of your particular friends, but she *does* seem to be a little opportunistic from time to time," Averie replied.

It was clear that he was debating how to answer that. "I understand Lady Carrie," he said at last. "I know what to expect of her, which makes my life easier. I never make mistakes with her."

Which was the most interesting answer he could have given, though the most obscure. "Now that I have a reason to think about it, I'd guess you rarely make mistakes with anyone," Averie replied.

His smile came, warm and amused. "I am on my guard, Lady Averie, but it is clear to me that I am constantly making mistakes with you."

Now her chin came up. "Oh? And what have these many errors consisted of?"

He shook his head. "I'm an officer in a foreign army, and I've been given entree into a social world that I will never be able to call my own. Anything less than utter submission to the system is an error."

"So let me put it to you again—"

Without asking, without even signaling his intent, he abruptly pulled her into his arms and swept her onto the dance floor. He was significantly shorter than Morgan; they could stare into each other's eyes almost without having to tilt their heads. "You seem different from all the others," he said, as if that was an answer. His voice was offhand, and the bright music made all conversation seem unimportant, so it was hard for Averie to tell how seriously he meant the remark. "That leads me to expect you to behave differently. Which leads *me* to behave in ways I should not."

She was almost bewildered—and almost exhilarated. "You have been nothing but courteous to me," she replied. "Never once inappropriate."

"I have been too honest," he said.

"I would hardly consider that offensive."

"Dangerous," he amended.

They were twirling through the dance, completely oblivious to what music played, who else might be near them on the floor. Averie thought she had never in her life been so absorbed in a conversation. "Dangerous to you?" she asked. "Or to me?"

That smile again. "I can't think of any way in which my existence poses a hazard to you."

"I cannot imagine, in turn, that I offer any threat to your well-being."

"It is the consequence of saying what is in your head, or in your heart," he said, and now his smile was missing. "It leads you to expect something in return."

She thought about that while the motion of the dance led them to separate, circle each other, and join hands again. "And that's how I've failed you? By not meeting your honesty with my own?"

"On the contrary," he said very softly. "That's how you've been dangerous. Precisely *because* you have been so truthful. I sometimes wonder if you've ever told a falsehood in your life."

She cast down her eyes with an assumed contrition. "I have lied to Lady Selkirk more times than I would like to admit."

He laughed, genuinely amused. "I suppose I was referring to dishonesty on a somewhat grander scale than white lies you might tell your chaperone."

She lifted her eyes again and gave him a straight look.

"So let me be very clear," she said. "You find me dangerous because I speak to you openly, and this encourages
you to respond in the same way. Because I treat you as
a friend."

"As an equal," he said.

That startled her so much she almost came to a halt,
but he kept his hold and guided her into the next turn.
"How are you not my equal?" she demanded.

"In every way that can be enumerated," he said.
"Don't pretend you don't understand the distinctions of
class, culture, wealth, and military rank."

"I treat everybody the way I treat you," she said.

His smile reappeared briefly and was gone. "I know."

"And no one else seems to think his life will be ruined."

"Perhaps everyone else is quite safe."

"But what do you want from me?" she demanded.
She really was at a loss now. "Shall I behave differently?
Treat you with coldness and disdain? Follow Carrie Dryser's lead, and speak to you only when there is no one
else more interesting in the room?"

"I hope you do none of those things."

"Then what?"

He inclined his head a little. She had the sense
that this whole conversation had been difficult for
him—that, at the same time, he passionately wished it
had never begun and desperately hoped it would not
conclude. She thought he had not intended it to take

this direction but knew he would have no choice but to answer her now.

"I hope you understand if I perhaps do not seem as open as you would like," he said finally. "If I am too formal. If I am too severe. It is my way of repairing damage."

The music stopped, and he dropped his hands. Averie stared at him, trying to remember the last time she had been so frustrated when a tête-à-tête had been ended by a final chord of music. "You don't want to be my friend," she said baldly.

"I do want to," he said. "But I cannot be."

Before Averie could answer, Lana grabbed her elbow. "Averie! Edna says they are serving some kind of special sweet out in the courtyard. Should we all take a break from dancing?"

Averie tore her eyes away from Lieutenant Du'kai's face. "Yes, it's really delicious. Grace spent half the day making it."

Lana tugged on her arm. Most of the other dancers were already streaming out the door, and the musicians were folding up their instruments. "Well, we don't want to miss it! Hurry up."

Averie allowed Lana to pull her toward the door, but she turned back to offer Lieutenant Du'kai a parting comment. "You have no idea how stubborn I can be," she said. "I don't think I can accept that."

His face showed both laughter and resignation, but he did not answer, merely gave her a correct bow. Lana was whispering in her ear. "Doesn't Ket Du'kai dance divinely? He is almost my favorite of the officers."

"Is he?" Averie whispered back. The air outside was so much cooler than the air inside that she had to pause a moment to revel in it. Or maybe she had just gotten a bit too overheated during that final dance. "I think I saw you paired up with Lieutenant Lansdale more than once."

Lana laughed, sighed, and shook her head. "As well moon after him as fall in love with—with—a Chiarrizi!" she said. "Come on. Let's sample some of this marvelous dessert. What a perfect way to end a simply wonderful evening!"

CHAPTER
ELEVEN

The consensus among all the officers' families seemed to be that General Winston's party was the standard by which to judge all future social events. The following day, visitors dropped by every hour to offer their compliments and repeat the gossip. Lady Selkirk was so pleased that she scarcely bothered to reprimand Averie for her choice of attire and the underhanded way she had introduced it. For the moment, at least, Averie was a social success, and Lady Selkirk was all smiles.

But that afternoon, it was hard to be quite so jubilant. Word came that there had been another attack on the Aebrian encampment up by the Maekath Mountains. Two soldiers had died and half a dozen had been wounded. Averie's father and Morgan moved up their travel plans and departed the very next morning, taking many of the troops with them. Lieutenant Lansdale was gone, Lana gloomily informed Averie. Lieutenant Du'kai had been called up as well. They were left with Major General Worth, Captain Martin, a handful of enlisted men, and strict instructions to stay within a circumscribed quadrant of the city.

For the next few weeks, life in Chesza looked to be very dull.

Later, Averie thought that if she hadn't had Lana and Jalessa to keep her company, she would have gone slowly insane. First, of course, there was the worry. Were her father and Morgan safe? What about all their other friends—Rufus Gaele, Jamie Lansdale, Ket Du'kai, *all* of them, none to be singled out more than another? But it was impossible to spend every hour of the day in a state of agitation; boredom set in quickly enough. And boredom was even harder than anxiety to keep at bay.

Lana came by daily, or Averie went to the Worth house. Edna and her sister, and even Carrie Dryser, joined them frequently, for their own lives had become just as narrowly defined. They gossiped and wrote letters home and played board games, but mostly they passed the time sewing. Jalessa had brought a cartload of fabric, and she was helping all of the girls design their own *tallahs*. In the normal course of events, none of them cared much for setting a stitch, but all of them became caught up in the pleasure of creating their new wardrobes. The pattern was easy to follow, the fabric was forgiving, and the end result was so desirable that they all worked away with enthusiasm.

The other occupation that kept Averie busy was teaching Jalessa the Aebrian language. It hadn't even occurred to her that Jalessa might be interested in learning until they were alone one afternoon about three days after the soldiers had departed.

"Isn't Edna funny?" Averie said. "When she told that story about her father's aunt—! I thought Lana would start crying, she was laughing so hard."

Jalessa smiled. Her hands were still busy as she sewed a new *tallah* for herself, but Averie was just reclining lazily in one of the more comfortable *maroya* chairs. "I didn't catch the details," she said.

"Of course you did! She was sitting right next to you! She was—" Averie stopped abruptly. "We weren't speaking Weskish, were we? Edna's little sister isn't very good at it, and so we—but, Jalessa, how rude! I'm so sorry!"

"It doesn't matter."

Averie sat up. "I could teach you Aebrian, if you like," she offered. "At least, I *think* I could. I've never tried to teach anybody anything before."

Jalessa considered that with the same seriousness she brought to everything. "I would like that," she decided. "I know a few words already."

"Really? What can you say?"

"Water," Jalessa said carefully, getting the syllables right but the accent wrong. "Help me. I do not speak your language."

"Well, that's a start," Averie said. "Let's see, how did I learn Weskish? I think we began with verbs."

So she conjugated a few key verbs for Jalessa, and when that got tedious, she went around the *maroya* and named everything. *Table. Chair. Window. Curtain. Floor.* Then she started on colors. *Red. Blue. Black. Green.*

Lady Selkirk had taken to her room with a headache, so Averie let Jalessa join her for dinner, and the lessons continued over the meal. *Plate. Glass. Fork. Spoon.*

"The plate is blue," Jalessa said when they were about halfway through the meal.

Averie clapped her hands. "Yes! That's exactly right! I think you're going to learn Aebrian much more quickly than I learned Weskish."

When Lana came over in the morning, she proved quite willing to join the new project. Flighty as she was, Lana turned out to be an adept teacher, giving credit to a Xantish servant she'd had in Port Elise. "I had to teach her *everything*, because she didn't speak a word of Aebrian when she arrived," Lana said.

Lana stayed through dinner, and Lady Selkirk joined them, still wan from the aftereffects of a migraine. Averie guessed that she would be too lethargic to put up much protest if Jalessa took her meal with them. And indeed, Lady Selkirk was still in enough pain that she almost didn't seem to notice the despised foreigner sitting right next to her.

Until Jalessa spoke, in her flawless and soothing Weskish. "There is an herb that the Chiarrizi use to fight such headaches," she said. "I have a little in my room."

The march of expressions across Lady Selkirk's face was almost comical. *What is this person doing sitting beside me at dinner? How can such laxity be allowed? But oh, if she can cure my headache . . . Can I trust her heathen potions? But my head will not stop throbbing. . . .* "Indeed, I would be most grateful," Lady Selkirk said in a weak voice.

As Jalessa exited, Lana remarked, "My mother had a stomachache the whole first week we were here. Our seamstress brought her some kind of tea—it smelled awful—but my mother felt better the very next day."

Lady Selkirk's face cleared up. Again, Averie could read the thought in her head. *Well, if foreign medicines are good enough for Lady Worth—!* She had to wonder if Lana had made up the story on the spot, and she hid a grin. "Often these local remedies work to cure local ills," Lady Selkirk said in a pious voice.

They pushed the food around on their plates until Jalessa returned with a packet of what looked like dried seeds. "Mix these in with your bumain," she suggested, sprinkling a few on Lady Selkirk's plate. "I think you'll feel better in half an hour."

So Lady Selkirk obediently mashed up the drug and swallowed the mixture, then sat there looking like a puppy hopeful of a treat. Grace brought them dessert and tea, and the girls talked idly while the sunlight slowly drained away from the courtyard.

"Well, I suppose I'd better go back," Lana said with a sigh. "Shall you come to my house tomorrow, just for the variation?"

Averie yawned and nodded. "It is one of Jalessa's free days, so I'll be even more bored than usual. I'll be by around noon."

"You know, my headache feels much better," Lady Selkirk announced. She was rubbing her temples as if to check for any residue of pain, but she was smiling. "I do believe it's gone." She smiled at Jalessa and addressed her directly in Weskish. "Thank you. You have done me a great kindness."

Jalessa responded with her own grave smile. "I was happy to serve."

In the following days, the most amazing transformation occurred. Lady Selkirk became Jalessa's patron. There was no other way to describe it, Averie thought. Lady Selkirk invited Jalessa to join them for every meal; she asked after Jalessa's family and occupation; she commented favorably upon Jalessa's clothes; she asked Jalessa's opinion on new recipes that Grace might learn. And she bestirred herself to improve Jalessa.

It began with Lady Selkirk taking an interest in the Aebrian lessons. "No, Averie, for goodness' sake, what a slipshod way you have of trying to teach something!" she exclaimed one afternoon. "You need a *system*. Here. Jalessa. Sit by me."

Averie was extremely annoyed, and she glanced at Jalessa to see if she was equally irritated but didn't feel free to express it. But, in fact, Jalessa seemed pleased, and she immediately pulled up a chair beside Lady Selkirk. "Let us review what you already know and then return to the very basics," Lady Selkirk said in her grand way, and the tutorial was under way.

That evening, when Jalessa came to her room to say good night, Averie instantly said, "You don't have to let her lecture you, you know. She's so domineering! I can make up some story about why you shouldn't become her student."

Jalessa was amused. "I didn't mind at all," she said. "In fact, I was glad that she might be beginning to like me."

Averie sniffed. "Who cares if Lady Selkirk likes them?"

"I *am* living in her house."

"It's my father's house."

"She considers it hers to run. If it pleases her to try to

educate me, I will do my best to meet her expectations. Then there will be harmony in the household, and all of us will be more at ease." Her smile widened. "And I may learn something useful."

"Well, if she's mean to you—and she can be *very* sharp-tongued—you just let me know. I won't have her treating you badly."

"I don't think she plans to treat me badly anymore."

Indeed, as the days passed, Lady Selkirk grew fonder and fonder of their Chiarrizi companion. She began offering advice on how Jalessa might straighten her posture or alter her style of dress. The strictures made Averie fume, but Jalessa seemed to accept them with gratitude, and even adopted many of Lady Selkirk's recommendations.

"She's quite bright—I am impressed at how quickly she is picking up the language and how well she responds to instruction," Lady Selkirk told Averie on the next day that Jalessa was gone. "I imagine she could learn anything she put her mind to."

"If only we had a harp here," Averie said. "You could teach her music, too."

"Don't be sarcastic, young lady. It's very unbecoming. *You* could stand to learn from Jalessa, you know—she's a very quiet girl, well behaved and restful."

Averie made a face, but since she couldn't bring herself to say anything to Jalessa's discredit, she was unable to answer.

"In fact, I think she would make a most excellent lady's maid," Lady Selkirk went on. "Once she has the language down—and I'm convinced that soon she will speak it with something approximating fluency—she could serve in almost any household."

"You mean in *Port Elise*?" Averie demanded.

"Of course I mean in Port Elise! I don't see much demand for ladies' maids here."

"Jalessa doesn't want to go to Aeberelle! She won't want to leave Chiarrin!"

Lady Selkirk looked surprised. Clearly she couldn't understand why any creature in the known world would not be thrilled at the prospect of moving to the most fabulous city in existence. "Why wouldn't she? A lady's maid—a good one—makes a fine salary and has a position of utmost respectability."

"But—her life is here! Her family!"

"You might ask her, Averie," Lady Selkirk said with great dignity. "She might be excited at the prospect of traveling the world. *You* were eager enough to do it."

"All right, then. I *will* ask her. And if she is not interested, you must promise not to badger her and try to change her mind."

"I would never do that!"

Averie snorted. "But if she *does* want to come back to Port Elise, she will come back and work for *me*, because *I* found her and I'm the one who's her friend."

Lady Selkirk replied in a honeyed voice, "Averie, my dear, I'm sure someone as intelligent and talented as Jalessa could find a *much* better situation."

To Averie's surprise, when she repeated this conversation the following morning, Jalessa was not at all offended. She stood behind Averie, combing out Averie's long wet hair, and grew very quiet. Averie watched her in the mirror, unable to guess what thoughts were going on behind her placid face.

When the silence had continued for quite a while, Averie said in a tentative voice, "She didn't mean it as an insult."

"No. For Lady Selkirk, this is a compliment of a very high order," Jalessa replied.

"But you wouldn't do it, would you?" Averie said. "You don't want to be a servant, I know."

Jalessa resumed her gentle combing and smiled at Averie in the mirror. "It has not been particularly difficult being a servant to *you*."

"Well, most fashionable young ladies are far more demanding than I am."

"And the money has been most useful. I have shared it with my grandmother and my sister, and it has brought them luxuries they did not think to have. If I went to Port Elise . . ." She shook her head, and the tails of the headscarves floated around her shoulders.

"I suppose money could always be sent back home."

Averie turned around in her chair, pulling her wet hair from Jalessa's grasp. "You'd consider it then? Really? I didn't think there was a chance!"

"Let us say, I would not reject such a notion without thinking about it a good long time," Jalessa replied. "I do not have to decide this very moment, do I?"

"Well, if you choose to come to Port Elise, I hope you accept a position with me!"

Jalessa smiled and turned Averie's head so she was facing forward again. "All of that is a very long way off," she said. "First let us just get your hair done for the day."

It was important to look good this morning, because they were finally getting out of the house.

Captain Martin had come 'round the night before with a note from Morgan and welcome news. "Your father says that they have taken care of the problems up near the Maekaths," he told Averie and Lady Selkirk. "And the city has been so quiet. Both Worth and your father think all the malcontents went north to plot rebellion. So you can explore more of the city tomorrow, if you like—but you have to accept my guard."

"Of course! How delightful! Where shall we go? Mualota Fountain?" Averie asked.

"I was thinking you might enjoy some of the sights in

the northwestern quadrant. I've just been by the Worth house, and I'm on my way to see the Harmons and the Drysers and the others. Everyone would enjoy an expedition, don't you think?"

Averie was so happy at the idea of getting to explore more of Chesza that she didn't even particularly mind that Carrie Dryser would be along for the fun. "When shall I be ready? I could go this very instant."

"I think tomorrow morning will be soon enough."

It had not seemed soon enough for Averie, but it had finally arrived. Averie dressed in a new gold and green *tallah* and matching headscarves edged with blue. It was no surprise, when the group gathered at the Worth house, that most of the young women were similarly attired. Their mothers and chaperones were all wearing proper Aebrian gowns, modified for the heat—all except Lady Harmon. She wore a *tallah* over her ample form, and she looked both supremely comfortable and completely at ease. After the women spent a few moments admiring one another's outfits, Captain Martin called the group to order.

"You shall ride in three wagons, and twenty-five soldiers will accompany us," he said. "We expect no trouble, but if trouble comes, I want you to do exactly as you are told. If one of my men tells you to lie down in the wagon, do it. If he tells you to jump from the wagon and run, do that instead. If we stop and walk around, I want all of you to stay with the group. No wandering off—and Lady Averie, that especially means you." She pouted, and everyone else laughed. "Are we ready? Then let's go."

Soon enough they were piled in the wagons and moving slowly through the Chesza streets. Most of the others had brought parasols to protect them from the sun, but Averie didn't bother. She sat at the edge of the wagon and gazed out, striving to see as much as she could. Yes—that was Mualota's great feathered spray off in the distance to their right. There were the familiar wood-and-terra-cotta buildings, the parched-looking trees, the occasional burst of colorful blossoms. Because she was watching for them, she saw everywhere the representations of the three wounded gods of Chiarrin. A one-eyed fish painted on a door. A small bronze statue in a shop window, featuring *seena* with an arrow through her breast. A three-legged *doena* racing across a yard, caught in rough stone. The broken gods of Chiarrin gathered to protect their people.

"I am so thirsty," Lady Worth remarked. "I didn't think to bring water."

"There is some in the wagon," Jalessa replied. "Let me fetch it."

"Excellent, Jalessa!" Lady Selkirk said in an approving voice, and only then did Averie realize that Lady Worth had spoken in Aebrian. "That girl is really a marvel," she added in an aside to her friend.

They all sipped from the cups that Jalessa handed around, but everyone was still hot. "I wonder how far Captain Martin plans to take us?" Lana whispered to Averie. "I mean, I very much want to be out of the house, but it is so wretched and miserable. We never went this far before."

Jalessa heard that, too. "You will like this," she promised. "It's not far now."

Indeed, five minutes later the wagons pulled out of a narrow street and into a long, open plaza that seemed empty except for the people bustling across the smooth stonework on the ground. The horses huffed to a halt, and Captain Martin came riding up beside them. "All out," he called.

"Here?" Lady Selkirk demanded, looking around with disbelief. "Why, there's nothing to even look at!"

But Averie had already figured it out. Curving from the west like a huge stone serpent, one of the Chiarrin aqueducts was on proud display across the length of the plaza. It was about shoulder height, encased in honey-white stone, and about as big around as three girls standing in a close circle with their arms around one another's shoulders. Bits of silver glinted at regular intervals along its underside, and Averie realized these were faucets. She further realized that all the men and women scurrying across the plaza were carrying buckets to haul away their water for the day.

"It's an aqueduct!" she exclaimed, scrambling from the wagon. "I've been wanting to see one!"

Lana and Edna were right behind Averie, but Carrie and the older women still seemed puzzled to think that *this* had been their destination. Soldiers fanned around them as the girls made their way across the plaza. Averie was sorry to see that the Chiarrizi moved aside to let them pass and watched them with cool, unfriendly expressions.

Jalessa fell in step beside Averie and Lana. "For those who live near a *correa*, it is the easiest source of water," she said.

"*Correa?* That's what you call an aqueduct?" Averie said.

"Yes." Jalessa smiled. "Often you will see children here, running so fast that half the water spills out of their buckets. It is typical for children to be responsible for fetching the family's water, and they must complete that chore before they are free to play."

Averie glanced around, and, sure enough, she saw a dozen boys and girls speeding up to the *correa*, opening the faucets, and letting the water pour into their containers. Some paused to thrust their faces into jets of water or splash their neighbors. One young girl simply ducked under the spigot and allowed the water to drench her. Nearby, men and women stood in clusters, laughing and talking, their buckets at their feet. The paving stones of the plaza were slick with wet footsteps and careless spills. Clearly, the Chiarrizi could waste water if they lived near a *correa*, Averie thought.

"People come here to visit with their friends, I suppose," Averie said.

Jalessa nodded. "It was fashionable, a few years ago, for young couples to get married at a *correa*. You still will come across a wedding here from time to time. All the friends and family members come and sit on the stones, and the bride and the groom arrive last. They step under the faucets and bathe while everyone watches—"

"Wait," Lana interrupted. "Bathe. You mean, get *naked* and bathe? In front of everyone they know?"

Jalessa looked surprised. "Yes. Of course they must shed their old lives before joining each other, cleansed and new." She paused. "This is not how people marry in Aeberelle?"

"*No!*" Lana and Averie said together. Lana added, "The very thought makes me want to remain a spinster forever."

Averie agreed heartily, but she liked the ritual itself, the idea that a newlywed couple should come together fresh and unused. She wondered how Morgan would react if she suggested they strip naked and scrub each other before they shared a marriage bed. She rather thought he would be shocked.

Jalessa was pointing to the far edge of the plaza, half

in shadow from a line of tall, wispy trees. "Vendors sell fruit and dried meat and other things a family might need for dinner," she said. "There aren't as many as you'd find in the market, but for the cook who's forgotten a spice, the vendors are very welcome."

The majority of the others had joined them by this time. "Can we buy something from them?" Edna asked.

"I'm sure they'd be happy to sell you whatever you like."

Averie glanced at Captain Martin, but he nodded, so they all passed under the *correa*, careful not to slip in the spilled water, and visited the merchants. Most of the girls, always mindful of their figures, bought bunches of wikberry or bumain. But Averie went from booth to booth, dribbling out coins at each one, and sampled a small round of cheese, a flat pastry filled with something sweet, and a strip of dried hodee meat. Lady Worth and Lady Harmon also showed some adventurousness in their food choices.

"I'll take some of this dried hodee home with me," Lady Harmon decided.

Of course, the food made them thirsty, but water was only a few steps away. Not wanting to get their skirts wet, Lana and the other girls turned on the spigots with caution, then leaned in to sip from their cupped hands.

"It tastes different," Lana commented.

Edna took another swallow. "You're right. Wilder, somehow."

"There are filters on the pipes that run to the big houses," Jalessa said. "The water is purified before you drink it."

Carrie Dryser opened her hands with a squeal and water splashed at her feet. "Oooh! You mean this isn't safe to drink?"

"Of course it is," Averie said. "You see all these other people drinking it."

"It might have flavors that are unfamiliar to you," Jalessa replied evenly. "I don't think it will harm you."

Carrie stepped away, and a few of the others mimicked her. "Well, I don't want to consume anything *impure*," she said.

Lana and Averie exchanged glances, and then each of them bent to slurp more water from their hands. Edna Harmon wet a handkerchief, wiped her face, and remarked, "I think I've consumed more than my share of impure foods and liquids, and some of them in Port Elise." That earned her a laugh.

"All in all, this has been most interesting," Lady Selkirk said, and seemed actually to mean it. Averie thought she must have been won over by the cultural commentary—or the fact that Jalessa had delivered it. "But I think it's time we were going back. It's so *hot*. I need to be inside someplace cool."

Edna offered her dripping handkerchief. "Pat your face down," she recommended.

Lady Selkirk eyed the wet cloth with some disfavor. "Perhaps not," she said.

Captain Martin had lifted his hand and was signaling the sightseers. "Back to the wagons," he called. "Time to go."

But Averie, like Lady Selkirk—like everybody—was hot. And she loved the *correa*. And she wasn't ready to leave. Reaching up to the nearest spigot, she turned it on full force and then, kicking off her sandals, dropped to her knees under the gushing water. She heard gasps and little cries of "mercy!" from the women around her, but she ignored them. She closed her eyes and turned her face up, straight into the onrushing spray. Her clothes were instantly drenched, her hair plastered to her head; she felt the water puddle in the lap of her *tallah*.

"Averie!" Lady Selkirk commanded, her voice horrified. "*Averie!* Stop that this instant! Get into the wagon, you dreadful girl!"

But Averie merely lifted her hands to feel the play of water on her palms. She opened her mouth and drank straight from the falling column of water. The *tallah* clung to her body in wet folds, but she didn't care. This was as close as she would come to bathing nude in the cleansing water of Chiarrin, washing away her old life, scrubbing her past from her skin. She opened her mouth again, and this time, instead of drinking, she laughed out loud.

CHAPTER
TWELVE

A week later, the soldiers returned. Lady Selkirk had spent most of that time not speaking to Averie, which suited the younger girl just fine, though she was even more bored than usual on the days Jalessa wasn't present. Major General Worth had decreed that it was safe to go to the market again, so Averie and Lana shopped three days out of seven. Captain Martin also finally agreed to take the two of them on another tour of the city, but even such excursions couldn't completely fill the long, dull afternoons.

And no diversion could compare to the happiness of having the officers back, all of them safe. Morgan and Averie's father arrived in the middle of the night, and she jumped from her bed to welcome them when she heard their voices in the hallway.

"Go to sleep, Averie, we'll talk in the morning," was

her father's greeting, but Morgan kissed her hard and told her he'd missed her.

Finally! Something to look forward to! In the morning, Averie helped Grace prepare a hearty breakfast, though the men didn't rise till almost noon. Averie, Lady Selkirk, and Jalessa waited in the *maroya* until the men finally made an appearance. Jalessa stayed quietly in a chair in the far corner of the room, but Averie and Lady Selkirk had their own little tables set up and joined the others for the meal.

"So. Tell us," Averie demanded. "What happened?"

Her father swallowed a bite of dried hodee. "A few rebels operating at the base of the Maekaths," he said. "We shut them down. Found the gunpowder right away but couldn't locate their camp, though we were chasing men all over the mountains."

"Did you ever learn where they'd gotten the gunpowder?" Lady Selkirk asked.

Morgan nodded. "Yes, and that's a problem, because there could be more of it." He sipped from his juice. "The crates were stamped in Weskish. Looks like the Chiarrizi have friends."

Averie was nodding, for that made sense—if Chiarrin had a long history of trading with Weskolia, why wouldn't the two nations be allies in war as well?—but everyone else seemed horrified. "In *Weskish*! But I thought we had a treaty with Weskolia!" Lady Selkirk exclaimed.

The general snorted. "A bad treaty," he said.

"And the Weskish technically haven't broken its provisions," Morgan added. "They agreed not to make war on us or our colonies, but that doesn't prevent them from making alliances with independent nations. Which Chiarrin was until we arrived."

"Then they must stop making alliances with Chiarrin right now!" Lady Selkirk said. "No more gunpowder—no, and no aid of any kind!"

Morgan shrugged. "It's not so simple. The Weskish would say that we have invaded a country in which they had a stake already. They would claim that *we* have violated the treaty, not them."

"Well, it sounds as if we have," Averie said. Everyone looked at her in surprise; it was rare she could bring herself to pay attention to conversations about politics. But this involved Chiarrin, and she found it quite easy to follow. "And if I were Weskolia, I'd be angry," she added. "What's to keep them from saying we stole their land?"

"It's not their land. They had only commercial interests here," her father said testily. "Weskolia trades with ports all over the globe! Does that mean we can't go to Larall or Keftak City if we choose? No! Chiarrin has never been a Weskish colony."

"Just a Weskish trading partner, is that it?" Averie said. She was determined to put this together correctly. Her father nodded curtly, and she went on. "But suppose the Weskish want to keep Chiarrin as a trading partner? Suppose they don't want us here?"

"The Weskish are not going to go to war over Chiarrin," Morgan said in a kindly voice, as if trying to reassure her that she was safe.

She brushed this aside. She wasn't afraid; she was curious. "Maybe they don't want to go to war, but they don't want us here, either," she said. "If I was a Weskish king, I'd give the Chiarrizi all the gunpowder they wanted. Yes, and if I was a Chiarrizi rebel, I'd be over in Weskolia right now, looking for weapons and other support!"

Morgan frowned. "Well, you're neither Weskish nor Chiarizzi," he said shortly. "Don't forget where Aeberelle's interests lie."

Averie shrugged. "Well, I wouldn't want anyone sailing into Port Elise and taking over my city, so I don't blame the Chiarrizi for trying to fight us," she said.

"Averie!" Lady Selkirk exclaimed.

Unexpectedly, her father was nodding. "Right. Any nation is going to defend itself. Can't blame the people for that. But Chiarrin doesn't have the resources to protect itself, and it was only a matter of time before someone took over the country. Chiarrin is too temptingly placed to remain a sovereign nation for long. We got here first, and we'll stay. But we've got to cut their connection with Weskolia, that's for certain."

"No weapons have come into the harbor," Morgan said. "We've controlled it for eight months."

Her father nodded again. "Over the Soldath Mountains, perhaps, though that's a hard pass to cross. Might be time to run some patrols in the northern half of the country."

"That stretches us a little thin down by the Maekaths," Morgan observed.

"We have plenty of troops," Averie's father said. "We just need to redeploy."

Lady Selkirk looked dismayed. "Does that mean you'll be leaving the city again?"

"Probably, but not for a few days," General Winston replied indifferently. "We need to make some tactical decisions first if we're going to head up to the Soldath Mountains."

The conversation veered to other topics, and the men excused themselves shortly after the meal. Averie was bored again until Lana arrived, repeating news her father had shared.

"He said there were skirmishes up at the Maekaths every night," Lana whispered to Averie as they braved the heat outdoors for a private conversation in the courtyard. "There were three Aebrian soldiers killed, did you hear that?"

"No! How dreadful!"

"No officers. Still, I would think their families will be

just as sad to learn they've died—and so far away from home, too, in such a strange place!"

"How many Chiarrizi died, did he say?"

Lana shook her head. "No, but it must have been quite a few, because he mentioned that the enlisted men were grumbling about having to dig the grave big enough. It's the heat, he said—you can't just leave the bodies where they've fallen."

"That's *awful*," Averie responded. "Do you think a hundred of them died? Five hundred? How terrible for *their* families! And perhaps none of them wanted to be soldiers, but they had no choice when enemies appeared on their own soil."

Lana opened her blue eyes very wide. "You sound almost like a dissenter. One of those crazy people who stands on street corners in Port Elise and claims that everything the government does is wrong."

Averie rearranged her skirts, hoping to make herself a little cooler. Even in the shade, it was so hot the shadows seemed to be panting. "Well, it doesn't make sense to me," she said frankly. "Why should Aeberelle invade Chiarrin? Why should we take land that belongs to someone else? Why did we invade Xan'tai all those years ago? Just because we wanted to? I can't take your pearl ring just because I want it. My father would never take Morgan's jacket just because he wanted it. So why can we take over countries? I don't understand it."

Lana sighed. "I don't understand it, either," she said. "I suppose that's why Aebrian women aren't meant to be soldiers."

But they're meant to be soldiers' wives, Averie thought. *And that means that I had better understand it soon enough.*

Averie didn't see Morgan until much later, when she returned to the courtyard after the heat had begun to dissipate. The men had been gone until well past dinner, no doubt plotting strategy with Worth and the senior officers. Averie had been just about to go to her room when the door from the *maroya* opened, and Morgan stepped outside.

She stood up, and he came directly toward her, taking her in a tight embrace and kissing her most satisfactorily. In the back of her mind, she was a little relieved. She had wondered if her comments earlier might make him want to scold her instead of hug her. He drew her down beside him on the bench and spoke with his mouth against her hair.

"I missed you before, when you were all the way in Port Elise," he said. "I thought it would not be so bad this time, because you were so much closer! But it was worse. The thought that you were just a two days' ride away . . . I kept wanting to jump on my horse and gallop to Chesza."

She smiled in the darkness, for that was gratifying to

hear. "Well, I missed you, too, but partly because it was very *dull* to be practically confined to the house," she said. "We were so happy when Captain Martin took us on an expedition!"

"Where did you go on this outing?"

"To the *correa* in the northwestern quadrant."

"The what?"

"That's what Jalessa calls the aqueducts."

He pulled back to gaze down at her. "You *are* going native, aren't you?" he murmured. "You wear Chiarrizi clothes and learn Chiarrizi language—"

"Well, it seems useful."

"And you take up Chiarrizi causes," he added in a meaningful voice.

That was certainly a reference to the conversation during the meal. "I feel bad about all of this," she said in a low voice. "Morgan, we have taken over another country! I suppose I never really thought it through before, but it just seems—well, it's *wrong*, I think." Now she was the one to gaze up at him. "I'm sorry if that makes you angry."

He took advantage of her upturned face to kiss her swiftly on the mouth. "Of course I'm not angry. Such emotions prove what a good heart you have," he said. "War can be an ugly business. I am rather relieved to learn you do not like it much."

"Yes, but then it bothers me that *you* like it," she said.

He tilted his head from side to side in an equivocal

motion. "I can't say I like it," he responded at last. "I see it as necessary in certain situations. If, as you say, ships came sailing in to Port Elise Harbor, you would want us to be able to fight, wouldn't you?"

"Of course I would! I would want us to be able to win, too!"

He laughed and laced his fingers with hers. "Well, we would," he assured her. "The Aebrian military is second to none."

"But no one in Chiarrin came sailing into Port Elise," she said. "Why did we just . . . take it over?"

He tapped a finger on her knee, through the soft folds of the *tallah*. "This is Aeberelle." He traced his finger halfway up her thigh and tapped again. "This is Weskolia. Over here"—on her other leg—"this is Larall, this is Khovstu. Chiarrin is right here. Now way over here"—he pointed to his own knee—"that's Xan'tai and the southern islands. We have colonies in Xan'tai, and Weskolia and Khovstu have colonies in the islands. Larall would like to gain a foothold in all of those places. For any country looking to establish itself in the eastern hemisphere, the best launching place for a navy is—can you guess?—Chiarrin. We knew Weskolia had been making overtures for years. We knew Khovstu had been overhauling its navy. We knew we had to get here first. Or Larall might make an alliance with Khovstu, Khovstu might invade Xan'tai, *Weskolia* might invade Xan'tai, all treaties to the contrary—"

"But why do we care about Xan'tai?" she asked patiently.

"Because it's ours."

"But it didn't used to be. It used to be a sovereign nation. Maybe it wants to be a sovereign nation again."

"It might want to be, but if Aeberelle pulled out today, Khovstu would be there tomorrow," he said cynically.

"Then we're protecting the Xantish?"

He laughed. "In a manner of speaking. We're protecting our Xantish interests."

"But—"

"Averie. Aeberelle is the most powerful country in the world. And the wealthiest. Your father owns shares of three Xantish companies, and they've supported Weymire Estate for decades. You wouldn't be buying a single emerald in the Chesza market if not for your father's foreign investments. You have an elegant and enviable lifestyle, and most of it is made possible because of Aeberelle's colonies in exotic lands."

She pulled away from him, greatly disturbed. Well, of course she had known her father's wealth came from commerce, but she had never actually considered how the money was obtained. "I don't think I like that," she said uncertainly. "I think I would rather not have emeralds if that would keep places like Chiarrin from being attacked."

He nodded calmly. "So you would see us return

Xan'tai to home rule and pull out of Chesza and hand back all the other countries that Aeberelle has taken over."

"Yes, I would," she said firmly. "I would give up my luxuries—I would even give up Weymire Estate if I had to—if that meant preventing war on foreign soil."

"And if that meant that a thousand independent ship captains lost their trade, and the shopkeepers who rely on their merchandise had nothing to sell, and the shop owners' sons and daughters starved to death, and the mills in northern Aeberelle went silent, and all of the mill workers and their families went hungry because they had no jobs? You would condemn all of *them* to privation because of your soft heart?"

Her brows drew together in a frown. "No, but I— surely that would not all happen—would it? I mean—it must be simpler than that," she floundered.

He took her hand and kissed it very gently. "In fact, it is much more complicated than that," he said. "But I am impressed that you are trying to understand it."

She laughed shakily. "It is giving me a headache."

"No, no, your headache comes from sitting out too long in the Chesza sun," he said teasingly.

In truth, her skull was beginning to pound, whatever the reason. She leaned her cheek against Morgan's shoulder and allowed him to play with her fingers. "Do you really have to leave again so soon?" she whispered.

"I'm afraid so," he said in a brisk voice. "We can't let the rebels dig in. We need to make it clear that we've got five times the manpower and the firepower. I'm afraid we're in for a bloody time of it later if we don't show a certain ruthlessness now."

Even as he spoke, Averie felt her whole body grow chilly. She looked down at his fingers, once again interlaced with hers, and she thought, *He has been killing people with those hands. He plans to kill more of them.* The thought made her so sick that she could only offer monosyllabic answers for the rest of the conversation. Quickly enough he noted that she must be exhausted, and he solicitously shepherded her back into the house. At her bedroom door, she accepted his kiss on her cheek, then she slipped inside the room, but she did not lie down upon her bed.

Instead, she sat at her window the rest of the night, watching the shadows of the courtyard and listening to the fountain make its merry pattering sound. Not until Jalessa came to find her in the morning did she rouse enough to shake her head and say she wanted to stay in her room all day. Alone. She slept till midway through the afternoon, but even when she rose, she did not feel rested.

CHAPTER
THIRTEEN

I t turned out that Averie's father and Morgan would
be in Chesza a full week before heading north to
the Soldath Mountains. Averie, still disturbed by
her conversation with Morgan and all the new thoughts
that she had entertained, was so quiet and so well behaved for the next few days that Lady Selkirk was in
transports.

"I always knew your levity and high spirits would
settle down someday and you'd be very well-mannered
girl," her chaperone said.

Morgan and her father didn't seem to notice her with-
drawal, and Lana was always so vivacious herself that she
could make conversation for both of them. But two days
later, Jalessa asked Averie why she was so sad.

They were sitting in the *maroya*, enjoying one of Lady
Selkirk's rare absences. They had been working on a few

of the more difficult concepts in the Aebrian language, but Averie had found herself too listless to continue the lesson.

Jalessa's question caught her off guard. "Sad? Oh, I don't think that's the word for it," she said.

Jalessa sat patiently, her hands folded in her lap, and said, "But something is unsettling you. Something heavy weighs on your mind."

Averie smiled. "In Port Elise, you would never say that to someone so bluntly! It would be considered rude."

"In Chesza, it would be considered rude to see your *sova* in trouble and not ask what that trouble might be." Jalessa waited a moment, and when Averie did not answer, she prodded a little. "Is it Colonel Stode? Have you disagreed with him?"

Averie shook her head. "No—not exactly, no. Though lately I do find that . . . sometimes the things that matter to him don't seem as important to me," she said. "But he never seems to get annoyed when I don't understand him."

"Perhaps you are the one who should be annoyed when he doesn't understand *you*," Jalessa said quietly.

Averie managed a smile. "Yes, and from time to time I *am* a little frustrated with him! But Morgan is not my problem now. Or at least not truly."

"But there is a problem."

Averie looked at her helplessly. How did you explain

your disgust with imperialism to someone who had suffered at the hands of the imperialists? "I love Chesza,"
she whispered. "And yet I am beginning to believe that
we have done a terrible thing by coming here."

Jalessa's face sharpened. "Ah," she said. "Yes, that
is a dreadful burden. To question the morality of those
whom you feel you should admire. And to feel helpless
in the face of their power and their certainty."

Averie felt great relief to hear her inchoate thoughts
put so succinctly into words. "Have you ever felt this
way?" she asked. "Just—repulsed and horrified at the
world?"

"More than once," Jalessa said.

"And how did you make yourself feel better?"

Jalessa considered. Averie thought that Jalessa was
one of the most serene people she knew. She did not
rush to judgment; she did not get stirred up over small
things; she rarely let life dismay her. "Sometimes I tried
harder to understand what seemed wrong," she said,
"and I found it was not so terrible as I had originally
thought. Sometimes I decided it was worse, and I walked
away from those who made decisions that I could not
abide." She smiled slightly. "Sometimes I decided to do
something to change the world."

"I can hardly walk away from my father or Morgan,"
Averie said.

Jalessa didn't answer, but she watched Averie from

those wise, complex eyes. Averie felt herself first flush and then turn pale.

"I've thought about it," she whispered. "I've wondered what it would be like if Morgan was no longer in my life. I don't want him to die, of course, but if he did—or if he decided not to marry me—what would I do then?" She drew a deep, shuddering breath. "I don't think I'd choose to marry a soldier, if I were to do it over again."

"But you love Colonel Stode," Jalessa said in an uninflected voice.

"But I love him," Averie repeated. "Of course I will marry him."

"Then you must work harder to understand him."

Averie nodded and stared down at her lap. Today she was wearing one of her old underdresses, and a seam was coming undone. She pulled at a loose thread and watched her fingers. Jalessa waited in patient silence. "So what did you do?" Averie asked presently. "When you set out to change the world?"

"I was a little girl. The woman who lived in the house next to my mother's kept a whole flock of birds in a coop out back. I thought she treated them badly. So one night when everyone was sleeping, I crept out and opened all the cage doors and set them free."

Averie clapped her hands. "I like that story! I would have done the same thing."

Jalessa laughed. "Well, I don't know that I really made

things better. More than half the birds were still there in the morning. They were domesticated, you see, and they didn't know how to fend for themselves. My mother was very angry, and she devised punishments that lasted the rest of the summer, or at least that's how I remember it."

"But some of the birds got free?" Averie asked. "And never returned?"

Jalessa nodded. "Some got free."

"Then it was worth it."

Jalessa, still amused, tilted her head to one side and regarded Averie. "That's what I always thought," she said.

The conversation had made Averie feel much better. She stood up, feeling hungry for the first time in days. "Let's find Grace," she said. "I want something to eat."

The next morning, Lady Worth arrived with Lana, both of them brimming with excitement.

"There's to be a festival in the marketplace in a few days," Lana announced as soon as they had joined Averie, Lady Selkirk, and Jalessa in the *maroya*. "And my father says we can go!"

Lady Selkirk instantly looked suspicious. "What kind of festival? And I think you'd better check with General Winston first."

"Oh, but it seems like the kind of thing that should be completely harmless," Lady Worth replied. "Music and dancing. My husband said it was actually a good sign that the Chiarrizi planned to hold the event even while we occupy the city. He says it shows that they are learning to accept our presence with less resentment."

"But what is the festival for?" Averie asked.

Jalessa answered in her soft voice. "It celebrates the turning of summer. *Kyleeta.* The hottest time of the season. Soon the days will begin to cool off, the nights will lengthen. The festival gives thanks for the season that has been and looks forward to the season that will be."

"See? That sounds very innocent," Lady Worth said.

Lady Selkirk sniffed again. "Music and dancing. And alcohol, no doubt."

Jalessa was smiling. "Vendors do offer fermented wikberry juice and other spirits that tend to make the young men . . . rambunctious."

"I thought so," Lady Selkirk said.

"But it is a very friendly festival," Jalessa went on. "I have never seen *kyleeta* night spill into violence." She smiled at Lana and Averie. "And the dancing is fun."

"Oh, can we go, can we go, can we go?" Averie pleaded.

"You'll have to ask your father," Lady Selkirk said, "and I'm sure he'll say no."

Lana sighed and slumped back against the cushions. "Even if we could go, we don't know how to do any of the steps," she said.

"I could teach you," Jalessa said. "Some of them are very simple circle dances. Even the children join in."

"I'll ask my father," Averie said. "The minute he comes home tonight."

In fact, her father already knew about the *kyleeta* festival, for some of the enlisted men had requested permission to attend. Like Major General Worth, he believed the celebration sent a signal that the Chiarrizi were beginning to accept the presence of the Aebrians, so he was disposed to view the event with favor.

"But, General!" Lady Selkirk exclaimed over dinner. "Scarcely more than a month ago, the attacks in the marketplace! And you have just ridden back from what I understand to be a war zone not a hundred miles from here!"

The general nodded and helped himself to more mashed bumain. "My feeling is that there's a small group of malcontents who've mounted the attacks, and they've pulled out of Chesza entirely," he said. "Even the eastern quadrant of the city has been quiet these past few weeks. Those who are left are the sensible people who want to make peace with the Aebrians and resume their normal lives."

Averie bounced in her chair. "Then can we go to the festival? Can we *please* go?"

Morgan was frowning. "Sir, I'm still not entirely sure—"

"Oh, couldn't let 'em go without an escort, of course," the general said, looking thoughtful. "Even if our women weren't to attend, we'd want troops there, just to prove that we won't brook violence in the city. But if we send fifty men to guard the perimeter and a handful of officers to stick very close beside the ladies—well, I think it's safe enough."

"*Safe* isn't the word that comes to my mind," Morgan said a trifle grimly.

Her father shrugged. "Well, if we won't let them out of the house from time to time, why even allow them to come to Chesza?" he asked reasonably. "May as well just have them stay in Port Elise and send picture postcards of the Chiarrizi countryside."

"And there are days I wish we'd done just that!" Lady Selkirk snapped.

But Averie agreed completely with her father. "Yes! Exactly! I am here to see Chesza, and I'm *so glad* that you will let me see it!" she exclaimed. She jumped from her tall chair and dove through the folding tables to plant a kiss on his cheek. He laughed and looked, for once, pleased with her. She turned and held her hands out to Morgan. "And you'll come with me, won't you? You'll be the escort that stays very, *very* close to me?"

"Averie Agatha Winston," Lady Selkirk reprimanded, not liking the suggestive tone.

Morgan smiled, but he did not look happy. "Of course."

She returned to her seat and continued her dinner with positive relish. "Jalessa is going to teach us some of the simpler dances that are performed at *kyleeta*," she said. "Why don't you join us tomorrow and learn some of the steps with Lana and me?"

Morgan looked affronted. "I think I have more pressing uses for my time."

She gave him what she hoped was a soulful look. "Then perhaps tomorrow evening. When it cools down in the courtyard. I can teach you whatever I learn."

That did make him smile, though it made Lady Selkirk frown, misliking Averie's tone again. "Well, General, if you're sure," she said in minatory accents.

"I think the experience will be good for everyone," he said.

Accordingly, three days later, Lana joined Averie and Jalessa in Averie's bedroom, and they put the finishing touches on their festival dresses. All of them wore red, to signify celebration, and all of them planned to twine a ribbon of scarlet through their headscarves.

"That's such an unusual color for you," Lana observed to Averie. "It makes you look so pale."

Averie instantly put her hands to her cheeks. "Too pale? I can add some rouge."

Lana shrugged. "Who will be able to see your face in the dark?" She smiled. "Anyway, you look delicate.

Interesting. Colonel Stode will be enthralled."

"And which officers will be enthralled by Lady Lana Worth?" Jalessa murmured.

"All of them, I hope!" Lana replied. Both girls laughed, but Averie noticed that Lana sighed soon after.

The sun was almost down, and shadows were slanting across the courtyard, when the three of them were finally ready. They headed to the *maroya*, where Morgan and an escort of enlisted men were waiting to accompany them to the fair.

But Morgan was deep in conversation with Averie's father and someone who looked like a courier—exhausted, bedraggled, and earnest. Morgan didn't even glance over when the girls entered the room, though Lady Selkirk and Lady Worth instantly approached to assess their attire.

"Well, I can't say I approve of young girls dressing like savages, but I must admit there is nothing indecorous about these particular fashions," was Lady Selkirk's grudging comment. She herself was wearing a black dress in a very Aebrian style, but she had added a red lace shawl that showed she was trying to get into the spirit of the celebration, Averie thought. "Lana, that is a very good color for you. Averie—"

"I know," Averie said. "It doesn't flatter me."

"But it's still a very pretty dress," Lady Worth said, smiling.

Averie was watching Morgan, who was frowning and gesturing. "What's wrong?"

Lady Selkirk glanced back over her shoulder. "A ship sailed in this afternoon with news. I haven't been told yet what the courier had to say, but both your father and Colonel Stode seem uneasy."

"Not more fighting in the northern stretches, I hope," Jalessa said. Her voice was neutral, but Averie thought, as she had several times before, that Jalessa must be even more anxious than Averie was at the thought of violence on Chiarrin soil.

"I wouldn't think so. Such news wouldn't come by ship," Lady Worth said.

At that moment, Morgan broke off his conference and came striding across the room to join the women. He was wearing his dress uniform, and his dark blond hair had been carefully styled; he looked most stern and handsome. "Averie, Lady Lana—you are both quite lovely tonight," he said, but Averie thought the compliment sounded rote.

"Morgan, what's wrong?" she burst out.

"Weskish ships spotted passing much too close to the coast for us to be happy," he answered readily enough. "We're sending off warships of our own to track them down." He spoke in Aebrian, too rapidly for Jalessa to follow.

"Do you think they plan to attack us?" Lana asked in alarm.

He gave her a look that was almost scornful. "No, of course not. But are they bringing fresh supplies to the Chiarrizi? Maybe. In any case, I'm off to investigate."

"You're going?" Averie wailed. "But Morgan—!"

He kissed her quickly on the forehead. "I know. The festival. I've sent for another couple of officers to take my place. You can still attend. Just . . . just be careful."

She clung to his arms, not letting him slip back to resume his urgent conversation with her father. "This is worse than having you leave for the Soldath Mountains! How long will you be gone?"

"I don't know. A few days. I wouldn't think we'd engage in any fighting, though, even if we sight them. Too many disastrous consequences to *both* sides. But it will do them good to know we won't allow them to slip unobserved into our waters."

"Then *you* be careful," Averie said, tugging him close enough so he could kiss her on the mouth. He obliged, but very briefly, and pulled back with a laugh.

"Too many watchers," he said, though all the women were smiling at the romantic gesture, and none of the men seemed remotely interested. "Enjoy your festival. The soldiers are gathered outdoors." And he bowed and withdrew to join her father.

Averie sighed. "Now I'm sure I will not have half as much fun as I was hoping," she said. "But let's be on our way."

The instant the women stepped outside, the waiting soldiers snapped to strict attention. Averie counted ten uniforms before she had a chance to sort out how many were enlisted men and how many were officers.

"Lieutenant Lansdale," Lana breathed in her ear. "Oh, I didn't dare *hope*!"

Averie laughed, but a few seconds later, she could have echoed the sentiment just as fervently. For there beside the wagon, offering a gesture that was halfway between a bow and a salute, was Lieutenant Ket Du'kai. Come to escort them to *kyleeta* night.

CHAPTER
FOURTEEN

The marketplace was absolutely mobbed. The soldiers made a tight phalanx around the women, but even so, over the blue-clad shoulders, Averie could see an amazing press of people. Men, women, boys, girls, infants in their mothers' arms, old men being gently led by their grandsons, young women hand in hand and giggling into each other's ears, smiling young men roving together in packs. Everyone wore clothing edged in red, or stitched with red, or with dangling crimson ribbons down the back. And everyone looked happy, Averie thought—broad faces creased with smiles, hands waving in excitement, feet barely able to contain their impulse to dance.

The festival scene was fairly well lit by lanterns strung on wires across the broad plaza and hung on poles around the perimeter. Still, the looming darkness added a definitely reckless air to the whole carnival atmosphere. The feeling was enhanced by the enticing mix of scents wafting across the plaza: sweet smells of sugared confections, spicier aromas of cooked meat, the sharp odor of alcohol.

But what really set the tone for the festival was the music. Averie had never heard such instruments or such melodies. There were drums, or something deep and percussive like drums, but rapping along at such a delirious pace that the other instruments had to dip and skirl and dash along to keep up. And who could tell exactly what those other instruments were? There seemed to be pipes of some kind, though with a reedy and ethereal sound. Averie caught the pluck and glide of what might be stringed instruments. Then there were sounds that seemed to be made by bells—or cymbals—or something shivery and atonal, and she couldn't tell what made *that* noise, either, but she thought it added a descant of gaiety to the whole bright cacophony.

"I love this music!" she called to Lana, and Lana nodded enthusiastically back.

Lady Selkirk seemed less enthralled. "Really, it's all sort of . . . vulgar," she said, nearly shouting over the noise. "Not like proper music at all."

Lady Worth smiled as she swayed a little to the frenzied beat. "No, quite *im*proper, I daresay," she replied. "But I rather like it, too."

Jalessa pointed out various attractions. "On that side are the booths selling food. Over there, wikberry juice. And here in the middle is where there will be dancing."

"Dancing," Averie and Lana said together.

"Let's try to get as close as we can," Jalessa added.

They edged through the crowd, which grew thicker as they got closer to the center of the plaza. Eventually, Averie made out a dais where all the musicians had congregated, and she stared in fascination as her party inched forward. One old man appeared to be shaking a long, thick pole; a younger man was bent so low over what looked like a black metal cauldron that his face had entirely disappeared inside it. A woman about Averie's age was skipping across a lumpy surface, and every time her heavy shoes hit one of the strange bumps, a silver chime rang out. These were musicians? These were their instruments? What gloriously exotic creatures on marvelously strange contraptions!

"Where do people actually *dance*?" Lana was crying into her ear. "There's no place for them! There's hardly room to stand!"

Indeed, their little group had finally come to a complete halt because they could force their way no closer to the stage. People were everywhere, shoulder to shoulder. Impossible to imagine indulging in a waltz or a cotillion here!

"Ask Jalessa," she called back.

But at that moment, the music changed—slowed—took on a different cadence altogether. A murmur swept over the crowd, and there was a sort of surge as they all moved even closer to the stage. Lady Selkirk looked around in alarm; the soldiers stiffened their backs and tried to hold a circle open around their charges. But there was nothing to fear. As the musicians swung into their new melody, the revelers began to clap along, stamping their feet and swaying back and forth. Instantly, Lana and Averie joined in, feeling the pulse of the music rise up as from the earth itself and burst out through their palms in an irresistible heartbeat. Lady Worth started clapping along a few moments later, and even Lady Selkirk tapped her fingers against her thigh in perfect time.

Averie glanced around the ranks of the soldiers to find them still holding their firm positions, though most of them were nodding their heads along with the beat. Lieutenant Du'kai kept his hands on his weapons and his eyes on the stage—but his shoulders swayed slightly with the beat, and his face showed a deep and genuine pleasure.

She squirmed past Lady Worth and one of the soldiers to come stand beside him. He smiled down at her. "This is wonderful," she called over the music.

"The best of Chesza, I think," he shouted back.

"I haven't seen you since the party," she said. He cupped his hand to his ear as if he hadn't been able to hear, and she raised her voice even more. "How are you doing?"

"I've been busy," he replied in the same loud voice, smiling again. It was ridiculous to try to carry on a conversation under such circumstances, and she thought he was amused that she would even try. "You?"

She was determined to talk to him. The last time she had seen him, he had told her he could not be her friend. She would prove him wrong. "Were you up at the Maekaths?"

He nodded.

"Did you see any fighting?"

"No."

She was surprised at how relieved she was to receive this answer. She did not want Lieutenant Du'kai to be slaughtering rebel Chiarrizi. Well, in truth, she did not want anyone to be killing anyone. "My father thinks the Chiarrizi are beginning to accept the presence of the Aebrians."

He shrugged.

She was annoyed. He did not want to be drawn into a discussion about the occupation, but he might like her next topic even less. "Did you ask to be named my escort tonight?" she shouted.

That caused his smile to reappear. "No! In fact, I tried to beg off."

She could not tell if he was teasing or speaking the

truth, and she scowled at him. "Even if that's true, it's not a gentlemanly thing to say."

He laughed. "Actually, I was eager to see the festival, so I was glad to come."

Which, again, was not the answer she wanted. He knew it, too, because his brown eyes were bright with understanding. She tossed her head and felt the ends of the headscarves flick her neck. "I wanted Morgan to come, but he was called away."

"So I heard."

"Lana and I have been practicing the steps of the Chiarrizi dances—the simple ones," she said. "Can we join in when they start?"

He glanced around the mob of people and shook his head. "I cannot allow you to do anything that takes you more than a foot away from me."

Well, that didn't sound so bad. "You could dance, too."

Another smile. "If I knew the steps."

She remembered how smoothly he had glided around the impromptu dance floor in the *maroya* the night of the party. "I'm sure you could pick them up very quickly."

He shook his head again. "I can't imagine how anyone in this mob can actually find room to dance!" he said.

She had come to much the same conclusion. "Well, we're certainly staying long enough to find out."

As it happened, they only had to wait another five

minutes. The music changed again, and a happy excla-
mation seemed to escape all the revelers at once. There
was a certain pushing and resettling of the audience,
and then suddenly the whole crowd seemed to break into
separate and moving patterns. Lieutenant Du'kai called
out a sharp command, and there was a scramble among
the soldiers. Averie found herself suddenly standing with
her back to Ket Du'kai and his arms lifted on either side
of her as if to fend off attackers. Lieutenant Lansdale
had similarly encircled Lana, while other soldiers had
flanked the chaperones.

But there was no need for alarm, as they could see at
once. The crowd had merely formed itself into several
large, sloppy rings, and they were beginning one of the
slow circle dances that Lana and Averie had been practicing. The chain of dancers made its first lazy loop right
in front of them, snaking its way past those who had
chosen to stand and watch, and absorbing a dozen more
who decided to join in.

Jalessa raised her voice over the insistent music. "Averie! Lana! This is one you learned!"

"I know!" Averie cried back.

For an instant, Lieutenant Du'kai's arms actually
tightened around Averie from behind. "It's not safe," he
said, his voice a murmur against her hair.

She gave him the look of mutiny that had always cast
her caretakers into despair and twisted free of his hold.

Grabbing Lana's hand, she pulled them both into the circle. On her left, a Chiarrizi man caught her hand in his, damp with sweat. On her right, Lana laughed out loud as she clutched the hand of a woman next to her and executed the dance steps flawlessly. Both of them were quickly breathless and exhilarated. This was nothing like pacing around the *maroya* as Jalessa hummed. This was a modulated frenzy—a driven, joyous exuberance. Averie felt rash, a little mad, swept up in color and delight.

When they had made one full turn of the circle, new dancers broke into their ranks—Ket Du'kai on Averie's left, Jamie Lansdale between them, and an enlisted man on Lana's right. Averie gave Lieutenant Du'kai a swift warning look, but he smiled slightly and shook his head as he followed the other dancers. He would not try to pull her away; he could tell how futile it was. Her stubbornness had forced his hand.

Now her pleasure in the dance was complete. She returned him a radiant smile but did not attempt to speak as she paced through the measures. Step, back, half turn, sway, step, foot forward, foot behind, step. He didn't try to mimic the dancers, just shifted to the left when the motion pulled everyone along and paused when they twisted or tapped their feet. His hand on hers was much tighter than Lieutenant Lansdale's. He watched her as if he expected her to bolt to the other side of the plaza, and he was determined, this time, to stop her before she could get free.

She had no particular desire, at the moment, to get free of Ket Du'kai.

The music changed again—new dance—and he jerked his head up and glanced toward the stage, looking hopeful. But she laughed and shook her head, tugging him now in the other direction, for this dance was performed from left to right. Resigned, he followed her, never relaxing his grip. Lieutenant Lansdale stumbled, caught out of sync, but Lana laughed and towed him along.

The third dance took them back the other way, drew them in toward the center of the circle, and puffed them back out again. Averie raised her hands over her head when the music gave its cue, lifting the officers' hands along with hers, then she swung them back down hard with a swooping motion. On the other side of Lieutenant Lansdale, she could hear Lana laughing out loud. This had been their favorite of all the dances when Jalessa taught them in the *maroya*.

Averie took a peek over her shoulder, just to watch the whole great mob of people swaying and stepping in the same general rhythmic patterns. She wondered what the dance would look like from the vantage point of the dais—or even higher—from the treetops or the sky. What would it be like to see the circles turning beside circles, great colorful gears churning out merriment and music? From the ground, all she could see were bobbing heads and floating hems and clasped hands sweeping up and back down like flowers suddenly unfolding. She faced forward again, still smiling.

The music came to a halt with a few resounding chords, but the silence was instantly filled with applause and cheers. Ket Du'kai did not join in. Instead, he put his hands on Averie's waist, clearly ready to snatch her out of the way if trouble should descend in any form. And indeed, the whole crowd was redistributing itself, maintaining its design of circles curled against circles, but clearing out space in the middle of each ring for the next set of dances to be performed.

"What's this?" Lieutenant Du'kai said in Averie's ear.

"Now I think we just watch for a time."

He replied in words that she did not understand, but they sounded heartfelt and relieved. She had the impression he had just thanked his Xantish gods, and she gave him a look that was half mischief and half reproach. He responded with a crooked grin.

When the music started up again, it was a little slower, a little sweeter. Couples crowded into the center of the circle and spun around in motions that seemed close to something Averie recognized as true dancing. She was surprised to see a good-looking young man invite Jalessa into the circle. Jalessa looked surprised, too, but not at all unhappy. He took her wrists in one hand and held them above both of their heads. His other hand rested on her waist and drew her intimately next to his body. Jalessa watched him, her lips parted in a breathless smile, but they did not exchange any words as far as Averie could see. She watched closely, thinking this was not much different from a waltz in that the partners mirrored each other's steps and the man seemed to determine exactly where those steps would go next. *I could do that,* she thought.

Almost as if she could read Averie's mind, Jalessa turned in her partner's arms and searched the ranks of the onlookers. Spotting Averie, she broke into a smile and dodged the other dancers to pull her partner to Averie's side.

"Would you like to try this?" she said into Averie's ear. "Just let him hold you and move along with him."

Close up, Jalessa's friend was extremely attractive, with brown curls escaping from the edges of his headscarf and pale green eyes against deeply tanned skin. He was smiling at Averie in a way that made her blush, just because it was so very male and appraising, but she couldn't keep herself from smiling back.

"Oh, I'd *love* to," Averie replied, and Jalessa laid her partner's hand in Averie's.

Not so fast. "I don't think so," Lieutenant Du'kai said, tightening his grip.

"You'll be three feet away," she said, and shrugged out of his hold. Jalessa's friend instantly wrapped his fingers around her wrists and drew her into the circle.

This dance proved to be quite unlike any she had ever enjoyed in a polite Aebrian ballroom.

The Chiarrizi man clipped her wrists together with one hand and held them up so that their own arms formed a sort of canopy over their heads. He put his other palm at her waist, and she could feel the heat of his skin through the folds of her *tallah*. The music had slowed still more, to a lazy, sinuous beat that still seemed to run with an undercurrent of urgency. Her partner pulled her so close their stomachs almost touched. With each dark spike of music he lightly brushed his body against hers in what even Averie recognized as a fair imitation of a sexual rhythm. It should have been frightening, but it wasn't. He was smiling down at her, a challenge and an invitation on his face. *Are you afraid, foreign girl? There is so much I could show you if you would only follow me. . . .*

She stared back up at him and allowed him to move her through the crowded circle however he wished. Mostly they advanced in small, incremental steps, practically locked into position by the sheer numbers of other couples occupying the same space. Everyone around them swayed with a similar deep intoxication, as if the music itself was hypnotic. Averie could not look away from the Chiarrizi's intent gaze. His fingers around her wrists made her feel she was in some way his captive, but in a deliciously wicked way. His hand on her hip pulled her against him, suggestively, in time with the music.

She had spent some wondering what it would be like when she finally joined Morgan in the marriage bed, but she had never been entirely sure she would enjoy that experience. With this man, this stranger, whose face was full of promise and whose hands were full of knowledge, she had no doubt. He would be a magnificent lover.

She almost blushed as the thought took possession of her mind. But then she tossed her head and stared boldly back at him, letting him see, by the expression on her face, that she understood what he was conveying by his own. She remembered Jalessa telling her that men and women in Chesza did not wait for marriage to find out how they pleased each other in bed. They must do more than dance, she realized, but surely this was one of the tests. *Indeed, you please me very much, native man,* she thought deliberately as he led her through another cramped quarter turn. *In other circumstances, at another time, we might both find out just how much.*

He had no trouble reading that thought. His lips widened in a smile of pure speculation, and his hand guided her even closer. For a moment, she allowed herself to press against him, feel the shape of his body beneath his *tallah,* but then her good sense got the better of her, and she laughed and pulled back. He laughed, too, and his green eyes glittered. He did not seem disappointed, just even more curious.

The music came to a close with a wail from some unidentifiable instrument, and Averie felt as if she had shaken awake from a particularly engrossing dream. Her partner retained his hold on her wrists but let her hands fall down between them, and he made a gesture that had more than a little in common with a bow. Surfacing, he gave her another knowing smile. Now she did feel a flush heat her cheeks as she reviewed her behavior, though she wasn't exactly sorry. So she returned him a smile of her own, gently disengaged her hands, and turned toward the circle of watchers to find her own party.

Lieutenant Du'kai was literally a step away from her, on the very perimeter. He must have followed them around the circle for the entire duration of the dance. His expression was impossible to read, but Averie was pretty sure he wasn't feeling admiration. If he was shocked or angry, he hid those emotions as well. But his eyes were even darker than usual, and his face was completely unsmiling.

"Where's Lady Selkirk?" she asked in the quiet between musical numbers.

"She and Lady Worth are fetching refreshments, accompanied by soldiers."

Well, *there* was an unexpected stroke of fortune! Lana and Jalessa had witnessed her Chiarrizi dance, however, and now they elbowed their way through the onlookers to Averie's side. Close behind them came Lieutenant Lansdale and four of the enlisted men. Predictably, Lana appeared to be thrilled, but Jalessa's expression was more thoughtful.

"Averie!" Lana squealed. "What a beautiful man! But such an improper way to behave! You looked quite shameless."

Averie grimaced and threw Jalessa an apologetic look. "Oh, I know, but there is something about that music—! And, my goodness, *yes*—what an attractive man. Jalessa, I'm sorry if I conducted myself in an unbecoming way."

"I hope he did not offend you," Jalessa replied. "He is a very self-assured man, and he likes women very much. I did not think to warn him to treat a young Aebrian girl with a little more"—she seemed to search for a word— "coolness."

"Well, I enjoyed myself," Averie said frankly. "Thank you for giving me the chance to dance as the Chiarrizi do."

The musicians practiced a few tentative notes, and, behind her, Ket Du'kai spoke rapidly, as if aware he didn't have much time left for argument. "Perhaps we have had enough Chiarrizi dancing for one evening."

Lana and Averie instantly announced that *they* had not, and Averie added, "We can't leave without Lady Worth and Lady Selkirk, and they're nowhere in sight."

"I believe I could find them quickly enough," Lieutenant Du'kai replied.

The players hit their notes, and it was instantly too loud to continue the debate. "Just a few more songs!" Averie shouted over the music. "Surely you're enjoying yourself, too!"

He looked down at her, lips parted as if to speak, but he said nothing. He closed his mouth and watched her a little while longer. For a moment—just a second—she felt as breathless as she had in the embrace of the Chiarrizi man, as certain that she was attractive, unique, alluring. What had he planned to say? she found herself wondering. *Yes, Lady Averie, I enjoy myself any time I am by your side.* He said nothing. But he did not, for the longest time, look away.

A pinch on her arm made Averie turn her attention from Ket Du'kai to Lana, who was enthralled with the new set of dancers. Averie craned her neck to see over. Ah—this was a different kind of exhibition altogether. A single man cavorted through the clear space, leaping and spinning in such a lively fashion that his *tallah* swirled around his knees. The crowd clapped along again, shouting out praise and appreciation. He soared through the circle twice more, came to a halt, reached in with his left hand, and dragged a middle-aged woman out from the ring of onlookers.

They traded places. She stood still for a moment, hands on her hips, and then she launched into a dizzying display of footwork, moving so fast and turning so rapidly that she almost became a blur beneath the lantern light. Cheers and applause accompanied her entire performance. When she was done, she slipped into the crowd and tapped a young boy on the shoulder. He glided into a twisting, tilting, spinning display that Averie thought might be the most difficult piece of the evening.

In the next ten minutes, three more individuals took the stage, each offering a distinctly personal performance. Averie had pushed her way to the very front of the circle—Lieutenant Du'kai perforce beside her—and watched with amazement. She wondered if every Chiarrizi could offer a routine of such complexity, or if there were only a few who possessed such skills, and those were the ones always selected from the crowd at any festival.

Jalessa's attractive friend was next up—no surprise that he leapt and whirled through a brilliant acrobatic display. To follow him, he chose a woman who looked about Jalessa's age, though with an angular face and an air of sharp impatience. She performed a slashing, angry dance, using a slim rod as a prop. She spun to a halt in front of Averie, and reached out with her rod to tap Ket Du'kai on the shoulder.

For a moment, no one moved. Du'kai seemed frozen, staring at the Chiarrizi woman, whose expression was surely a cross between challenge and mockery. The music still played at its frenetic pace, but, for a moment, silence seemed to descend on their own small group. Averie half expected Jalessa to hurry forward, to make explanations. *Oh, he is a foreigner. He doesn't understand our ways.* But of course, the Chiarrizi woman knew that already, could tell by the soldier's face and uniform that he didn't belong, in this city, in this plaza, in this dance.

Averie was shocked beyond measure when Ket Du'kai gave the Chiarrizi woman a tiny bow and squeezed past her into the circle.

Now a murmur of excited speculation swept through the crowd. Everyone pushed even closer, and the rhythmic hand-clapping grew louder. Averie was too stunned to clap, to do anything but stare. She put her hand out blindly, as if to aid her balance, and found it taken in a comforting clasp. Lana had pushed up behind her and was peering over Averie's shoulder into the clearing.

Then Du'kai began to move. His performance was nothing like that of the Chiarrizi, nothing like anything Averie had seen in an Aebrian ballroom. He had taken something from his pocket—a wallet, perhaps—and he tossed this in the air as he turned in a circle below it, kicking out first one foot, then the other, as if leaping over a series of rolling hazards. Someone in the crowd whistled and tossed him an item that looked like a small orange. Du'kai caught it deftly, sent it spinning above his head in counterpoint to the other object, and continued turning and kicking as the items rose and fell. Now one of the spectators lobbed a piece of bumain; a third Chiarrizi darted into the circle with what looked like a couple of wooden dolls. Each of these Du'kai threw in the air, juggling them with an easy precision as he continued to slowly spin beneath them, head tilted back, legs kicking out, body perfectly balanced between opposing motions.

"Ho!" someone cried in warning, and shoved a large, heavy ball from the perimeter of the circle straight at Du'kai's feet. The Xantish man timed his jump perfectly to skip over it, still handling the objects rotating in the air. Clearly this was part of the act, even Averie could tell at once; clearly, his feet were supposed to be just as busy as his hands. The other Chiarrizi could see that as well, and within minutes, through some unfathomable magic, the spectators had gathered all manner of assorted rolling objects that they proceeded to shoot across the clearing to one another, directly in his path. At one point Averie counted seven separate balls and wheeled children's contraptions crisscrossing the constricted space in the dancer's circle. Du'kai cleared all of them with ease, meanwhile adding two more objects to the items he was tossing in the air. Averie had never seen such a display of coordination, concentration, athleticism, and dexterity. She was so afraid that he would drop something, or trip and fall, that she scarcely drew a breath for the whole time he stayed inside the circle.

She didn't know how he would extricate himself from the various fusillades, but fortunately he didn't have to. The music barked to a crescendo and crashed to a halt. Ket Du'kai caught his juggling articles with a few quick twists of his hands and sidestepped the last few toy carts shoved in his direction. The crowd erupted into applause and furious cheering. The lieutenant offered a deep and loose-jointed bow, and came up grinning.

His eyes went straight to Averie. She stared back at him, trying desperately to read the expression on his face.

"Well!" said Lady Selkirk's voice, and Averie nearly jumped out of her shoes. She hadn't realized the older women had wended their way back from the refreshment booths. "How extraordinary! Where do you suppose he learned to do such tricks? And *why*? Quite impressive, of course, but not very useful."

"Oh, well, when was anything like theater ever actually useful?" Lady Worth replied. "It is merely entertaining, and that was most entertaining, you must admit."

"This whole evening has been splendid!" Lana exclaimed.

Lieutenant Du'kai joined them at this point, although he had to fight through a mob of well-wishers to do so. His face wore its usual pleasant smile; he did not seem at all ruffled or embarrassed or even sweaty after a vigor-

ous display on a hot night. "That is an old-fashioned performance skill that some of the more traditional Xantish
learn, though the art is dying out in most of the cities,"
he told them, as if he had been asked for a bit of trivia
about his native land and had shown them a dull sort of
sleight of hand. "It didn't really suit the celebration here,
but I couldn't think of anything else to offer."

"It was *wonderful*!" Lana said. "I was so impressed."

He smiled at her. "My father and my uncle could
juggle twice as many pieces and leap over great obstacles
moving quite fast," he said. "My talents in this area are
only average, and I have had little time to practice in
recent years."

Two more Chiarrizi came up to slap Lieutenant Du'kai
on the shoulder and call unintelligible but obviously com-
plimentary words in his ear. "You seem to have pleased
this audience, at any rate," Lady Worth remarked.

The lieutenant glanced around, as if counting the
members of his party, and then addressed the older wom-
en. "I think we have lingered long enough to both watch
the performances and offer our own," he said. "It is time
to go, don't you think?"

Averie and Lana instantly and vociferously protested,
but Lady Selkirk said, "Oh, indeed, yes," and even Lady
Worth was nodding. "It's so hot," Lady Selkirk added,
as if that had anything to do with whether or not they
should stay.

"But I am convinced there will be more dancing," Averie wailed. "Or—something even *better* than dancing!"

"There might be, but you shall not be here to see it," Lady Selkirk said, and began a determined march away from the center of the plaza, pushing her way through the crowds. Lady Worth and Jalessa were a few steps behind her. Still protesting, Averie and Lana allowed their escorts to shepherd them back to where their conveyance was waiting.

There was no chance to talk to Lieutenant Du'kai, though Averie glanced at him from time to time as they made their way through the festival mob. He always seemed to be looking away when she turned to gaze at him, either scanning the crowd for trouble or leaning over to make a comment to one of his men. Not until they were at the wagon, the women settled on benches and the men on horseback beside them, did Averie manage to catch his eye. And then she felt that it was deliberate, that he had paused in the act of turning his horse toward home, and permitted himself to give her one long, meaningful stare. His expression matched the one he had worn when he stepped out of the circle, when he had gazed straight at her as if daring her to read the thought in his head.

Only a moment the look held; then he urged the horse forward and signaled his men to follow. Averie sat the entire ride back to the house in abstracted silence, barely bothering to reply to Lana's chatter. She spent that whole time analyzing what Ket Du'kai might have meant to convey to her by the expression on his face.

You are not the only one who can fall under the spell of the Chiarrizi, perhaps he had been saying. *You are not the only one who knows how to put aside formality and give way to exuberance. You are not the only one who can dazzle. You are not the only one who knows how to misbehave.*

CHAPTER
FIFTEEN

I n the morning, both Morgan and Averie's father
were gone. Jalessa had taken one of her free days,
and Lady Selkirk was so tired from her excursions
the night before that she scarcely spoke over breakfast
and returned immediately to her room to nap. Averie
wandered from the *maroya* to the courtyard, feeling
bored and a little depressed. She took off her shoes and
perched on the edge of the fountain. The bright sound
of the chiming ball sounded unusually harsh; the water
felt unpleasantly warm under her splashing fingers. The
sun, just past noon, beat down relentlessly. It was too hot
to sit in the direct sunlight, but for the longest time, she
couldn't summon the strength to rise and seek a place in
the shade. She just dabbled her hands in the water and
let the sun bake her face and wondered why she felt so
lost and dismal.

An afternoon nap did not cure her of her unaccustomed megrims. In fact, she almost had a tantrum as she unwound herself from the tangled sheets and kicked them to the floor in a fit of rage. It was so *hot* in here. The tinkling of the fountain outside her window made her seriously consider slipping off her clothes, climbing out her window, and plunging naked into the water. Then she thought perhaps it would make more sense simply to turn on the taps in her bathing room and stand under the spray.

She followed this more sedate plan, lingering under the faucet so long that she finally got tired of standing, and sank to the tiled floor with the water still beating down on her head. *Finally* she felt a little better as the water washed away her melancholy. Still, she couldn't bring herself to rise to her feet, shut off the tap, and rummage through her clothes for a clean *tallah*. Closing her eyes, she drifted back to sleep.

She might have slept forever if not for the annoying noises sounding a short distance away. She turned to her side, reaching for a pillow, and woke confused to find herself on hard, wet tile, drenched to the bone. Where was she? Why was she so *wet*? Who was calling her name and knocking loudly at the door? She struggled to get up, but her head was so heavy—her head was *pounding*—and her feet couldn't find a purchase on the slick floor. She sat back, panting a little, resting her head on the wet wall. Well, in a minute, then. She would just sit here quietly and collect her thoughts.

The noise at the door grew louder and more urgent, and then suddenly there was an ominous cracking sound. *Someone's broken in,* Averie thought, unalarmed. She heard Sieffel's voice and then the excited counterpoint of women's voices, worried and sharp. Footsteps, the creak of another door opening, and then Lady Selkirk stepped into the room and shrieked. The sound hurt Averie's head, and she closed her eyes again.

"Grace! In here! Gracious glory, she looks half drowned." The water abruptly ceased running. Lady Selkirk must have shut off the valves. "Averie. *Averie.* Grace, quickly—bring me her nightshirt! I think she must have been taken ill."

Averie felt a moment of light relief—of course! she was sick!—just as her head started pounding again. She squeezed her eyes shut even tighter. Behind her closed lids she could sense the flicker of shadows, and she heard the low murmur of Grace's voice.

"We'd better dry her off—she'll be shivering with chill if she's been in the water this past hour and more."

A soft towel was rubbed over Averie's face and chest; cool hands pressed themselves to her cheeks. "No chill," Lady Selkirk said, and her voice was grim. "She's burning up with fever."

"That's worse," Grace said, and her voice sounded

apprehensive. "Something she picked up at the festival last night?"

"I suppose so. I've had a headache all day myself. And Lady Worth sent a note around this afternoon saying Lana had been mopey and tired all day and that she didn't feel too strong either. But this—this seems much more extreme."

"Can we get her to the bed between us?"

"Dressed first," Lady Selkirk said firmly. "Averie. Averie, you will have to stand up now, and we will put your nightshirt over your head. Come now. Be good."

By dint of wheedling and tugging, the two women were able to coax Averie to her feet, slip a nightdress over her head, and guide her back to bed. She collapsed there with a sigh. The pillowcase felt cool against her cheek—finally, something that was not *hot*—but it warmed up quickly against her skin. She tried opening her eyes but found the lids too heavy. So she merely lay there, listening to the conversation around her.

" . . . can we do for her?"

"Lady Worth might know . . . here a month longer . . ."

" . . . quinine, but . . . worse? How to treat . . . foreign diseases . . . no business living like this! . . . back in Aeberelle!"

" . . . so hot . . . keep her cool . . ."

" . . . drink something?"

" . . . don't want her to throw up . . ."

"Oh, I wish Jalessa were here!"

I wish Jalessa were here, too, Averie thought. *Jalessa would know what to do.*

The next few hours passed in pain, incoherence, and darkness. Someone tilted liquid down her throat, and she promptly vomited it back up. Once started, she could not stop retching up everything in her body, which made her feel even worse. And she was so *hot.* Grace laid wet towels across her body, but that helped only a little. She twisted and turned in the bed, whimpering, and fell into small fits of sleep, only to wake again, still miserable. Now and then she opened her eyes but shut them again right away. The sunlight hurt her head; even the candle-light, once night fell, burned too brightly. There was nothing to do but keep her eyes closed and give herself up to chaotic dreaming.

Daylight brought a new assault on her senses. She buried her face under her pillow to keep out the unendurable light, but then she felt so smothered she could not breathe. Her bones were bars of molten metal; her stomach felt like it had been wadded into a hard ball by someone's unforgiving hand. She shut her eyes and tried to lie still.

Voices seeped into her consciousness some time later.

" . . . still sleeping? How's her fever?"

"High. Maybe higher than yesterday."

"I've sent a note to her father, though I cannot guess how quickly it can be delivered all the way to the Soldath Mountains. He will be most distraught."

"And Colonel Stode?"

"Somewhere on board ship! Who knows where? This dreadful country . . ."

". . . note from Lady Worth . . . everyone well in that household . . ."

"Good news, I suppose, but I am most worried for *this* household. . . ."

The voices retreated to a murmur, or else Averie fell asleep again. She was jerked from a fevered dream by a fresh set of sensations—a new voice in the room, new hands on her forehead, a fresh and vaguely familiar scent.

"Averie. Averie, can you hear me?" It was Jalessa's voice, though it took Averie a moment to recognize it. Or maybe it took her that long to realize that Jalessa was speaking Weskish, and then to remember what the words meant in that other tongue. "Open your eyes if you can do so."

It took a powerful effort, and Averie couldn't focus properly, but she blinked her eyes open long enough to see Jalessa's broad face hovering over hers. The Chiarrizi girl, usually so placid, looked distinctly alarmed. But she gave Averie a wide smile.

"Good. You can understand me. Can you speak?"

Averie shook her head, just the minutest gesture, her hair against the pillow.

"Try. You didn't try," Jalessa said. "Say my name."

Averie had to think about it a long moment first. "Jess-a."

"Good! I've sent Grace and Sieffel to the market to fetch some drugs that will make you feel better."

This word Averie could remember a little more quickly. *"No."*

"Yes, I know. I know, you think you will throw up again, but you need to take this medicine. You need to, Averie, do you understand? Or you may die."

"Jalessa!" The sharp hiss came from Lady Selkirk, who did not believe in honesty with invalids.

"She might," Jalessa said, turning her head to address Lady Selkirk. "And she must know. She must know she must *try*, or she is lost."

Die? Averie thought. She was so tired that the threat did not seem as fearful as it normally would. *I'm only eighteen. But I could die?* She tried to summon terror, but all she could manage was exhaustion. She let her lids drift shut again.

Jalessa shook her roughly by the shoulder. "No! Averie! You cannot sleep! You have to stay awake long enough to swallow the drugs. Averie, look at me."

Oh, too hard. Averie tried but almost immediately gave up. Her body felt curious—like ash, like something that had burned and now was so light it could float on the faintest breeze. If she stretched her fingers and toes, she might lift herself off the mattress merely because she did not possess enough weight to stay in place—

Her cheeks stung with two hard slaps, and she grunted in pain and surprise. *"Jalessa!"* came Lady Selkirk's horrified voice, and then another sharp blow landed. Furious and helpless, Averie fought to open her eyes and found Jalessa's face inches from hers, set and afraid. The Chiarrizi girl's strange eyes were dark with concentration.

"Averie. You cannot sleep. Look at me, *mua sova.* Focus on me. As soon as you take the drugs, you can close your eyes again."

Averie wanted to speak, wanted to complain, wanted to say she was hot, she hurt, she understood, she didn't care, but she couldn't force any of the words out. But she tried, she tried harder than she had ever tried to do anything in her life, to keep her eyes open and her gaze fixed on Jalessa's face. Jalessa nodded and slowly lifted her hands to the back of her neck, appearing to undo the catch of a necklace. Yes—seconds later, she held a thin chain, dripping between her fingers. She caught one of Averie's fevered hands in hers and closed it around the attached charm. This was no smooth pendant of gold or opal. This felt like a spiny seashell or a bramble notched with thorns.

"Feel her? That is *seena*," Jalessa murmured, squeezing her hand so tightly over Averie's that Averie could feel the arrow from the wounded bird digging into her own palm. Those other pointed edges must be the goddess's beak and talons and outstretched wings. "She is struck through the heart, but she will not die. She will not surrender. Draw strength from her strength, Averie. Feel your pain as she feels hers."

Indeed, the sting of those pinpricks was just enough to keep Averie awake, clutching to consciousness. She kept her hand curled tightly around the little goddess, while Jalessa watched her, nodding from time to time.

If only she could speak! Averie tried to think of the simplest words that would convey the most complex questions. "What—sick?" was the best she could do, but Jalessa nodded again.

"It is a common enough fever among the Chiarrizi, mostly affecting children. Adults either get very sick or have just a few hours of discomfort and recover quickly."

Averie remembered some of the snatches of conversation she had overheard between Grace and Lady Selkirk. "La-na?" she managed to ask.

Lady Selkirk answered. "She had a slight fever yesterday but is much better today, her mother says. Weak and tired, but not nearly as unwell as you."

"*Ky—kyleeta?*" Averie asked next.

"That is probably where you picked up the infection," Jalessa said. "Though it is not the season for this fever, and I did not think to warn you to take precautions."

Averie swallowed, suddenly aware of how thirsty she was. Suddenly remembering something Jalessa had said a few moments ago. "Die?" she whispered.

"Of course not!" Lady Selkirk said heartily. "You're young and quite strong. Even when you were a child, you were never sick more than a day or two at a time."

But Jalessa's face told a different story. So did Jalessa's words. "Yes," she said quietly. "The fever can be fatal when someone is as sick as you are." She saw the question in Averie's eyes and added, "More than half the time."

"Jalessa!" Lady Selkirk breathed. "Surely not!"

Jalessa patted Averie's hand, still wrapped around the *seena* charm. "So you see why you must stay awake, *mua sova, mua lota*. You see why you must take the drugs I give you. You must hold tight to the goddess and put your faith in her."

Averie could form no more words, but she nodded her head ever so slightly.

Lady Selkirk, who was standing anxiously at the side of the bed, jerked her head to one side. "I think they're back," she said, and opened the door. Indeed, a moment later, Grace came hurrying through, carrying a black pouch.

"Keep your hands on *seena*," Jalessa instructed Averie,

then rose to confer with Grace and Lady Selkirk. Averie watched in some trepidation as Jalessa stirred a powdery mixture into a glass of water from the nightstand.

Impossible that they expected her to sit up and swallow all that. But that was exactly the case. Lady Selkirk and Grace helped Averie struggle into an upright position, though the motion made her head feel like it was exploding. She clutched the goddess charm tighter, felt all the filed points pierce her skin, thought about how her own blood would paint the arrow tip that had gone through *seena*'s breast. Jalessa put the glass to Averie's lips and tilted the liquid down her throat. Averie choked and swallowed.

"Think about what it will be like when you are back in Aeberelle," Jalessa said. "Think about your friends there, and all the stories you have to tell them about Chesza. You do not want to die before you have returned to Port Elise! You do not want to die before you have married Colonel Stode."

"Think of your wedding," Lady Selkirk added helpfully as Averie took another sip, and another. "You will have such a pretty dress, and your father will buy you a set of pearls. *Everyone* in Port Elise will attend."

The medicine did not taste nearly as bad as Averie had expected—it actually had a citrus flavor that was pleasing to the tongue—but there was so much of it. Averie felt her eyes flutter shut. Jalessa's free hand closed over Averie's, causing the edges of the *seena* charm to dig even deeper into her palm.

"You don't want to die before nightfall," Jalessa whispered with some intensity. "You don't want to die before you see Colonel Stode again."

That made Averie open her eyes and swallow more. Slowly she finished the glass, and Jalessa was smiling as the older women laid Averie back on the pillow.

"In three hours you must drink some more," Jalessa warned, smoothing Averie's hair back from her face. "But you may sleep now. You were very brave. I am quite proud of you, *mua lota*."

She reached for Averie's hand as if to retrieve her necklace, but Averie tightened her fingers. "Keep?" she begged.

Jalessa gazed down at her. "You want to hold on to *seena*? You may, as long as you promise to drink the medicine when it is time."

Averie nodded. "Not want . . . to die . . . before . . ." The words trailed off.

"You can tell us later," Jalessa said. "Now Lady Selkirk and Grace are going to get some sleep, and I will sit with you until it is time for your next dose. You sleep now."

"If you're sure," Lady Selkirk said doubtfully, but Averie could hear the weariness and longing in her voice.

"Go. I will stay with her."

"I'll be back once I've rested."

There were the sounds of footsteps retreating, the door opening and shutting, quiet voices fading down the hall. Averie snuggled into the pillow, closed her hand as tightly as she could on the goddess charm, and thought, *I don't want to die until I have kissed Ket Du'kai.*

Light, dark, pain, medicine, whispered conferences in the room, cool towels along her forehead, light and darkness again. Averie lost any sense of time as the fever ran its course. There was only physical sensation and disordered dreaming. Drink, sleep, endure.

Until one hour she opened her eyes and suddenly knew who she was and what had happened to her. It was night; she lay in her shadowed room straining to make out the details. The gauzy curtains were pulled back to admit a light evening breeze and the tinkling melody of the fountain. It was so still in the room, so dark. Was she alone? No, for there was the black shape of a cushioned chair pulled up beside her bed, and Averie could make out the outline of a person sleeping in it. She couldn't tell who it was.

"I'm—I'm awake," she said in a shaky voice. "Who's sitting there?"

The shape moved and sat up, resolving itself into Jalessa. "Averie?" she said, her voice still burred with sleep. "Did you speak?"

"Yes—I'm awake. How long have I been sick?"

There was no light to see by, but Averie could hear the delight in Jalessa's voice. "Five days. But listen to you! You sound quite like yourself."

"I've been very bad off, haven't I?"

Jalessa leaned forward to lay her hands on Averie's cheeks and forehead. "The fever's gone. Just like that. That's the way it always goes. It disappears like a match flame blown out." She settled back in her chair. "Yes. You were very bad. Yesterday we had almost given up hope."

Averie swallowed, for that was a frightening thing to hear. "I still feel . . . so odd. Like I could float out of the room."

"That's from so many days of lying here with nothing to eat. Let me get you some juice. But once the delirium fades, you're out of danger. The weakness will pass soon."

Averie lifted her head just enough to drink from the glass Jalessa held to her lips. It was excruciating to make even that much effort, but the juice tasted better than anything she'd ever had in her life. Her whole body ached, but it was not the same pain she could remember enduring for the past nightmarish week. "My father and Morgan. Do they know I've been ill?" she asked when the glass was empty.

"Colonel Stode sailed back into harbor yesterday

afternoon, having received an urgent note from Lady Selkirk. Your father . . . was unable to leave his post at the Soldaths, but he requested constant updates. As soon as the house stirs, we will send a messenger to tell him the good news."

Averie tried to see Jalessa's face, but the room was too dark. "You're the only reason I didn't die, aren't you," she said flatly.

Jalessa shrugged. "Any Chiarrizi would have known to give you the same drugs."

"You gave me *seena*, too."

There was a smile in Jalessa's voice. "Ah, many other Chiarrizi would have asked the goddess to watch out for you, as well. She looks after the sick and injured."

"You say that," Averie replied in a quiet voice. "But I know better. You sat with me. You held my hand. You saved me."

The other woman was silent for a moment. "It would have been a terrible thing if you had died," she said at last.

"Thank you, Jalessa," Averie whispered. "*Mua dei, mua sova.*" Emotion overcame her, or maybe it was the weakness, but she felt herself starting to cry. Except she was too tired, too wrung out, too empty to cry. Her eyes burned, and she bit her lip. "What would we have done without you . . . ?"

Jalessa leaned forward again and wrapped Averie's

hands in a comforting grip. "Thank me in the morning. For now I think you need more drugs and more sleep. You will feel much better when you wake up."

"But I'll still be grateful," Averie said, so quietly the words might almost have gone unsaid.

CHAPTER
SIXTEEN

The next few days passed with all the irritability Averie historically experienced when recovering from illness. She was rarely sick, but at those times she was a dreadful patient. She tried hard not to quarrel with Grace or Jalessa or Morgan or Lana, all of whom tried mightily to entertain her and succeeded mostly in annoying her. Instead, she reserved most of her bad humor for Lady Selkirk, who at one point exclaimed, "I almost rue the day Jalessa saved your life!" and stormed out of the room. Averie was ashamed of herself after that and made a greater attempt to be agreeable to her visitors.

Morgan seemed likely to be the first to benefit from her improved manners when he arrived two hours later. "Is it safe to come in?" he asked, peering around the door.

Averie sighed. "I hope so. I will need to apologize to Lady Selkirk soon."

Morgan advanced into the room, kissed her on the cheek, and sat in the chair beside the bed. "You will need to apologize to all of us," he said cheerfully. "Even your father, who is not here. In his last memo to me, he mentioned that your notes were full of complaints and whining. Pretty impressive when you can sense a scowl from hundreds of miles away. Yes—like that one. Exactly."

That made Averie laugh, and her expression lightened. "Well, I *hate* lying in bed all day. And I itch and I ache and I'm *hungry*, but as soon as I eat something I think I will throw it up again, and all in all I am not very happy."

"No," said Morgan seriously. "But at least you're not dead. To think of losing you . . ." He took her fingers and played with them, looking down at their entwined hands. "Well. That's something I wouldn't like to relive any time soon."

She squeezed his hand; her strength had returned enough to allow her to do *that*, at any rate. "Well, now you know how I feel when you put on your uniform and sail for some dangerous part of the world," she said. "Afraid that I might lose you forever."

He smiled slightly. "Yes, but that's a soldier's job, to face battle and bloodshed," he said. "The job for a beautiful young lady is to give a soldier something to fight for. Which means he needs to know she is safe." He took a deep breath. "You've been here two months. I'm wondering if it might be better for you to go back to Port Elise now, instead of staying six months as you planned."

She almost snatched her hand away. "Port Elise! How am I any safer there?"

"How are you not?" he shot back.

"I could just as easily succumb to a fever in Aeberelle," she pointed out. "People die every day from inflammations and infections!"

"Yes, but in Aeberelle we have physicians who know how to care for them, not—not—local witch women who mumble heathen prayers over a few mashed herbs!"

He spoke with such venom that Averie blinked. Did he dislike Jalessa so much? "Yes, but the mashed herbs saved my life, Morgan," she said softly.

He shook his head. "And I am grateful to Jalessa, grateful beyond words, but horrified that she was needed for such a task. The thought of risking you again in such a fashion—well, it turns my blood to water."

She struggled to assume a dignified and serious pose, not an easy thing to do under the circumstances. She said, "But Morgan, it is not the last time I will be at risk if I follow you to exotic locations around the world."

He stared back at her. His handsome face looked tired, as if he had not slept—or, if he had, as if his dreams had been as bad as hers. "Then perhaps you should not plan on following me," he said.

She opened her eyes very wide. "What—you want to send me back to Port Elise now and keep me there the rest of my life?"

He rubbed the back of her hand with his thumb. "Well—not quite so baldly as all that, but—I wasn't in favor of bringing you here anyway, you know," he added in a rush. "I don't think a war zone is the place for women, and so I told your father."

Now she did draw her hand away from him, slowly, icily. "Morgan. I always understood that there would be times I couldn't travel with you. But I never planned to stay behind, fretting about you, knowing you were having adventures while I was just . . . just . . ." She gestured helplessly. "Leading a meaningless existence."

"It's hardly meaningless to be overseeing our estates and, if we are so fortunate, raising our children," he retorted. "How can you be angry at me for wanting to keep you safe?"

"How can you understand me so little as to think that *safe* is what I want?" she flung back at him.

He made a gesture of frustration. "This is madness. All you do is quarrel. If I said I wanted you to stay in Chesza, you would find some reason to disagree *then*."

Hurt, she said, "I've been sick. I know that makes me difficult sometimes—"

"You are *always* like this," he replied. "Or, at least since you have been in Chesza. It seems we agree on nothing."

She could hardly argue with that, but she thought that was his fault, and not her own. "Well, we certainly don't agree about me going back to Port Elise," she said stiffly. "And I will *not* do so."

He came to his feet and stood looking down at her a moment, his face troubled. "No, I don't suppose you will," he said. "Well. It certainly seems like you're getting some of your strength back. I hope you continue to feel better."

And he marched smartly from the room—leaving her feeling much worse, indeed.

She did not repeat this conversation to anyone, not even Lana, because she thought she might burst into tears before she could choke it all out. Such a distance that had come between Morgan and her! What had happened? Could it really be Chesza that had divided them? She had been quite pleased with him while she made the trip to Chiarrin—so excited about the prospect of seeing him again. What had gone wrong? She had always been flighty and high-spirited, but that had never bothered him before. And she had always been stubborn—

anyone would attest to that!—but maybe she had never set her will against Morgan's before. Maybe he had always thought he could provide her sober, thoughtful counsel, and she would gratefully accept it.

Maybe she had thought she could, with her merry heart and casual ways, lighten his somberness. Maybe they had each expected the other to change without taking into consideration the fact that both of them liked themselves very much the way they were.

She did not know, in the following days, exactly what the consequences of their latest disagreement might be. Was their betrothal broken, or were they merely at odds?

Should they be polite to each other or attempt, over meals and chance encounters in the hall, to mend their differences?

It scarcely mattered, as it turned out. Averie almost never saw Morgan in the next few days. Her father was still gone, and Major General Worth required Morgan's almost constant attendance. No more evenings before the fountain, courting. No more stolen kisses in the corridor. Civil exchanges over the few meals they had together, mostly for Lady Selkirk's sake, and bitterness in secret, or so Averie imagined.

She thought the heaviness in her chest might be attributed as much to heartache as to the lingering effects of illness, but in public she only ever admitted to the latter.

Despite her uncertain romantic state, Averie's body continued to improve. Lady Selkirk believed she was still too weak to venture out again, so Averie became quite the hostess, holding court almost daily in the *maroya*. Lana was there every morning, of course, but Carrie Dryser, Edna Harmon and her sister, and some of the older women dropped by on a regular basis to see how Averie was getting on.

Now, two weeks past *kyleeta*, the weather was beginning to turn, and the mornings were cool enough to be pleasant. The Aebrian women had fallen into the habit of gathering at the Winston house for breakfast, sitting outside in the shadow cast by the eastern wing of the house. After Sieffel had set up folding tables, Grace would carry out fruit and bread and hodee cheese. The older women would sit in the shade, fanning themselves and pretending that it was a degree or two cooler than it had been the day before. The girls fluttered around the sunnier portion of the courtyard like so many impatient butterflies, wearing their *tallahs* and whispering gossip.

The most interesting information was always obtained during these gatherings.

"Did you *hear*?" Lana demanded one morning as she and Edna and Averie strolled through the sunshine. "One of the enlisted men has gone missing."

"Gone missing?" Averie repeated sharply. "You mean, missing in battle?"

"No," Edna breathed, glancing over her shoulder in the direction of her mother, who was deep in conversation with Lady Worth and Lady Selkirk. Probably discussing the same choice tidbit. "Left without leave in the middle of the night."

"Left for where? There's no place to go."

"He's in love with a Chiarrizi girl," Lana whispered.

"No!"

"Yes! He's been meeting her in secret—oh, for weeks, they say. Now she's going to have his baby. He asked permission to visit her family, and of course it was refused. Now he's gone—*and* all his personal items."

"*And* all his reputation," Edna added. "If they find him, he'll be court-martialed."

"But then— Will he— Does he intend to stay in Chiarrin?" Averie asked blankly. "I mean, forever? He does not plan to return to Aeberelle?"

Edna shrugged. "Who knows? He can't have been thinking clearly. To give up everything! For a girl he scarcely knows! In a foreign country, so far from home . . . I cannot imagine it. He must have been made lunatic by the heat."

"Colonel Stode was very angry, my father said," Lana put in. "Apparently this was a man the colonel thought had great potential, and to see him throw it all away . . . he was deeply disappointed."

Averie kept her voice neutral. "I think there are a

number of things about Chesza that have caused Morgan great disappointment."

"My father doesn't like the place either," Edna said, nodding. "He says it's strange. Slippery and hard to understand. But I rather like Chiarrin."

"Oh, so do I," Lana said. "Except for the heat, and even that doesn't bother me if I can wear my *tallahs*." They all giggled.

Averie instantly sobered. "Well, I am sorry for this young man—this soldier. What a hard choice he has made, between everything he has known and loved his whole life and a completely fresh and unfamiliar world. That can't have been an easy decision."

Lana shrugged. "Unless he didn't *like* that old life and has been looking for something else." Averie and Edna stared at her, and she hastened to go on. "Many men join the army because they are poor, or they are second sons with no hope of inheritance. That does not mean they like being soldiers. We don't know why this man joined. We don't know, for certain, why he has left. He might not be so unhappy as we think."

There is never any knowing with certainty what is going on inside someone else's head, Averie thought, eyeing Lana with new respect. *Maybe coming to Chiarrin was the best thing that could ever have happened to this man.* Much as she loved Chesza, she was fairly certain she would not be able to say the same thing for herself.

The shocking decision of the enlisted man was the topic of conversation that night as well, when Captain Gaele and Captain Martin came by after dinner. They were accompanied by Carrie Dryser and her mother, both of whom seemed less interested in Averie's health than in getting out of the house on a lovely evening. The older women stayed indoors, comfortable in the *maroya*, while the younger women and the officers enjoyed the air in the courtyard. Carrie and Captain Gaele strolled around the fountain while Captain Martin sat beside Averie on one of the stone benches.

"Terrible business," he said, shaking his head. "Hurts morale, makes all the men restless, puts everyone on edge. What will the general do if he's caught, that's what the men want to know. And what if he's not caught? To think of leaving one of your own behind, gone native— that makes men uneasy. That makes them rash. I've seen this more than once—the minute one man deserts, two or three follow suit."

"How will you stop them?" Averie asked.

"That's the hard thing. You can impose curfews at the barracks, but what about the men out patrolling? They can slip away into the night. You can double up the men on watch, but suppose both want to slip off? We have been constantly switching the partners, but it's still a chancy business. Colonel Stode is working tirelessly to keep everyone in line, but I'm afraid it's been rather a drain on him."

"We haven't seen much of Morgan in the past few days," Averie said calmly. "And I agree, he looks quite weary."

"Well, I'm not surprised." Martin nodded once. "Good man, Morgan Stode."

The other two came waltzing up just then, laughing, of course—everyone laughed when Rufus Gaele was nearby. "You two look so grim!" Carrie exclaimed. "I told Captain Gaele that he must put his energy into charming Averie from the dismals. I will take gloomy Captain Martin off so that Averie has a chance to recover her spirits."

Despite Averie and Captain Martin instantly disclaiming any tendency toward melancholy, Carrie managed to draw the serious man away with her and leave the smiling one behind.

"Here's a tale I wager you haven't heard yet," Captain Gaele said, and plunged straight into a complicated story about two soldiers, an angry hodee, and a small Chiarrizi boy. Obligingly, Averie allowed herself to be entertained, but very little of her attention was on the recital. Instead, she was watching Carrie as she put her hand on Captain Martin's arm and leaned very close to him. The other girl seemed to have given up her pursuit of Captain Gaele to concentrate on the more eligible Captain Martin. Cynically, Averie wondered if the small Aebrian community might soon be able to celebrate news of a pairing far more suitable than that of an enlisted man and a Chiarrizi woman.

The next thought came unbidden to her mind. *What an excellent wife she would make for Morgan, for they are both ambitious and she would be entirely committed to his career. Not wayward or difficult like I am. She would be a much easier bride.*

"Don't you see?" Captain Gaele ended up. "Or don't you think it's funny?"

She turned to give him a wide smile and, for the moment, all her attention. "I was trying to think of a story to tell you in return," she said gaily. "And I just remembered one! Back on Weymire Estate . . ."

They talked easily for another quarter hour until Lady Dryser poked her head out and called to Carrie that it was time to go. By this time, Averie's head hurt and her back hurt and her heart hurt, and she was more than willing to see her company disappear.

It was another four days before Ket Du'kai came to the house. Averie had given up the notion that he might drop by. She even believed she understood, mostly, why he stayed away. Too much revealed during those hot dances at the marketplace, too much unsaid that still seemed written brightly on the air. In his place, she might have avoided the Winston house, too.

When he did come, he arrived with Morgan and stayed for dinner.

Averie had slept late that afternoon and hurried into the *maroya* for the meal without bothering to brush her hair or change out of her crumpled *tallah*. So she was caught between pleasure and dismay when she stepped into the room to see the two dark blue uniforms stationed on either side of Lady Selkirk. Morgan, actually here for a meal!

Ket Du'kai beside him.

Averie glanced around quickly, but there was no sign of Jalessa, even though this was one of the evenings she would stay overnight at the house. The Chiarrizi girl never took her meals with them when Morgan was present, though neither of them had ever said aloud that Morgan did not like her to join them. But this was one night Averie would have liked to have a little support and companionship.

She sought her seat immediately, feeling a traitorous weakness, but managed to smile at the others and gesture for them to find their places. Years of training came to her aid as she began to play the gracious hostess. "A welcome surprise to see both of you," she said. "I hope that means the day was a good one, with no particular disasters."

Lieutenant Du'kai laughed, and Morgan grimaced. "For a wonder," Morgan said. "No rebels attacked the market, no deserters slipped off during patrol, no Weskish warships were spotted in our waters, *and* we got a letter from your father saying all is quiet by the Soldaths and he is on his way back, bringing all the troops."

"A very good day!" Averie exclaimed. "Worth celebrating indeed!"

Ket Du'kai gave her one quick glance and a brief nod. "You're looking well, Lady Averie," he said. "Have you entirely recovered from your recent illness?"

She laughed and waved a hand. "Oh no, I intend to remain wan and pitiful for a while longer," she said. "I had no idea how kindly people treat you when you're an invalid. They bring you presents and are most solicitous of your comfort. And when their company bores you, instead of having to endure it politely for another hour, you merely say, 'Oh, I am so sorry, but I feel dreadfully weak. May I be excused?' and you go back to your chamber to read or nap. It is really the most delightful existence."

Even Morgan appeared to find this amusing. He gave Averie an ironic smile and said, "I suppose you shall be addicted to disease from now on and find yourself succumbing at every convenient moment."

"Well, you know, I think I would, except that the *actual* sickness is so gruesome that I can't bear the idea of going through it again," she said. She sipped her water and changed the subject. "But tell me how you have been! Captain Gaele and Captain Martin dropped by the other evening, but I haven't seen an officer since, and I have no idea what is going on in the world."

Morgan cut his meat. "The world seems to be coming to grips with the notion of peace," he answered. "The trouble at the Soldaths has calmed down, there have been no uprisings near the Maekaths, and Chesza itself has been very quiet."

"I have not heard of any troubles in the eastern quadrant for weeks now," Lady Selkirk said.

Morgan nodded and swallowed. "Worth thinks that Chesza is tired of turmoil and we'll see no more uprisings here. If we can secure Chesza, we can concentrate on the middle of the country, and more quickly bring Chiarrin under our control."

Does that mean you believe it is safe for me to stay in Chezsa? Averie wondered. She glanced at Lieutenant Du'kai, intending to draw him into the conversation, and found him with his gaze fixed on his plate and his face unsmiling. Her stomach clutched in a moment of sympathy. Was he thinking that these were the sorts of conversations Aebrian officers had held when they were trying to subdue Xan'tai?

"Well, I'm in favor of any move toward peace," she said lightly. "Lieutenant, did you try some of that bread? It's delicious."

"Any more news about that unfortunate man?" Lady

Selkirk asked. "The one who has"—she paused delicate-ly—"disappeared?"

Morgan wiped his mouth. "Not a trace of him. At first, Worth was worried that he might have fallen in with the rebels and would tell them military secrets."

"Heavens! Did he know any secrets?" Lady Selkirk exclaimed.

Morgan looked impatient. "Patrol patterns, weapons caches, those sorts of things. So we moved equipment and altered some routines, but there's been no trouble. Whoever he's run to, she doesn't seem to have friends among the fighters, and that's good news."

"What was he like?" Averie asked. "This young man."

"He was a soldier in the *Aebrian army*," Morgan said, as if that was a complete description. "Bound to duty and to honor—both of which he's betrayed."

Ket Du'kai spoke up in a low voice. "He was Xantish."

Morgan glanced at him sharply. "He was. But there have been fine Xantish soldiers in the Aebrian army for generations now, and I would not have expected this be-havior from one of them any more than I would have expected it from an Aebrian man born and bred."

The lieutenant shrugged. "Chiarrin is nothing like Xan'tai, but it is more like Xan'tai than it is like Aeber-elle. He might have been homesick. He might have been unhappy." He shrugged again. "He might simply have fallen in love with a girl."

"I don't see what harm comes of it, if he hasn't discussed military business," Averie said.

Morgan hastily laid down his napkin. "There's plenty of harm! It sets a bad example in the barracks, it undermines morale, it weakens the chain of command. An army operates by directive and response. If men don't obey rules, they won't obey orders, and if they won't obey orders, the army cannot function. Even a slight infraction can have grave consequences." He glared at her. "And this is *not* a slight infraction."

Well. Something else on which she and Morgan disagreed. No surprises there. But she hated for them to be quarreling in front of others. "Perhaps we can find happier topics to discuss," she said in a quiet voice, "for the sake of our guest."

In situations like this, Lady Selkirk could always be counted on. "Heavens, yes!" she exclaimed. "When will the general be back? Soon, I hope."

Conversation for the rest of the dinner was stilted, but at least it wasn't incendiary. Averie was sure she wasn't the only one who was glad when the meal came to an end. The dishes hadn't even been cleared away before Morgan was on his feet. "Promised Worth I'd be back this evening," he said.

Lieutenant Du'kai also rose. "I'll accompany you back to quarters." He did not even look at Averie, though she was sure he could sense her dismay. All this time without a glimpse of him, and now he was leaving after having barely exchanged a word with her! Perhaps he had not even wanted to come, she thought glumly. Perhaps Morgan had insisted. Perhaps Morgan had wanted an extra presence at the dinner table to keep from falling into any casual intimacies.

It was more and more depressing as she considered every possibility.

"Well." Averie stood and escorted her guests slowly through the *maroya*. "I'm so glad you could join us, Lieutenant. Morgan."

At the door, Morgan paused to kiss her on the cheek, then pulled back to give her a serious look. She stared back at him, unsure of what she wanted to read on his face or what she wanted to convey with hers. In a few moments, the men had slipped out into the night.

Lady Selkirk was yawning. "I don't think I slept more than two hours all night," she said. "I'm off to bed. Call me if you need anything."

Once the tables were folded and Grace was back in the kitchen, the house seemed literally deserted. Averie wandered disconsolately through the *maroya* and finally headed out to the courtyard, leaving the door open behind her. Sitting on one of the benches, she watched the fountain playing silver in the moonlight. This was the time of day when it was most obvious that the fever pitch of summer was past, for the air felt silky and actually cool against the skin. Averie could imagine a time she might want to fetch a shawl to protect her against the chill. How cold did it get in Chesza? She would have to ask Jalessa.

She kicked her toes lightly against the stone paving. Not that there was much likelihood she would be in Chesza long enough to see the seasons turn again.

She heard footsteps in the *maroya* and glanced up in time to see the silhouette of a man step out into the courtyard. "Morgan?" she said, flooded with sudden gladness. It had been so long since he had found the time to join her in the evening! Had he come back to scold her or kiss her? She was not sure it mattered.

She rose to her feet but realized immediately she was wrong. This man was shorter, slimmer than Morgan, almost her own height, moving quietly through the darkness. "No," he apologized, and she instantly recognized his voice. "It's Ket Du'kai."

CHAPTER
SEVENTEEN

Now a different emotion washed over Averie, prickly and uncomfortable, hard to define. She put her hand against her throat. "Lieutenant," she said, and managed to keep her voice absolutely polite. "Did you leave something behind?"

"Colonel Stode did. Some papers. In the *maroya*, he said. He asked me to come back for them and gave me his key. I didn't feel I should just sneak through the house looking for them, but no one was in the front room. And I saw this door was open. . . ."

His voice trailed off. She realized they were staring at each other, though there was so little to see in this imperfect light.

"I often sit out in the courtyard at night," she said in a quiet voice. "It has become my favorite place at my favorite time of day."

"When I am off duty, I sometimes walk to Mualota Fountain at night," he said. "There is a soothing motion to the water. And a sense of holiness to the place."

She nodded. "Yes. I would not have thought to put it that way, but that's exactly right. It is almost as if all water is holy in Chesza, because it is so precious."

Lieutenant Du'kai came a step nearer, almost as if moving against his will. "So how are you feeling?" he asked. "You seem so thin."

She laughed softly. "Over dinner, you said I looked well."

She could hear the smile in his voice. "You are most luminous, for an invalid." A slight change in tone. "But you *do* look like you've lost weight."

"I have," she said. "I don't entirely have my appetite back."

"They told me you almost died."

He spoke the words starkly, with no pretense at his usual grace. She nodded jerkily. "That's what they told me, too. I know I have never felt so strange." She hesitated, then said, "I missed you, while I was getting well. I thought you might— We are friends, so I— Didn't you want to know how I was doing?" Hard as she tried, she could not keep the hurt and betrayal from her voice.

He inhaled sharply. "Lady Averie, I inquired after you every day. I practically had paid spies in the household to tell me, on an hourly basis, how you fared. I know when your fever broke and I know when you first opened your eyes. I have thought of you every hour since—" He pressed his lips together and looked away.

Now she was the one to step closer. Her head was singing with excitement; she thought her hands might be trembling. "Since . . . I fell ill?" she prompted. "Since . . . we went to the *kyleeta* festival? Since we danced together at my party?"

He was still looking away. "Since we met aboard ship more than two months ago," he whispered.

For a moment, she could not get any air. She was close enough now to touch him, and she did so, but gingerly, laying her fingertips along the bend of his elbow, feeling the stiff fabric of the uniform against her hand. Just so did Morgan's jacket feel when she took his arm, but oh how different the man inside the uniform, the emotions inside the girl! "Ket," she said timidly. "I know it's wrong, I know it's impossible, but I have thought about you every day, too."

His head jerked around. He stared at her in the dark, and his hand came up, warm and reassuring, to cover hers. "That is good to know—you have no idea how good—but it changes nothing," he said.

Her hand twisted till she could lace her fingers with his. "Wait— But— If we could just talk for a moment! This might not be the time, with Morgan waiting for you and Lady Selkirk only a few feet away. . . ."

She thought she saw him smile. "There *is* no place and time to have this conversation," he said gently.

"But I—"

"Shhh." He kept his hold on her hand and put his free hand against her mouth. "It's an old story, and there are no new words. But there is no place for me in your world, and I do not expect you to try to find one. I don't ask anything from you at all."

"But what if there is something I want to give?" she whispered against his fingers.

He smiled again. "I am wise enough to make sure you keep it to yourself."

She drew back from his hand, intending to protest, and he swiftly bent and kissed her. His mouth was tender against hers, gentle, and it lingered, as if he could not bring himself to pull away. Averie shook her hand free and put both arms around his neck, drawing him closer. Now his kiss was harder, but still sweet, still the awe of a man tasting wonder and not the greed of a parched man finding water. He placed his hands on her waist as if to keep from wrapping them around her back and crushing her to his body.

A moment longer the kiss held. Then he abruptly lifted his head, though his hands did not fall away. "But not as wise as I should be, apparently," he said, his voice threaded with rue. "There is something about you, Lady Averie, that undermines all my defenses."

Her hands had drifted down to settle on his arms. She stared up at him, leaning a little forward, silently asking for another kiss. He was the one who held them apart. "I don't know enough about war to have any defenses at all," she said.

He laughed. "And this is a war, or would be, if Colonel Stode guessed or even thought that I—" He shook his head. "Lady Averie—"

"Stop calling me that."

"Averie," he said gently. "I must go. And I must never, I see, be alone with you again for even five minutes. This is a story without a happy ending. I cannot bear to read too many more of its chapters."

"Just tell me—" she started, and bit her lip.

As if compelled against his will to ask, he said, "Tell you what?"

"If things were different. If I were not betrothed to Morgan. If—"

"If you were not the general's daughter, if you were not a beautiful heiress, if you were not a member of the Aebrian aristocracy while I am a landless Xantish officer? If things were different, neither of us would be who we are."

"But if they were," she whispered. "Would you love me then?"

Swiftly, he bent and kissed her again, then dropped his hands and stepped away. "I love you anyway," he said. "And I am not sorry that I do."

He bowed very low, gave her one last piercing look as he straightened up, then spun on his heel and marched back into the *maroya*. She stared after him, unable to move. She didn't know if he stopped to search for Morgan's papers or if he headed straight for the door, wanting to leave this place as fast as his feet could take him.

He loved her. He had said it; she knew it was true. He *loved* her, and oh by all the water in Chesza, she loved him, too. But this was no cause for spinning joy, as Morgan's declaration had been two years ago. Her heart was leaden, her hands cold; she felt wrapped with doom and despair, not delight.

She loved Ket Du'kai, and she would never be allowed to have him.

She pressed her hand to her mouth, pushing back a whimper, or maybe a scream. Her other hand went out as if to touch a wall for balance. She felt dizzy enough to topple over. She must get inside. She must get to sanctuary. She tripped through the doorway, stumbled down the hall—one hand still over her mouth, one knotted against her stomach. At her own doorway she paused, then hurried on, down the dim corridor, around the bend, and through the back wing of the house. Into the servants' quarters.

Faint light seeped out from under the door to Jalessa's room. Averie knocked and called out Jalessa's name at the same time, frantically rattling the door. Quickly,

Jalessa opened it, her uncovered hair loose around her shoulders, concern on her broad face.

"Averie! What's wrong? Are you sick again? Did something happen?"

A relief just to be in the room, to feel the strong arms around her, guiding her to the narrow bed. Averie sank onto the mattress and doubled over, sobbing into her knees. Jalessa's hands went seeking through the curtain of her hair, feeling Averie's forehead, her cheeks, patting her wrists.

"What's wrong, *mua lota*? Sit up. Here, lean against me. Tell me what happened."

Averie allowed herself to be pushed upright, pulled against Jalessa's shoulder. "He was here—he came back after they both left," she hiccuped. "And he said—and he *kissed* me—and I don't know what to do! I think I love him, I *know* I love him, but it's so complicated. And then Morgan and I have been fighting and I—I don't think I can marry him! But how can I not marry him? Everyone expects it! And how can I have changed my mind? Like that? All of a sudden? Jalessa, everything is so terrible!"

Jalessa actually seemed able to follow this completely incoherent speech. "Lieutenant Du'kai was here tonight," she said in her calm voice.

"Yes," Averie whispered.

"You love him, but you are promised to another man."

"Oh, yes."

"And in Aeberelle, no one breaks such promises?"

Averie shook her head, feeling the motion of her skull against Jalessa's shoulder. "Some people do. Terrible people. Mean people. Everyone despises them."

"So instead they marry where they have not given their hearts?"

Averie rubbed her eyes. "Marriage isn't about hearts—not often, anyway," she mumbled. "It's about land and family connections. I was one of the lucky ones. I fell in love with someone it would be good for me to marry. At least . . . I thought I did."

Jalessa pushed back some of the hair hanging in Averie's eyes. "And you no longer love the handsome and honorable Colonel Stode? Who sat beside you and wept when you were so sick he thought you would die?"

Averie started crying again. The tears were so bitter her eyes burned. "How can that be?" she sobbed. "I have *always* loved him! Here in Chesza I have seen a different side of him, but *he* isn't different. Have *I* changed so much? I don't *want* to change! I want to be the person I was before!"

Jalessa stroked her hair with a slow, soothing motion. "You have to be the person you become, no matter what events change you," she said. "The heart grows and stretches, just as the body does, and you cannot stop either of them. But you have some choice, with the heart. You can hold on to some things—you can throw others away. But it is very hard. Very hard to be who you wish you were, instead of who you are."

Averie closed her eyes. "I don't know that I can marry Morgan," she said, her voice faint. "But even if I don't, that doesn't mean I can ever . . . ever marry Ket Du'kai. So why ruin one man's life if it does not bring me any closer to another?"

Jalessa kissed her on the temple, the way a mother might kiss a crying child. "You must decide where the greatest chance for misery lies—for yourself and for everyone else—and then you must choose the other path," she said. "What seems so hard tonight will not seem easy tomorrow. But different answers may present themselves in time. Sometimes the only way out is through a thicket of pain. But it is still a way out."

Averie nodded and drew a deep, tremulous breath. "I don't think anything will change, no matter how many days or weeks I wait," she said in low tones. "But thank you for listening. There is no one else I could tell this story to."

She pulled herself free of Jalessa's half embrace and came shakily to her feet. Jalessa walked her to the door, her face concerned. "Do you want me to stay with you tonight?" the Chiarrizi woman asked.

Averie managed a weak laugh. "No, no, you've missed

enough sleep for me already, thank you very much. I'll be better in the morning, I'm sure I will."

Jalessa pushed another strand of hair behind Averie's ear. "And in the morning, Lieutenant Du'kai still will have kissed you," she said.

Averie caught her breath and her eyes misted over again. "Yes," she whispered. "Whatever else happens, I have *that* to remember forever."

The morning ushered in no clarity of understanding, but at least it did bring Lana to the Winston house, bouncing with her usual vitality. "Let's go to the market!" she invited. "You haven't been for weeks, and surely you're well enough by now."

Both of them enjoyed the excursion, despite the fact that none of the soldiers in their escort held a special place in Averie's heart. The air was just enough cooler to leave them pleasantly warm instead of nearly fainting with the heat. They strolled through the haphazard wagons and munched on dried fruit and generally had a most agreeable day.

Lana stayed for a noon meal, and then the girls sat in the courtyard while Lady Selkirk retired for her customary nap. *This was the very bench I was sitting on last night when Ket came back and kissed me,* Averie thought, glancing down at the smooth stone. She was tempted to tell Lana the story, but she hesitated. A few unwary words to her mother, to Edna Harmon, and Lana could accidentally rip apart Averie's fragile peace.

She approached the topic obliquely. "So Lieutenant Lansdale wasn't in your escort today," Averie said.

Lana sighed theatrically. "No! He's been sent up to the Maekaths."

Averie tried to make her voice mischievous. "What would you do if Lieutenant Lansdale ever mustered the nerve to kiss you?"

Lana uttered a little squeal. "I'd kiss him back, of course! But he never will."

"But what if he—what if he declared his love for you? Told you he wanted to marry you? Would you even consider it?"

Lana was shaking her head even harder. "I wouldn't. I couldn't. My mother's sister married for love, some farmer's son who works his own land. Everyone else has cast her off entirely, of course, but my mother still goes to visit her a couple times a year. You can't imagine—she doesn't even pretend to be happy. None of her old friends speak to her, and her husband is this . . . this . . . well, I suppose he was handsome when she married him, but he's surly and fat and silent now. And that's her life! I mean, I know that I could marry a handsome officer from a good family, and he could turn brutish or dull, and that would be sad, but at least I would have my *life*. My family and friends wouldn't cast me off. At least I would not be so isolated and miserable and *alone*. I think that's why my mother takes me with her, when she visits," Lana added with a laugh. "So that I never forget. So that I am never tempted to make the same mistakes. My mother looks at me and thinks I am the type of girl who will make foolish choices, and she wants to make sure I always remember how bad those choices can be."

Oh no. Averie could not confide the tale of her illicit kiss to Lana. "Well, I just wondered," she said lamely.

"Do you know who I *would* like to hear a declaration from, though?" Lana went on. "Captain Martin. I know everyone thinks Rufus Gaele is so much more delightful, but I think it would tire me out, after a while, to always have to be laughing at his jokes. Captain Martin is more restful. And I think he's kind, though he seems so stern."

Averie could easily enter into the spirit of this particular pastime. "Carrie Dryser has her eyes on him, so you'd better work fast," she said.

"I know! How can I catch his attention? Would your father host another party?"

"Just what Lady Selkirk was talking about the other day!"

So they put their heads together and talked fashion and food, and the hour passed pleasantly enough. But Averie felt curiously sad when Lana finally departed—still burdened, still uneasy, still curled protectively around tender and ungainly secrets.

CHAPTER
EIGHTEEN

Her father was back from the Soldaths that afternoon. He came striding through the house, searching for Averie, and when he found her, he took her up in a hug so hard it left her breathless. Some of the breathlessness was from surprise, though; he usually was not a demonstrative man. When he released her, he kept his hands on her shoulders and stared down at her with something like a frown.

"Don't ever want to get letters like that again for the rest of my life," he said gruffly. "Hearing how sick you were. You be careful, now. No more diseases."

She laughed, because how could someone promise not to get ill? And she hugged him in return. "Well, you must be careful, too, not to get hurt in any fighting."

He grunted. "Not me. Old generals like me die in their beds."

Both her father and Morgan would be home for dinner; that meant Lady Selkirk wanted something special for the meal. She and Averie and Grace conferred in the kitchen, deciding on a menu.

"And there will be five for dinner, Grace," Lady Selkirk said.

Averie looked up. "Five? Will we have company?" *Ket Du'kai?*

"I mentioned to your father that Jalessa eats with us when we dine alone, and he thought it would be appropriate to have her join us tonight so that he can thank her."

Averie was torn between being pleased and feeling apprehensive. "I think . . . I don't think Morgan approves of her presence at the table."

Lady Selkirk sniffed. "Colonel Stode needs to realize just how valuable Jalessa is to this household." It was the first time Averie could remember hearing Lady Selkirk criticize Morgan even mildly.

"I don't want his disapproval to make Jalessa uncomfortable," Averie said.

"It is just for one night. A special occasion. I am sure we can all behave civilly."

Indeed, *civil* was the best word to describe dinner that evening, Averie thought cynically. Morgan was coolly polite to Jalessa, who sat as far from him as possible and said almost nothing. Nonetheless, to make her feel welcome, they all spoke in Weskish and discussed almost painfully trivial topics. Conversation about the weather lasted all the way through the main course, until Averie asked her father for a travelogue instead.

"So tell us what the countryside was like up by the mountains," she said.

"Flatlands, then mountains," he said, and took another bite of meat.

"The Maekaths are red, the Soldaths are blue," Jalessa added.

"I would like to see them sometime," Averie said. "I would like to travel through all of Chiarrin."

"Not any time soon," Morgan put in.

Averie glanced at him. "Why not? I understood that the rebels had surrendered."

"They've certainly quieted down here in the city, and we've got the Maekaths firmly under control," her father said. "But there are still some fighters in the hills. I envision a few bloody skirmishes ahead, though for now we've pulled the troops out of the far northern passes."

Lady Selkirk, with what she must have thought was great delicacy, widened her eyes and looked between the general and Jalessa as if to convey the idea that this might not be an appropriate topic with a Chiarizzi sitting right at the table. Averie smothered a grin and asked, "But the city is safe?"

Her father nodded. "Seems to be."

Averie sat up straighter in her chair, almost knocking her little table over. "Then can I see the rest of it? The parts I've had to stay out of so far?"

Morgan gave her a swift look. "It might not be *that* safe," he said.

But her father was nodding. "If you like. Bring a couple of enlisted men with you, but I don't expect trouble."

Averie smiled at Jalessa. "Then will you take me? I want to go back to the fountain, and to the eastern quadrant of the city and—and—anywhere else!"

Jalessa didn't even glance at Morgan. "I will," she said. "Any day you like."

After the meal, for a wonder, the men did not instantly slip off to discuss battle strategy, but sat in the *maroya*, relaxing. That might have been because Jalessa quietly excused herself, and so they did not have to be on their best behavior. Once she was gone, Lady Selkirk broached the idea of another dinner party.

"Lord, do we have to?" her father groaned, but he agreed to it readily enough. He glanced at Averie and grinned. "Gives the officers something to look forward to, a chance to flirt with pretty girls," he said.

"And the girls look forward to the flirting just as much," she replied.

It wasn't long before her father pushed himself to his

feet, declaring he was off for bed. Lady Selkirk was already writing lists of things to do before the party.

"I'm just going to sit in the courtyard a few moments," Averie said, and stepped outside. She had been settled on her favorite bench for a few minutes when the door opened again to admit a tall shadow. This time there was no mistake; it really was Morgan. But he hesitated, standing a few feet away and watching her in the darkness.

"May I join you for a few moments?" he asked at last.

"Of course," she said. She kept her voice perfectly level, but she felt nervous. Unsure of herself, of what she might want to say to him now that they finally had a few moments' privacy. Unsure of what she might want him to say.

He sat close enough for her to feel the heat of his body, but he didn't touch her. Neither of them spoke for so long that the night insects, frightened away by his approach, began to make their usual scratch and skitter.

Morgan was the one to break the silence. "We don't seem to understand each other as well as we once did," he said.

Averie made a small motion of dissent. "Or maybe we never understood each other all that well before."

He considered. "That could be true. We each believed the other person thought . . . differently than they do."

Averie didn't want to say the words. Her stomach clenched and left her almost too breathless to speak. "I am starting to wonder if I am the wrong wife for you," she said.

It was a long time before he replied. "And it seems clear that I am not the right husband for you," he said at last. "Though I wish with all my heart that was not true."

"We are so much at odds," she said.

He nodded. "I foresee a lifetime of quarrels and misunderstandings."

She almost laughed. "And I behave badly when people try to make me act a certain way, you know I do."

She heard a smile in his voice, under the pain. "And I can be very insistent. Which would only make you behave worse."

"Oh, I don't need excuses. I behave badly when there is no cause at all."

Now he took her hand, very gently, and raised it to his lips. "No," he said, his voice almost a whisper. "You behave most delightfully. You have been—in so many ways—the greatest joy of my life."

She leaned close enough to put her other arm around his shoulder. She was crying, and she could feel her tears wet the shoulder of his uniform. "I loved you the first time I met you, when I was eight years old," she said, her voice muffled against his jacket. "I talked about you for days. I told all the servants I would marry you."

He had put his free arm around her waist; he rested his forehead on top of her head. "We could still try," he said, his voice as choked as hers. "If you wanted."

She hesitated, for that seemed easier, at the moment—remembering that they had once loved each other and forgetting that they no longer did. "I would rather try to break apart with as much ease and kindness as we can," she said into his shoulder. "If we can do this without cruelty and without too much pain." She took a deep breath. "I think, if we don't, there is more pain ahead of us than what we are feeling now."

He nodded but did not lift his head, and so they sat that way for a few more moments, both of them collecting their thoughts and their scattered emotions. Eventually Morgan raised his head and Averie straightened up, but he kept his hold on her hand. "I would rather not tell your father, just now," he said. "Or anyone."

She nodded. "No. I agree. There is no reason."

"Perhaps once you go back to Aeberelle—"

She laughed. "You are *determined* to have me sail home!"

"But this was always just temporary. You were never going to stay longer than a few months."

She sighed. "I know."

"So perhaps—once you return—or right before you go—then we can let people know, very quietly. It will not be so difficult, then, to face people, once we are apart."

Still difficult but not, she silently agreed, so absolutely wretched. "I am willing to make that bargain," she said. "We will tell no one of our decision until we are parted, or about to be. And we will be good to each other while we still share the same roof."

He leaned in and kissed her on the forehead. "We will be good to each other afterward, too," he said. "Friends, no matter where or when we meet."

"That I will agree to as well," she whispered.

He kissed her forehead again, then her mouth, but so lightly it was barely a kiss at all. Then, disentangling his hand, he left her swiftly and went into the house. Averie sat in the courtyard a long time, listening to the fountain, listening to the night creatures, listening to her heart. All of them offered a muted but ceaseless cacophony, devoid of wisdom. None of them had quieted down by the time she rose and sought her bed.

After that, of course, it was impossible ever to feel truly comfortable with Morgan. They spoke with a subdued and painful courtesy whenever they were together at meals, but it was easier for both of them to be apart, so she began rising too late to join the men for breakfast and would not have been surprised if Morgan had started to skip dinners. The drawback was that there wasn't much other company to be had. Ket Du'kai did not return for a surprise visit. Averie had never had much patience with Lady Selkirk, and Lana had been confined to her house with a twisted ankle. Jalessa was practically the only person left who had any time for Averie—and that suited Averie just fine. It was almost a relief to be able to spend most of her time alone with the Chiarrizi girl.

So they embarked on a series of excursions. The very day after the sad conference with Morgan, they headed out to Mualota Fountain. It was just as Averie had remembered, a proud spume of water falling over nine black stone statues. There was one-eyed *kayla*; there was *doena*; there was wounded *seena*. Averie clutched her own *seena* charm on its silver chain and offered a silent thank-you to the goddess.

Accompanied by two enlisted men, they maneuvered through the press of people and made it to the basin's edge. The *seena* statue looked parched and hot. Averie scooped up water with her hand and dashed it over the bird's small head—a second time—a third. When she glanced over at Jalessa, the other girl was smiling.

Another day took them to the eastern quadrant of the city, the area that had been so restless ever since Averie arrived. This time, they were accompanied by four soldiers—*so much for talk of cease-fires,* Averie thought—and moved through streets that still seemed to steam with a sense of danger. The long, connected rows of independent dwellings seemed dirtier, smaller, less cared for.

Here and there Averie saw rooftops missing some of their bright tiles, windows and doors that were stripped of paint or hanging half off their hinges. Now and then they passed a block of buildings that appeared desolate and empty, but once, when Averie studied the windows as they rode by, she saw a face staring gravely out. Not entirely abandoned, then, but who would live in such a place? The desperate? Or the dangerous?

The driver turned the wagon down another street, following Jalessa's quiet directions. These buildings were even smaller, though better cared for. Now and then, in all the dreary expanse of poor existence, there would be a small plot of green, a colorfully painted door, a bright red curtain hanging in a window. Harder to fight for such tiny marks of grace in such an environment, Averie knew, and more important to do so.

"Here," Jalessa called, and the wagon came to a halt. Averie looked around. They were on a narrow road whose buildings crowded so close to the street that it was almost possible to touch the window frames from their seats in the cart.

"What's here?" Averie asked.

"Where I live," Jalessa replied.

Averie caught her breath, for it had never occurred to her to think that Jalessa might be truly poor. She had taken the job as Averie's maid willingly enough, but Averie had not realized the extra money had weighed so heavily in Jalessa's calculations. But Jalessa was poor and lived in a tense and dangerous part of town, and she never complained or showed any worry for her own safety.

"I've wanted to see your room for a long time," Averie said. "I'm glad you thought to bring me here."

Jalessa was smiling slightly, as if she knew very well what thoughts were circling in Averie's head. "Then let's see it."

A single soldier accompanied them inside. The door to Jalessa's room was painted scarlet and opened onto a cramped space with low ceilings and small windows. Averie took three steps inside and pivoted slowly to take it all in. Against one wall was a narrow bed and a boxy piece of furniture that probably held clothes. Next to another wall were two stools, two folding tables, a neat pile of dishes, and a small clay fire pit. Against both other walls were bolts and bolts of fabric. They were arranged by color and, possibly, quality—a pile of reds and crimsons leaning against a stack of oranges and umbers, melting into a tower of greens and blues and purples. Averie turned slowly, absorbing the prismatic effect. It was like being suddenly shrunk from her ordinary size and set inside a casket of carefully tumbled jewels.

"This is wonderful," she breathed. "And you live here? *Sleep* here? I would think all the colors would keep you awake at night!"

Jalessa laughed softly. "It is not the color that makes it hard to sleep, but the knowledge of how much work must be done to cut and sort and sell the cloth," she replied. "I have neglected my labor lately, as I have come to work for you."

Averie clapped her hands together. "I know! I will come with you one day and help you sell your cloth in the market!"

"Neither your father nor Lady Selkirk would think that was a good idea."

"But it would be fun! And I would learn—oh, valuable lessons of some kind. Math, certainly, as I tried to measure out lengths and charge by the ell! And I might even learn something about the cut and quality of fabric. All I know now is whether or not I like something."

"Well, and that's the most useful lesson of all," Jalessa said. She approached one of the stacks and stroked her hand down the variegated textures. These were a collection of purples, ranging from midnight grape to flirty lavender. This pile was almost in the middle of the room, as if it had mostly recently arrived and not yet been catalogued. Perhaps the newest to arrive from some weaver in the northern parts, Averie thought. Then she remembered that purple was the color of mourning. Perhaps these fabrics were in the center of the room because they were the most in demand. Perhaps the people of Chesza were all grieving as they watched their men fall to the Aebrian soldiers, as they gave up their hopes of fending off the invaders and instead sued for surrender and peace.

It didn't seem likely, after all, that the Chiarrizi would want to buy their fabric from a Aebrian girl.

A few days later, Jalessa took Averie to a temple that honored the goddess *seena*. Averie had continued wearing the *seena* charm on its silver chain, though she kept it under her *tallah* so that her father and Lady Selkirk didn't notice it. Averie had not asked if she could keep it, but Jalessa had not requested it back. Jalessa had never offered a comment on the necklace at all.

The temple was a small open building on the very edge of the city, so far north that Averie could barely see the plume of Mualota Fountain rising behind her. This building was unlike anything else she had seen in Chesza. For one thing, its walls were unfinished, or else the broad openings between pillars and portions of wall were meant to be gigantic doorways. For another, there was no roof, just arching stone that made a crisscross pattern of pale color against the cloudless sky.

Inside, the place was practically an aviary. A few thin, twisted trees held up slim branches to that distant sky, and every limb was heavy with birds. Averie just stood in the middle of the place and stared. The air was filled with anxious twitters and happy chirps and liquid, plaintive songs. The stone floor underfoot was buried under feathers of every imaginable shade, as rich and varied as the fabrics in Jalessa's tiny room. The odor of bird droppings and molted down should have been overpowering, and yet the scent that drifted through this open-air shrine was pleasant, if pungent and unfamiliar.

On the perimeter were a few benches occupied by a handful of Chiarrizi, their heads bowed in supplication. In the center of the building was a tall metal statue—*seena*, the arrow through her breast detailed and awful in this large depiction—her wings spread as if she were about to take off in a brave but chancy flight. Her beak pointed up toward the open sky, and her eyes seemed luminous with pain.

Visiting birds perched on her outstretched wings, on her narrow beak, on her short tail feathers, and called to each other with their urgent news.

"I love this place," Averie said, turning slowly on one foot to examine it all.

"People come here to pray to the goddess and lay their burdens at her feet," Jalessa said. Her hand rose and briefly touched Averie's hair. "I came here every day when you lay sick, and begged her not to allow you to die."

Averie nodded sharply. "Should I leave her something—an offering? Money? What would please her?"

"She likes food. Fruit or bread. As you see, people

lay wikberries and bumain at her feet, and that draws the other birds, and thus *seena* is never alone in her suffering."

"I don't have any food with me."

"There are vendors outside."

Of course. Averie followed Jalessa through one of the great doorways to a small promenade where half a dozen merchants had set up their carts. Averie bought something from each of them and carried quite a bounty back inside the temple. Jalessa knelt at the foot of the statue and Averie followed suit, arranging all the items in her lap.

Jalessa picked a wikberry from Averie's assortment and took a bite before laying it on the ground right where the metal of the statue dug into the soil. "Eat a portion of everything you offer to the goddess, so as to truly share your fate with hers," Jalessa directed. She smiled. "Also, I think the half-eaten pieces draw the attention of the other birds more rapidly, and so *seena* is assured of more quickly having company."

So Averie took them up one by one—the wheel of cheese, the loaf of bread, the bunch of berries—sampled each, and lay the rest at the foot of the goddess. Overhead, the nearest birds screamed and chattered. One of them swooped down and snatched the bread before Averie could even place it on the ground. Jalessa nodded with approval.

"Your gifts are highly valued, if the goddess takes them directly from your hand."

"I only want her to recognize how humbly I offer my thanks."

"Oh, *seena* recognizes you, never fear," Jalessa said. "She might almost have noted you from the moment you set foot in Chesza."

Averie's hand went up to the *seena* charm under the front of her *tallah*. She whispered, "And I think she will follow me from the hour I leave."

CHAPTER
NINETEEN

In contrast to the days, which were filled with mystery and wonder, the evenings were marked by awkwardness, silence, and sadness. Dinners were especially uncomfortable, as Morgan and Averie tested their resolve to remain on friendly terms—and as Jalessa's position in the household continued to be equivocal. Morgan still disliked the idea of her joining them at mealtimes, and Lady Selkirk could not bear to exclude her. The unsatisfactory compromise they finally settled on was to have Jalessa sit by herself at one end of the *maroya*, picking at her food or working on a sewing project. The rest of them sat at their folding tables on the other end of the room and spoke in Aebrian.

Meals were much easier when they were joined by one of the other officers. If Captain Martin was present, Averie would make a special effort to mention Lana's name.

He seemed as oblivious to this maneuver as all the other men at the table, but Lady Selkirk noticed and nodded her approval.

Rufus Gaele was their guest the night the conversation turned to the topic of entertaining. "I have been making guest lists," Lady Selkirk announced. "But we need to settle on a date so Averie and I can begin addressing invitations."

"What, you're having another party?" Captain Gaele exclaimed. "Excellent!"

"Now that it's cooler, I think this one will be particularly enjoyable," Lady Selkirk said. "But when to schedule it?"

"Exactly four days from now," Captain Gaele said.

His answer was so prompt that Averie instantly suspected a story. "Why then, if you please?" she asked.

"Because Martin and Hawksley will be gone!" he said, eyes wide with innocence. "I'll have all the pretty girls to myself!"

"Shame on you!" Averie cried, laughing. "Now we will have to wait until *you're* gone before we schedule another event."

Lady Selkirk didn't bother with raillery. She was more focused on her calendar. "Gone for how long?" she inquired. "And gone why?"

"Up to the Maekaths," Averie's father said briefly. "Relocating the camp from the southern edge of the mountain to the northern. Going to be chaos, so we're sending a few more officers to oversee the move."

"And how long will they be gone?" Lady Selkirk asked again.

Captain Gaele counted on his fingers. "Well, they're leaving day after tomorrow. Two days to travel there, another day to walk about the camp and issue orders and start cursing because nothing's ready to go. A day to make the move. Another day to settle in and check to see what got lost in transit. Two days back. Eight days, maybe nine." He turned a serious expression on Lady Selkirk. "Very well. You don't have to have the party in exactly four days, but sometime in the next week. That's good enough."

"I am *not* planning my social life to suit your flirtatious soul," Lady Selkirk said, trying to keep her voice stern. It was clear she was amused, though; she quite liked Captain Gaele. "If I choose a night ten days out, will that give everyone time to regroup?"

"I think so," Morgan said, trying not to sound bored.

"I hope Lana's foot is healed by then," Averie said. "She'll be very disappointed if she isn't able to dance."

"The officers will take turns sitting beside her," Captain Gaele promised.

"General, unless you've got an objection, I think I'll start finalizing plans," Lady Selkirk said.

Averie's father nodded, clearly as bored as Morgan and making less effort to hide it. "No objections," he said. "Do whatever you think is best."

Talk turned to other matters then, and Averie toyed with the food on her plate. Captain Gaele had not said that Ket Du'kai would be accompanying the others to the Maekath Mountains. As far as she knew, he was still in Chesza, though she had not laid eyes on him since that interlude in the garden. Naturally he would receive an invitation for the party. Would he decline the offer, or would he risk attending?

Another party meant another new *tallah,* so the next day Jalessa and Averie returned to Jalessa's small room to choose new fabric from her extensive stores. Averie was surprised at the number of people on the streets—old and young, most of them carrying bundles over their arms or strapped to their backs.

"Look at all the people! Are they going somewhere?" Averie demanded.

"Many are participating in *sofehta,*" Jalessa replied. "It is a harvest festival celebrated in the northern parts of the country—where there is actually a harvest. Here in Chesza, there are no crops, but everyone has ties to families who work the land."

"It's too early for the harvest. Isn't it?"

"Perhaps in Aeberelle, which you say is much colder.

We have two harvests in Chiarrin, for the growing season is so long."

"It looks like practically the whole city is being emptied."

Jalessa nodded. "It is a very popular event. People like to travel to the country to celebrate it, for it is a festival that needs to be observed in open land."

"When will it be held?"

"In two days."

"Can I go? Will you take me?"

Jalessa shook her head. "I'm not going. And I would discourage your father from sending you. Sometimes *sofehta* tends to be a little more unrestrained than *kyleeta*. It is not the place to send a young gentlewoman."

Averie pointed at a family of five—a young mother, three small children, and a rather agitated father trying to contain the smallest ones, who showed a tendency to wander. "But they're going. If it's such a raucous affair, maybe toddlers should stay home, too."

Jalessa smiled. "That is the decision of their parents. I assure you, my grandmother would not have allowed my sister or me to go when we were that age."

Averie was watching a group of giggling teenage girls pass by. Two wore blue headscarves edged with scarlet and purple; the youngest wore a white headscarf twined with lavender. Averie glanced around, looking for more Chiarrizi on their way out of town. Yes, that old woman's headscarf showed purple twined with red; those boys wore gold and crimson and purple. Red for celebration, which made sense, but why the purple?

"Is *sofehta* a time of mourning, too?" Averie asked, pointing to an old man dressed all in violet, walking with a cane and slow determination down the narrow walk.

"The color is a sign of respect for the stalks and vines that are cut down in the harvest. Not true death, of course, and yet still a cycle of life coming to an end."

"And what happens at the festival? Is there dancing, like at *kyleeta*?"

"Some dancing," Jalessa said in a rather repressive voice. She sounded almost like Lady Selkirk. "And some drinking. And rough behavior. As I said, not suitable for girls."

"Well, I hate to miss anything that looks like it will be interesting," Averie grumbled. "When is the *next* festival? What does *it* celebrate? And can I go to that?"

So on the way home, Jalessa recited the whole Chiarrin calendar for her: the second harvest festival, the observances of midwinter and the onset of spring, the days set aside to honor each of the gods. Averie listened closely.

"I wonder how many of these I will be allowed to attend," she said.

"The midwinter fair is something you will enjoy, if you are still in Chesza."

Averie sighed. "I would like to say I will be, but I can't be sure. I was supposed to stay for six months, but things with Morgan are so strained—I may be leaving sooner."

"Then enjoy what time you have left, however much or little it may be."

The following day was one of Jalessa's free days, so Averie expected to spend most of it with Lana. But Lady Selkirk had other plans. "You will sit with me in the *maroya* and address invitations," she said. "And you won't complain, and you will use your very best handwriting, or you will do over any card that I do not consider perfect."

Over the evening meal, they showed the stack of envelopes to the men, and Morgan promised to distribute the ones addressed to the officers. "It will be a good diversion," he said seriously. "The last few weeks have been difficult, and everyone would like a chance to relax. We're going to organize a special mess for the enlisted men, too—just something to let them know we realize how hard they've been working."

"Will all the officers be back by then?" Averie asked casually, not mentioning any names. "Or will some of them have to stay up by the Maekaths?"

"Hawksley and Worth are most likely to be stationed there for another week," her father said.

"Excellent," Lady Selkirk said. "The two whom we are least likely to miss."

Even Morgan and her father laughed at this, though Lady Selkirk didn't appear to be aware of having said anything humorous.

Jalessa was back the following day, newly made *tallah* over her arm, and Lana hobbled over to the Winston house to watch Averie try it on. "I have been so *bored*!" she exclaimed, collapsing on Averie's bed. "I had to get out or die."

Averie loved the party attire, of course, and studied her face in the mirror from all angles. The deep gold of the fabric was accented with stripes of crimson, and the colors were striking together. "I hope your foot is better by next week, so you can dance," she said to Lana.

Lana practiced a curtsy and almost fell over as her ankle betrayed her. "And I hope Captain Martin solicits my hand half the night," she said, straightening up.

"And Lieutenant Lansdale?"

Lana smiled, sighed, and shook her head. "One dance, maybe."

Over dinner that evening, Averie described the new *tallah* in great detail, though neither her father nor Morgan seemed particularly interested. "You should wear headscarves, too," she said, inspired. "Gold and red. Think how well they would go with the dark blue of your uniforms!"

Her father merely snorted and looked away. Morgan laughed at her. "Yes, Aebrian soldiers in Chiarrizi hats," he said. "That would make everyone take us seriously! The people of Chesza *and* our own men!"

She smiled at him. It was the most natural and spontaneous exchange they had had in days. "I think you would look very dashing," she offered.

"Look like fools," her father said.

"Well, maybe for the next party."

After dinner, Averie took her usual seat in the courtyard to enjoy the cool air and the playful splashing of the fountain. She was surprised, pleased, and a little uncertain when the door opened again and Morgan stepped outside.

"May I join you a moment?"

She moved over to make room for him on the bench. "Certainly."

He sat next to her, but three inches away. "I'm sure your soiree will be very grand," he said.

"I think it will be fun, at least. I hope we can persuade the musicians to come back—everyone enjoyed the dancing last time, even though the space was so small."

"You will dance with me, I hope."

Her heart squeezed. "Morgan. Of course I will."

"Though you will be very popular. The hostess always is."

She smiled at him, though it felt painful. "And I wouldn't be popular if I wasn't the hostess?"

"Oh! Of course you would! I meant—"

She laughed, a little more lightly. "Anyway, you are always quite sought after, too. All the girls admire your height and your blond hair and your handsome face."

He groaned and put his head in his hands. "Lord, no. Back on the marriage mart. I had forgotten what it was like to be the target of scheming young girls and their matchmaking mothers."

She laughed more gaily this time. "Well, let me just make a prediction to you. The minute I sail for Aeberelle and everybody learns . . . learns . . . about us, Carrie Dryser will begin to pursue you with single-minded determination."

He lifted his head to look at her. "Carrie? Really?" He sounded genuinely surprised. "We're friendly, of course, but she—I mean, she's friendly to everyone."

Averie sighed dramatically. "Men are such blockheads."

"I don't really like her that well, to tell you the truth."

"Excellent! For I don't like her either. I'm sure you could do better. Maybe I'll start looking over the next crop of young girls when I get back to Aeberelle."

He didn't answer, and a silence fell between them. Well, it had been a stupid thing to say. She could not be the person he wanted; what made her think she would be able to identify, in someone else, all the qualities she lacked herself? And how melancholy, to consider other girls as candidates for Morgan's heart.

"Perhaps I won't," she said softly.

He nodded, smiled at her in the dark, and patted her hand. "Don't stay out too late," he said. "I'll see you in the morning."

And he rose and left without another word. Despite his advice, Averie sat there another hour at least, listening to the silver balls chiming in the fountain, listening to the night creatures chattering from the trees, and feeling just a little lost.

The entire house was dark when she went inside, so even Grace, Sieffel, and Jalessa must be sleeping, she thought. Averie felt her way down the unlit corridor to her room and undressed in the dark. Sleep eluded her completely, so after tossing and turning for another two hours, she finally got up again. Lighting a candle, she perched on a seat by the window and tried to read a novel that Lana had lent her, but it couldn't hold her interest. She leaned her head against the back of the chair, closing her eyes. Perhaps she was tired enough now to sleep. She let herself be soothed by the patter of the falling water outside, the spicy scents drifting in through the open window. If she crept very quietly to the bed without opening her eyes, perhaps she could indeed sleep. . . .

There was a sudden silence everywhere in the world.

Alarmed, Averie sat up, instinctively putting her hands to her ears, but she hadn't suddenly gone deaf. There was the faint noise from the evening insects, rasping and hoarse. There the sweeter call and echo of the night birds. Then what had disturbed her? What sound had been lost from the night?

The fountain. There was no sound of water falling.

Standing, Averie leaned out the window and listened more closely, but she still couldn't hear the familiar tinkle and splash. Had something clogged the pipe leading to the courtyard? Or—worse!—to the house? Carrying the candle, she hurried to the bathing room and tried all the spigots. They opened, but only air came out.

Well, this would be inconvenient in the morning when it came time to clean and cook.

Averie wondered if she should try to preserve what little water might still be on hand. Perhaps she could use her bedroom pitcher and glass to scoop up some of what was left in the fountain. She grabbed them from the nightstand and ran barefoot down the hallway, to the *maroya,* and out into the cool night.

The basin was still about half full, but losing water steadily. Averie was able to fill both containers before the level got too low. But something else about the night was strange. Her skin prickled with unease and she looked around, trying to figure out what was wrong. There was a scent, heavy and bitter—not a night-blooming flower, not an animal odor. Something wicked and huge . . .

She glanced up and saw a rim of red above the western edge of the house. Dawn already? But dawn would come from the east, and the red was visible over the northern roof, and the southern roof—

Fire.

Averie spun in a circle, staring at what she could see of the horizon line over the six wings of the house. The whole city was in flames.

Dropping both her pitcher and the glass, she stumbled into the house, through the *maroya*, through the kitchens, and straight for Jalessa's room. Jalessa would know what was wrong. Perhaps this was only a part of the *sofehta* festival; perhaps what Averie was seeing were the lights from distant bonfires, impressive but harmless.

She knocked wildly at Jalessa's door, which swung open almost immediately. Jalessa apparently hadn't been able to sleep either. She was fully dressed, and the whole room was warm with candlelight.

Before Jalessa could speak, Averie caught her arm and pulled her toward the window. The red glow was even more pronounced from this view, which faced outward onto the city. "Look—look! It's fire! I think there's a ring of fire, all around the city!"

Jalessa nodded, unperturbed. "Yes."

"Is it the *sofehta* fair, then? You didn't mention bonfires, but are they part of the festival?" Averie said, her heart slowing just a minute with hope.

Jalessa shook her head. "Oh, no. Chesza is ablaze. Every mile of the city."

Averie stared at her. Jalessa seemed so tranquil. So . . . so odd. "But that's terrible! And the fountain has failed; there must be some kind of obstruction in the pipe, so if the flames come all the way to our house, we won't be able to put them out."

"All the fountains have stilled. All the water into Chesza has been stopped," Jalessa said.

For a moment, Averie couldn't take in the words. Couldn't understand why Jalessa would say them, and so calmly. The water stopped—how? And if there was no water, and the whole city was on fire, the whole city would be lost! Why wasn't Jalessa screaming and running from the house, looking for friends, fighting to save her home?

Why was Jalessa dressed so strangely, in a bright crimson *tallah* and a headscarf of red and purple? "Jalessa," Averie breathed, her throat choked, "what is happening?"

Jalessa swept her hand up and pointed out the window. "As you see. The city is in flames, and there is no water to put them out. Chesza will be destroyed. And the Aebrians will be destroyed with it."

"*What?*" Averie whispered.

"While Chesza burns, the Aebrian encampment at the Maekath Mountains is under attack. I expect most of those soldiers to be killed. And the barracks in Chesza were the first buildings to be set on fire. Most of those soldiers will die, too."

Averie knew she should be shrieking, should be running from the room, calling for her father, for Morgan, for Lady Selkirk, but she could not move. She was frozen and horror-struck, nearly dumb with disbelief. "But— But, you— What did you—?"

"We have been waiting nearly four months for our chance. It came this week, when your soldiers left one camp at the Maekaths for another. We ambushed them before they arrived at their new location. And we tore down all the *correas* that bring water into the city and set Chesza on fire."

"You—you— The rebels did this? You are—*you* are one of the rebels?"

"Every Chiarrizi is a rebel," Jalessa said, her voice hard with contempt. "Every vendor in the market, every child in the street. Since the day the Aebrians arrived, we have been trying to determine how to destroy them."

Averie pressed her hands to her cheeks. Her fingers were marble cold. "But you didn't hate us. You didn't hate *me*. You were my friend!"

Jalessa said flatly, "I used you to get information from your father."

Averie stared at her. *What information?* They never talked military matters in the house; Averie herself had little idea what her father or Morgan did every day. And when the men were present, Jalessa never joined them anyway. She sat half a room away in the *maroya*, paying them no attention while they conversed in formal Aebrian—

Although Jalessa had been learning Aebrian—

Averie had taught her, Lady Selkirk herself had given Jalessa lessons—

The encampment at the Maekaths. The move to the other side of the mountain. They had been discussing that with Rufus Gaele a few short days ago—

"You. You told them," Averie said, her voice so low it almost was not vocalized at all. "You sat in this house and you heard our discussion and you told them—"

Jalessa nodded. "Everything."

"But you— But you—" Averie still could not credit it. Still could not take it in. "But you're my friend! *Mua sova! Mua lota!* How could you betray me?"

Now, for the first time, a sort of passion came to Jalessa's broad, smooth face. "Betray you! You are my enemy—you and your father and your friends. Why would I have anything but hatred for you? You are not in my heart. You are not *mua lota. Mua lota* is Chesza, and my husband, and my daughter, and my sister—"

"Husband! Daughter!" Averie exclaimed. "But you—

You never mentioned them! You never—! Why didn't you *tell* me? All you have done is *lie* to me!"

Jalessa laughed. "And why wouldn't I lie? Why would I tell you about my family, about the things I love? Why would I tell you that you met my husband—danced with him at the *kyleeta* festival, and thought yourself a Chiarrizi girl for catching the eye of a Chiarrizi man."

Shock upon shock. There was nothing about Jalessa that was familiar now—not her life, not her hatred, not her face. "But you saved me when I was sick," Averie whispered. "Didn't you love me then?"

"I could not let you die," Jalessa said. "If you were dead, I would have no reason to stay, and I did not want to leave this house."

It was as if Jalessa had put a dagger in her heart. Averie felt the pain deep inside her body and pressed her fingers to her chest. "But now you can leave," she said, almost gasping the words. "So now you are ready to see me die as the city burns around me?"

Yes, she expected Jalessa to say. That would certainly be in keeping with the rest of the conversation. But for a moment Jalessa did not answer. "Go to the harbor," she said at last. "The boats will be the last things to be set on fire. You may be able to win to safety aboard a ship."

And she turned away from the window, picked up one of the tapers, and held a candle to the curtain.

"No!" Averie screamed, but Jalessa stepped deeper into the room, tipping the flame against the bedsheets and a pile of clothing discarded on the floor. "No! No! What are you doing? How can you burn down this house? How can you—how can *any* of you—annihilate your own city like this? How can you do it?"

Jalessa was at the door now, pulling it open. The influx of air caused the flames to leap higher. "We are *seena* and *doena* and *kayla*," she said. "We are wounded, but we do not falter. We survive, and we go on."

There was a sudden frantic pounding down the hall—distant enough to be at the front door, loud enough to be a whole cadre of men. Jalessa glanced that way, her lips tightening. "I see some of the soldiers have escaped to bring news to your father," she said. "I had better leave another way."

"No—you can't go, you—" Averie panted, grabbing at Jalessa's arm, but Jalessa shoved past her and ducked out the window. Averie saw her, haloed briefly by the flaming curtains, and then, with a flirt of scarlet cloth, she was gone.

The room was well and truly beginning to burn.

"Father!" Averie shrieked, scrambling out the door, racing down the hall, suddenly finding her voice and power over her body. "Father! Morgan! Everybody! The house is on fire! *The city is on fire!*"

CHAPTER
TWENTY

The next three hours were a nightmare of heat, flame, ash, and motion. It turned out that a large contingent of Aebrian soldiers had survived the intended massacre at the barracks. At least a hundred of them were milling around outside the Winston house as Averie followed Lady Selkirk out the door. Her father and Morgan were already there, snapping orders and demanding reports. Her heart absolutely unable to beat, Averie scanned the faces of the soldiers, looking for the people she knew. There was Captain Gaele and Lieutenant Lansdale, but where was Ket Du'kai? Where was Major Harmon? Captain Martin and Major General Worth were up at the Maekaths—had they been slaughtered? Never to see Joseph Martin's handsome face again—and, oh, how awful, Lana's father . . . Both lost? Along with so many other men?

"To the harbor with the women!" Morgan was shouting to a cluster of soldiers awaiting orders. "There are five warships there! Man them all, put the women on board one, and take that ship out far enough to be safe from action!"

"I have sent men to the other houses, Colonel!" Captain Gaele shouted back. "The Worths and the Harmons and the others! They will all be taken on board!"

"Good! The rest of you, follow me!"

Lady Selkirk grabbed Averie's arm, for comfort or assistance, Averie was not sure. "Are we all out of the house?" Lady Selkirk called. "Grace, Sieffel—you will come with us."

The servants crowded closer. Averie was amazed to see that Grace carried a basket in one hand and Sieffel had bundles over his shoulder. Food or clothing or something else that would come in handy in an emergency, she thought. The servants were certainly much better at a quick evacuation than the gentry.

"Go! Go! Get moving!" Morgan ordered.

But Lady Selkirk clutched Averie even tighter. "Jalessa!" she wailed. "We can't leave her behind sleeping! She'll be burned up in her bed!"

Averie tried to answer and found herself unable to utter a word. But Grace spoke up in a reassuring voice. "We went by her room, my lady. It was empty, and the window was open. Looks like she escaped to safety."

"Oh, but I want her to come with us!" Lady Selkirk moaned. "I can't leave her like this, in a city that's coming down around our ears."

"Likely she has friends here she's worried about, and she'd rather be off with them," Grace said.

Averie could attest to that.

Just then, Morgan grabbed her arm, with even more force than Lady Selkirk. *"Go!"* he screamed. "We will join you later if we can!"

They ran—or tried to run. Lady Selkirk was a deadweight on Averie's arm; the streets were gritty with ash and debris; and everywhere fresh fires burst out from the windows of the buildings they passed. The air was too hot to breathe, but Averie didn't think that was what troubled her lungs so greatly. No, it was terror and worry and despair and loss. Those were the burdens that sat with such crushing heaviness on her chest. Where was Ket Du'kai? Already dead? What about Morgan, what about her father—what would happen to them? What about their own small band? Would they make it safely across the city? Would the warships, in fact, still be intact, or had Jalessa lied about that, too? Would the great sails be aflame, the hulls smashed in? Was there no way out of Chesza except by death?

Averie tripped, and a man's impatient hand dragged her up again, urged her on, even faster. She could not get over it, still could not understand the depths of Jalessa's duplicity. Her mind kept teasing at the puzzle, even as her feet pounded on, another block, another half mile. Obviously, there had been no such thing as a *sofehta* festival—or if *sofehta* was a real word, and not something Jalessa had manufactured on the spot, it meant something vastly different from a harvest fair. Every Chiarrizi in the city had known about the fire; those who were too old, too young, too infirm to help set the blazes had began their exodus a few days in advance. Every Chiarrizi was a rebel, so Jalessa had said—every child Averie smiled at in the streets, every vendor in the market, every dancer at the *kyleeta* festival. All of them had hated her, had hated her father, had schemed and plotted and worked to see them gone.

Jalessa had despised her from the beginning, then, from the very first day they met in the market, when she had helped Averie buy a pair of shoes. She had seemed friendly but a little distant, not at all as if she were trying to make friends with the Aebrian girls. Not at all as if she hoped one day to be invited into their households. Averie frowned. Perhaps that had not been the plan at first. Perhaps it was merely a quirk of fate that had seen Jalessa injured in the marketplace. How could the rebels have known that Averie would succor her, bring the wounded woman into her own home?

That must have been a lucky day for them, she thought, her feet running on and on while her mind plunged ahead just as hard, just as relentlessly. When Averie begged

Jalessa to become her maid—what a coup that had been for the rebels! If Jalessa had not been invited into her service, would another Chiarrizi have infiltrated the household? What about Lana's seamstress? What about the cook whom Lady Harmon boasted of having hired? Were they spies, too?

"This way," the lead soldier called, and they followed him in a tired, gasping group, around a low building partially obscured by smoke. The harbor was only another quarter mile away. Averie could see the silhouettes of the tall ships bobbing in the water, none of them alight with hungry fire—not yet, anyway.

Her mind went back to the false *sofehta* fair. Everyone wearing red and purple—how could she not have understood that? Celebration, death. Averie had never heard of a harvest festival that took death as its theme. But everyone in Chesza had worn appropriate colors for the event that was about to unfold.

Red and purple . . . Averie had seen those colors together before. That day in the market—the second day she had met Jalessa—the Chiarrizi woman had dug through merchandise in her cart to find special fabrics just for Averie and Lana. Jalessa had stood up, shaking out folds of cloth, just to get them out of the way—red in one hand, purple in the other. . . .

Averie came to a halt, there in the middle of the smoky street.

"Averie. What's wrong? Did you turn your ankle?" Lady Selkirk panted beside her. The soldier on her other side didn't even ask, just jerked her forward again. They continued on in their breathless, stooped, desperate run.

Jalessa had signaled with red and purple. She had known Lana and Averie were returning this day, because she had helped Averie make the transaction for her new shoes. Jalessa had told her friends, those who had somehow secured gunpowder and shells, she had told them that young Aebrian girls would be back at the market in a week. *If you want to break the hearts of the invaders, kill their women,* she might have said. *I will let you know when they are in the market and exactly where they are standing.*

But you! Won't you be injured in the blast? her husband must have replied. *No, I can't have it! We will not put you at risk.*

The risk is worth it, Jalessa would have answered. *There will be a wound through my heart, through yours, but we will use our blood to strike our enemies down.*

Or perhaps he had not even protested, that beautiful, reckless, passionate man. Perhaps he had nodded and helped her plan and cheerfully seen her off that morning, believing her death would bring them one step closer to freedom.

Mercifully, the harbor was not yet on fire, though the damp air at the water's edge felt gritty with cinder as well as salt. Coughing and crying, Averie and Lady Selkirk stumbled up the gangplank to one of the ships. Eager young sailors caught their arms, swung them on board, and demanded to know what was happening in the city. Averie let the escorting soldiers tell the awful news.

"This way, then—to the captain's cabin," one of the seamen said, guiding Averie past the mainsail. "You can rest there until we know . . . until we get orders . . ." He didn't know how to complete his sentence.

Shown to their new quarters, spare and cramped, she and Lady Selkirk collapsed and tried to order their thoughts. Ten minutes later there was a flurry of sound from above, and Lady Selkirk struggled to sit up. "Mercy! Have the Chiarrizi come to murder us?" she cried.

But it was nothing so alarming. Moments later, Lana and her mother burst through the door, sobbing and distraught. Averie launched herself into Lana's arms, and they clung to each other, incapable of speech. Over the next thirty minutes, all the other Aebrian women made an appearance before being taken to the quarters of the other ship's officers, displaced by their sudden arrival. None of them would sleep, of course—all of them would weep and worry and curse the impulse that had brought them to Chiarrin.

When the last Aebrian women stepped on board, the ship began to move, slowly edging its way out of the harbor. Averie pushed herself up from the narrow bunk where she had been lying, heavy and disconsolate, and opened a small porthole. The ship made a lumbering turn, and there it was, framed by the window: the City of Broken Gods. All of Chesza was one brilliant circle of fire, joyous and gorgeous, deadly and grim.

Everyone she loved was somewhere within that field of flame. She might never see any one of them alive again.

For three days, the ship lay at anchor a few miles out from the coastline, close enough for passengers to see the smoldering ruins of Chesza, too far to be surprised by a pursuing enemy vessel. The Aebrian women stayed confined to quarters, as much as possible. The captain had made it clear this was a warship and battle could be coming—if not with the Chiarrizi, then with the Weskish, who might be roaming these waters. He was happy to give haven to the refugees, but he was ready to fight at any minute.

Though they were not welcome on the main deck, always crowded with busy sailors, Averie and Lana still crept up there every day. They had discovered that, if they found a place along the railing and stood there very quietly, they would be allowed to stay as long as they liked. So they passed most of those three days pressed against the rail, gazing at the shredding smoke still lifting over Chesza. They spoke very little. Sometimes they held hands, so tightly that their muscles cramped against the bone. Sometimes they wept. Sometimes Averie would grow suddenly faint and hopeless, and turn to Lana, and lean against that thin shoulder; sometimes Lana was the one who would sag in Averie's arms. They only forced themselves to eat, once or twice a day, so that they would have the strength to continue the vigil in the coming hours.

On the third day, close to sunset, they saw movement among the remaining ships in Chesza Harbor. They clutched each other more tightly, mute with hope and despair, till they could make out the sight of the last four Aebrian warships hoisting their sails and slowly gliding free of land.

There had been enough Aebrian soldiers to fill all five ships from stern to bow. But, oh, what if these ships were empty, manned only by the crew, sent to sea because their captains no longer saw any reason to linger in the ruined harbor?

Averie leaned her head against Lana's so her pale hair mingled with Lana's dark curls. "Soon we will know," she whispered. "And we can start grieving."

All the women were abovestairs now, desperately scanning the faces of the men waving from the decks of the approaching ships. There were not very many. Edna Harmon shrieked and grabbed her little sister and went dancing in a clumsy circle when she spotted her father among the living. Carrie Dryser was sobbing in her mother's arms. Her father was not one of those shoving aside the other men, shouting across the water.

Neither was Morgan, nor Averie's father, nor Major General Worth.

Neither was Ket Du'kai.

"There's Rufus Gaele," Averie said suddenly. "Look! His head is all bandaged, and you can hardly see his face, but I know that's him."

"I'm glad," Lana whispered. "But I don't see my father."

Finally, after an agonizingly slow approach, the lead warship drew abreast, and sailors threw grappling lines across. Sailors swarmed over, securing the hooks and lines. More slowly, a few soldiers began to make their way across this makeshift bridge. A woman screamed and fell into her husband's arms. All around her, Averie heard high voices raised in frantic inquiry: *Have you seen my husband? Have you seen my brother? Did you leave my father behind in Chesza?*

"I don't see him," Lana said, and buried her face against Averie's shoulder. Averie closed her eyes and hugged Lana tightly and thought, *I don't see any of them.*

When she opened her eyes, Ket Du'kai was standing before her, his dark face grave and his brown eyes full of pain. She felt her body flash with a mix of contrasting fires—joy, relief, and overwhelming dread. She could not speak. Her lips formed a single word: *Who?*

"Colonel Stode lives, though he is injured," Ket said, speaking very fast. "General Winston is dead."

Averie felt those last four words as blows to the stomach. She staggered and almost fell over. The sound of his voice sent Lana spinning out of Averie's arms, and Averie had to catch at the railing to keep from pitching into the sea.

"My father," Lana breathed. "Is he—? My father—"

"Gravely wounded," Ket replied. "He is in the second warship, unconscious but alive."

"I must go to him." Lana stood straight, imbued suddenly with purpose and strength.

"We are readying the ships for a transfer of personnel," Ket said. "We hope to redistribute everyone as efficiently as possible and then set sail with all speed."

Averie found her voice, though it was very small. "Who else?" she asked. "Dead?"

Ket looked at her, and she could see his own hurt and loss underneath his compassion. "Captain Martin, Lieutenant Lansdale, Colonel Dryser, Captain Hawksley, and more than three thousand men," he replied.

Lana had gasped at the sound of Lansdale's name, and now she started weeping again. "So many!" she cried. "How terrible! How wretched! How could this happen?"

But Averie and Ket were still watching each other.

Both of them knew. "Because we were not wanted in Chesza," Averie said softly. "And the Chiarrizi would have done anything to see us go."

"They burned their own city," Lana said.

"They blew up the aqueducts. All of them," Ket added. "They practically brought down the mountain on the only road tying the northern country to the southern plains. They were willing to nearly wipe themselves out of existence in order to rid themselves of us."

"*Seena*," Averie whispered.

Ket nodded, but Lana looked at her in bewilderment. "What?"

"*Seena*," Averie repeated. "She takes an arrow through the heart, but she still lives. Chiarrin is *seena*. And *doena* and *kayla*. Chiarrin accepts the possibility of death, knowing it is the only way she can survive."

Lana sniffled and wiped a hand across her face. "I must go to my father," she said again. "I must find my mother, and both of us will go."

Without another word, she went darting off through the press of people still gathered on the upper deck. Averie and Ket Du'kai were left confronting each other.

"I am so very sorry about your father," he said.

Averie nodded, her throat closing up again. "I cannot absorb that just yet," she said. "I cannot understand that his death is real."

He nodded in return. "Colonel Stode's leg is shattered. The ship's doctors think it can be saved, but I expect he will require a cane for the rest of his life."

She tried to compose herself. "Is his soldiering life over, then?"

"It is too soon to be certain." He hesitated, then said, "It is Colonel Stode who is responsible for even this many men surviving. He organized the soldiers, took back the barracks, sent reinforcements to the Maekaths in case there were any who had escaped the slaughter—and there were a few. He showed bravery and intelligence, and he will no doubt be promoted for his actions. If he *can* continue to serve, the army will want him."

"I hope he can," Averie said. "He loves the military life."

"Days like this," Ket said, "it is hard to see how anybody could."

Averie glanced back at Chesza, taking a long last look at its smoking streets, its ruined walls. "You are a military man, so perhaps you can tell me this," she said. "We were routed from Chiarrin. Will we go back? With more men, a bigger army?"

"I don't know," he said gravely. "Chiarrin remains the prize it always was, worth some degree of bloodshed. But if we return, we may find Weskolia already ensconced as allies and protectors, all her warships lining the harbor. That is a battle Aeberelle may be forced to concede before it is even fought."

"I hope so," Averie whispered fiercely. "I hope no Aebrian soldier ever sets foot in Chesza again."

"But Aebrians may return, one way or another," Ket said. "As friends. Trading partners. Strange allies are born from commerce and opportunity." He turned a hand palm up. "You may be back some day, ready to buy and sell. The Chiarrizi might even welcome you then."

"No," she said, staring out at the water. "I will never return to Chesza."

"What will you do? When you are back in Aeber-elle?"

She made a helpless gesture. "Go to Weymire Estate, I imagine, at least for my period of mourning. And then— Oh, it is impossible to think of! A life without my father. I will inherit all his affairs, and I must try to understand his finances, and his commercial ventures, and his land management, and all the things I have never given any thought to before this."

"Colonel Stode will help you," he suggested. "Once you are married."

She turned back to him and felt an old, small grief stir under this new and massive one. "Morgan and I are not to be married after all," she said.

His head snapped back as if she had slapped him, and then he dropped his gaze as if to conceal whatever emotion might show in his eyes. "Then you have been piled with more than your share of losses," he said quietly.

"As have we all," she replied, just as quietly. She shook her head, trying to shake away darkness. "Now. Which ship is Morgan on? He is my dear friend still, and I will care for him while he lies wounded."

Ket pointed. For a mercy, it was the same ship holding Major General Worth; Averie would at least have Lana's company as this torturous journey progressed. "Someone will bring your things to you before day's end," he said.

She almost smiled. "What things? I left Chesza with scarcely more than these clothes."

He almost smiled back. "And someone will tell Lady Selkirk where you have landed. For you will most certainly want her comfort in this time of trial."

"She will be lost," Averie said, "without my father. I think she loved him, in her way."

"Then you will have to be kind to her."

Averie nodded. "I will certainly have to try."

There was no more to say. There was much more to say, but impossible to put any of it into words. They stood in silence a moment, and then Ket gave her a little bow. "Shall I escort you to the other ship? I believe the sailors are helping the civilians across the ropes, but the maneuver is tricky."

She shook her head. "I'm sure you have other duties. I won't take up any more of your time. Which—which ship will you be on for the rest of the journey?"

"This one, I think," he said. "Once we release the lines, we will probably not send people back and forth between vessels again. Unless there is dire trouble of some kind."

"Then I won't see you again until we dock in Port Elise."

He was silent a moment, and she glanced up to find his dark eyes watching her. "I will stand at the railing from time to time and look for you," he said. "You might come out now and then merely to lift a hand and assure me that you are well."

Again, she almost managed a smile. "I'll do that," she said. "Mornings, perhaps, when the day is calmest."

He made that little bow again, and impulsively she put out her hand. He took it in his and did not instantly release it. "I will look for you then," he said.

She nodded one more time, tugged her hand free, and turned to go. Three steps away, she turned back, that same hand pressed against her heart. "Ket," she said. "I am so glad you are still alive." And then, before he could answer, she picked up her skirts and hurried through the crowd, looking for Lady Selkirk, looking for passage to the sister ship, looking for the quickest way to Morgan's side.

Across the chancy walkway made of rope, Averie paused one more time to glance back at the coastline of Chiarrin. She felt so much pain that she almost wanted to check her body and see if she had sustained a physical injury, but she knew that her hurts had been inflicted only on her spirit. Her hand went to her throat and the clasp of the silver necklace she wore, and for a moment she was tempted to throw her *seena* charm into the ocean. The goddess had not simply rejected her; the goddess had schemed against her from the day Averie set foot in her city.

But then her hand fell, and Averie leaned for a moment against the railing, getting her balance on this new deck. Today, more than ever, she believed in the deity who would not yield, who struggled on against all hope, against all reason. Averie too stumbled on, gasping but determined, wounded to the heart, but still alive.

CHAPTER
TWENTY-ONE

The journey was endless, and endlessly sad. Morgan mended, but slowly. Others among the wounded men did not fare so well; many still suffered dumbly, and a number of them died. They were low on rations, the weather was bad, and the officers' quarters were cramped. And everyone was awash in grief and failure.

Averie could not bear to tell anyone about Jalessa's betrayal—not Morgan, not Lana, not Lady Selkirk. She did not believe she would have told Ket Du'kai even if he had been traveling on the same ship. She thought it was a secret she would carry with her forever, a dark memento stolen from Chesza and hidden away with all the other things she could never bear to lose.

The sight of Port Elise's tall crowded buildings, rising like mythological creatures from the endless expanse of the sea, was the first cause for smiling that any of them had had for what seemed like months.

"Home," Lana whispered one morning as she and Averie stood at the bow and gazed toward land. "*Home.* I will never leave Aeberelle again for any inducement whatsoever."

They had agreed to visit often and write even oftener. Averie planned to be at Weymire Estate as soon as she could organize herself to get there, but she knew there were matters she would have to attend to in the city first. She was no longer a promising heiress; she was a very wealthy young woman, as Lady Selkirk had reminded her at least five times a day for the entire voyage. She had duties. She had responsibilities. She had property and investments and advisors.

She had decisions to make.

They docked late in the afternoon amid grand chaos. Lady Selkirk had appointed herself Morgan's caretaker, and she shepherded him off the ship while Averie and Grace and Sieffel gathered their few personal items and arranged for transportation into the city. In the melee, it was barely possible to shout good-byes to Lana, to Edna, to the few remaining officers. But there was one farewell Averie was determined to make.

"I'll be right back," she told Lady Selkirk as Sieffel and a hired driver helped Morgan climb into the back of a hansom cab, and she plunged back into the milling mob.

Ket Du'kai was looking for her as hard as she was looking for him, and he found her first. She heard his voice shouting her name, and she turned, craning her neck to peer around the burly soldiers in her way. "Averie! Averie!"

She spotted him at last and pushed her way through the crowd. When she was close enough, he grabbed both her hands. "You are well? The journey was not too taxing?" he demanded.

"Taxing enough," she said. "You?"

"Glad to be back on solid ground and ready to turn over my burdens."

She nodded. She was gazing at him as if trying to imprint his face on her memory. She had glimpsed him most days of the voyage, when the warships were close enough that they could wave across the water, but it had been hard to make out the details of his features. His hair had grown much longer during these past weeks; the thick curls hung almost to his shoulders. He had allowed his beard to come in, and it gave his face a solemn, melancholy air. He looked, in many ways, like a wilder, stranger version of the man she had come to know.

In other ways, he looked more familiar than her own reflection.

"What happens to you next?" she asked. "Will you be stationed in Port Elise long? Will you be reassigned? Where might you go?"

His hands tightened on hers, and he stared at her with much the same hunger she knew that her own face was showing. "I might return to Xan'tai," he said softly. "My enlistment is up at the end of the month. I have been considering what I might do next. I don't think . . ." He paused, shook his head, and with difficulty continued. "I don't think I can endure any more postings like Chiarrin."

"No," she said. "I wouldn't think you could."

"And you?" he asked. "What happens now?"

"I will be about a week in Port Elise, I expect. Then on to Weymire Estate for at least a month. After that . . ." She shrugged. "I'll figure out the rest of my life."

"And Colonel Stode?"

"I will get him settled in Port Elise before I leave. I am sure his sisters will want to come stay with him, though the regiment will provide any care he needs." She squeezed his hands as it seemed he might drop hers. "Don't leave Aeberelle without coming to say goodbye."

"It would be a month at least before I am mustered out, I think."

"Come to me, then," she said. "At Weymire Estate."

He hesitated. "It will be harder to leave," he said at last, "if I see you again."

She laughed. "It's what I'm counting on. Promise me."

A moment, and then he nodded. "I promise."

She smiled again and released him. "Till then. *Kayla* feed you, *doena* guard you, *seena* give you courage."

"I will have to teach you about kinder gods," he said, his face shadowed.

"Yes," she said, backing into the crowd, "I think you will."

It was actually harder to say good-bye to Morgan, though Averie felt she left him in good hands. Both his sisters had come in from the country to act as his nurses, and they fussed over him with great affection. They also appeared to be enjoying the chance to visit old friends in the city and even spoke of staying in Port Elise for the next several months to pick up the threads of their social lives.

"They will act as your hostesses, if you choose to entertain," Averie told Morgan the day before she left for Weymire Estate. They were visiting in the parlor of his rented lodgings, which were very fashionable since Lady Selkirk had picked them out. Averie had come to return his mother's ruby ring to him, which had caused both of them to cry, though Morgan pretended he had merely gotten something in his eye. But they could not talk of their broken engagement, so they sipped tea and speculated about Morgan's future instead. "I think they would enjoy throwing some very lavish parties."

"The thought horrifies me," he replied.

She smiled. "You must start thinking about hosting dinners and balls," she teased. "Now that you have been promoted to undersecretary! You know the position is political as well as military, and politics always involve socializing."

"I think I shall plead weakness and injury for another six months at least," he said. "Will you come to my first party?"

She laid aside her teacup, gathered up her gloves, and came to her feet. Morgan's leg still bothered him, so she motioned him to stay in his chair. "If I can, I will," she said, and leaned over to kiss him on the forehead. "Good-bye, Morgan."

He caught her hand and held on to it as if to prevent her from leaving, as if he had one more question to ask, one more hope to voice. Then he gave her a twisted smile, kissed her fingers, and released her. She looked back only twice before she stepped through the door.

The days with the lawyers, the bankers, the land agents, the stewards, and everyone else connected with her father's estate were tedious and confusing—or would have been if Averie did not have very simple goals in mind. Sell the investments; sell every property except Weymire Estate; provide generous pensions for the long-time servants; ensure that a tidy little bequest was settled on Lady Selkirk, ostensibly from her father's will.

Free herself of all her obligations. Liquidate her assets. Turn her sizable fortune into ready cash.

Weymire Estate, when she finally returned there, seemed the sole spot of sense and tranquility in a world full of uncertainty, pain, and chaos. Averie slept late every morning for a week. She spent the days either riding across the sleepy green land with three dogs at her heels, or sitting in her favorite window seat, staring out at the rolling lawn. When she had the strength, she gathered the servants, invited the neighbors, and held a memorial service for her father. His body had burned in Chesza, but they buried one of his army uniforms and a cameo locket he had given to Averie's mother when they were courting. They set his marker in the family cemetery next to his wife's grave. Averie decorated both sites with wildflowers from the neglected garden.

Lady Selkirk had been astonished when Averie informed her that she no longer needed the services of a chaperone. "Although," Averie said very warmly, when Lady Selkirk looked hurt and insulted, "if I were to retain one, I would have no one but you. You always gave me the best care, and I'm sure I did not thank you nearly as often as I should have."

Lady Selkirk was mollified but unconvinced. "But a young girl like you! Unmarried!" she exclaimed. She had been shattered to learn that Averie had broken off her engagement to Morgan, and she continually brought his name up as if hoping to convince Averie to change her mind. "You cannot expect to live alone, even this far out in the country!"

"I don't intend to stay at Weymire Estate."

"Well, you *certainly* can't live in Port Elise by yourself."

"I know. I intend to travel."

Lady Selkirk stared at her openmouthed. "By *yourself*?"

Averie smiled. "I don't know yet. Yes, if I have to."

"Averie! You cannot! Your reputation! And, *Averie*! A young girl is so easily taken advantage of— No, no, no, you mustn't even think of it. You must listen to reason."

So Averie listened, and smiled politely, and showed Lady Selkirk to the door, and continued making her own plans.

Six weeks after Averie returned to Weymire Estate, Ket Du'kai finally came calling.

Averie had spent the day in the kitchen with the cook, the butler, and the housekeeper, discussing what portions of the mansion could be closed up while she was gone, and what portions should be kept in readiness against Averie's eventual return. They were all old friends as well as servants; they felt free to express their opinions. And all of them agreed with Lady Selkirk that Averie should not go jaunting off by herself to see the world.

The cook even volunteered to come with her, "since I've never seen any stretch of land outside of Aeberelle, and I'd like to, before I die." Averie thanked them all and declined their attentions.

She was in the parlor, drafting a letter to her father's attorney, when the butler brought the news that she had a caller. "A Xantish gentleman," he said, his voice disapproving. "He says he is called Ket Du'kai."

"I've been expecting him," Averie said, rather calmly, considering her heart was hammering with excitement. "Show him in."

He was dressed in serviceable but not particularly fashionable clothing, a jacket and trousers that looked comfortable for traveling. His hair had been cut and his beard trimmed, but she thought the real difference on his face was that some of the exhaustion and despair had lifted. Here was a man finally rested and at peace.

"You see I have come as you commanded," he said, bowing over her hand. "What a beautiful property this is. I was marveling at its size and grace the whole time I was coming up the walk. Before I go, perhaps you will give me the whole tour."

"Perhaps I will," she said, smiling. She drew him over to a striped divan set invitingly near a window and pulled him down next to her. He made sure he did not sit too close, though he did not release her hand. "You are out of uniform, I see. So you truly have left the army?"

"I have. And I have made my reservations on a ship bound for Xan'tai. I am sailing home in ten days' time."

Averie thought for a moment. "On the *Alabaster Eight*? I looked at her, too, but I confess I thought the accommodations would be crowded and inelegant. The *Southern Queen* seemed much more comfortable, and she leaves in two weeks."

Ket merely looked at her and said nothing. His face showed no expression; if anything, it appeared even more shuttered. She almost laughed at him, he was trying so hard to conceal all emotion.

"I am going to Xan'tai, too, you see," she added.

His hand tightened suddenly on hers, and then he released her. "I suppose I must ask you why?"

She tapped a finger against her lip, meditative. "Do you remember one of our first conversations as we sailed to Chesza?"

"I remember all of them."

"You told me that your dream was to fight for home rule in Xan'tai, but that a peaceful overthrow of the Aebrian government would take clever political maneuvering and a great deal of money. Well, I have a great deal of money. I will put it at your disposal so that you may initiate the clever political maneuvering."

Now he stared at her, completely at a loss.

Averie continued, "I keep thinking. Chiarrin today is

what Xan'tai must have been like a hundred years ago. I hated to see Chiarrin overrun by the Aebrian army, and part of me is glad that the Chiarrizi were able to fend us off—though the cost was so dreadfully high! Chiarrin saved itself, as Xan'tai could not. Very well. Perhaps with the right resources, and trying political battles instead of armed conflict, Xan'tai can free itself from Aebrian rule."

"That is what I hope, and what I will work toward," Ket said in a low voice. "But this is in no way your cause."

"It will be if I want to fund it."

"You cannot possibly plan to hand your cash over to Xantish activists."

"Well, no. But I can give it to *you*."

"No," he said, shaking his head. "It is lunatic to even consider making such an offer. I could never take your money."

"You could marry me for it," she suggested.

Now he was speechless again.

She went off in a peal of laughter. "If you could see your face," she said gaily. "And I thought by now you knew me well enough to never be shocked by my behavior."

He recovered, or mostly. "What you see is dismay that you have such a low opinion of me that you would think I actually *would* marry you for such a reason."

"Is there another reason why you might marry me?" she asked, her voice suddenly soft.

He looked at her a long time, as if marshaling his thoughts. "You know nothing about Xan'tai," he said at last. "In truth, you know very little about me. I would be every kind of rogue and scoundrel if I were to take advantage of your innocence and your generosity and your . . . your feelings for me, and accept any part of this proposal. But I am moved in a way that I cannot even express to think you would offer yourself and your estate to my country and to me."

She listened carefully, her head tilted to one side. "I don't believe," she said, "that you actually answered my question."

He almost smiled. "I refuse to encourage you in this madness by saying anything at all about the state of my heart."

Averie gave a tiny shrug. "Very well. I will book accommodations on the *Southern Queen*. Perhaps your sense of propriety will allow you to tell me how to contact you once I have arrived in Xan'tai. I believe we dock in the city of Neuri."

Now he looked both alarmed and a little admiring. "You cannot mean to set sail on your own for a country that is utterly strange to you!"

"Well, I will, if I can find no one to come with me. A few of the servants have offered, but I would rather travel alone."

On Ket's face, the alarm deepened and the amusement completely disappeared. "Entirely alone? Averie, you cannot. Truly. A solitary young woman to arrive by herself at the harbor in Neuri—that is a certain prescription for disaster."

"Perhaps you can be persuaded to meet the *Queen* when it docks."

He took her hands again, in a hard, urgent grip. "Averie! Don't be foolish. Don't throw away so much of your life on a whim—on a gesture. I love you—is that what you want me to say?—I love you, and I cannot bear that you would risk so much for me. You cannot marry me and come to Xan'tai and squander your money on a country you have never even *seen*. Yes, I know you are outrageous and impulsive, but truly, truly, this will not do. You must live the life you were meant for, not the one that sounds, at the moment, so romantic, and that cannot help but disappoint you."

"I have nothing left in Aeberelle, save for Weymire Estate," Averie said. She was very composed. She had expected the conversation to go somewhat like this, and, all in all, she rather liked the way Ket was responding. "My parents are both dead. I have no siblings. My close friends are scattered. I have broken off my engagement. Nothing holds me here. I want to go to Xan'tai—and I want to marry you. If I can attain only one of those objectives, well, then, I will go to Xan'tai. I don't see how you can stop me."

He watched her a long time, his dark eyes narrowed and searching. "So you really mean to come," he said.

"Oh, yes."

"I could change my reservations so that I travel on the *Southern Queen.*"

"That would be delightful."

He shook his head. "This foolishness about marrying me—I can't even discuss that."

"Not now, perhaps," she said in an encouraging voice. "But perhaps once we have arrived in Neuri. After the long voyage. We will know each other much better by then."

A glimmer of a smile crossed his face and was sternly banished. "I would see you live a year in Xan'tai first before you made any plans to wed a native," he said. "You are unfamiliar with its climate and its customs—you may find both of them disagreeable."

"A year is much too long," she said. "I would be willing to wait six months before I made such an important decision."

"Six months would certainly give you a tolerable overview of the country," he said. "But you cannot travel there alone, nor live there unchaperoned."

"I will *not* be alone. You will be on the ship with me."

He shook his head. "I won't be. I will stay here in Aeberelle and never again set foot in Xan'tai if you refuse to take a suitable companion with you."

This she had not expected—that Ket would overcome his amazement quickly enough to negotiate. She felt a frown gather on her forehead. "Who do you consider a suitable companion?"

His smile reappeared, stronger this time. "Lady Selkirk, perhaps."

"Lady *Selkirk*! Absolutely not."

He shrugged. "Then I find that I am not able to sail to Xan'tai in two weeks after all."

"I will go anyway," she threatened. "Without you."

"I suppose you will."

For a moment, they stared at each other, both stubborn, both unyielding, and then Averie made an infuriated noise deep in her throat. "Very well. I will bring Lady Selkirk—*if* she will come. And if she won't—"

"Then I'm sure she will help you find someone equally respectable," Ket said.

"I hardly think Lady Selkirk—or anyone!—could be ready to sail in two weeks' time!"

"Then perhaps we should postpone our departure."

I don't want to was the response Averie longed to make. But that was childish. That was something a petulant girl would say, and she was a young woman of means, preparing to set out on the greatest adventure of her life. She must be reasonable, resourceful, and rational if she was going to get what she wanted.

"Then perhaps we should," she answered with dignity. "After all, we hardly want to rush along absurdly when there are so many important matters to decide."

Ket smiled and bent over to kiss each of her hands in turn. "I think the next six months will be the most tumultuous of my existence, and you should know that my life has not been particularly uneventful till now."

Averie could not contain her own smile. "I would venture to say that your life will not be entirely settled even once that period of time has elapsed," she said.

He laughed. "It depends on how those months unfold, I suppose," he said. "We shall see."

Averie laughed in return and lifted his hand so that it brushed the back of her cheek. She knew he wanted to kiss her but was trying very hard to maintain some sense of decorum in the mad whirl that she had created around him. He did not look alarmed anymore, however. He looked much the way she felt: excited, hopeful, on the brink of marvels.

She answered, "We shall see, indeed."